A Place to Call Home

Jessica Berg

Author's Acknowledgements

There are several people who have made this book possible. First, I'd like to thank my husband who put up with the endless hours of my writing, deleting, and rewriting.

Secondly, I'd like to thank the ones who read my book over and over again, making sure it was the best it could possibly be. My mother, Barbara, Carie Flemming, and Stacey Weglin will always have my gratitude for their expert opinions and honest advice.

Also, no acknowledgment page would be complete without giving all to God. He is the One who has given me a special talent and made me brave enough to publish my work!

Cover Art Designer: Ruthie Madison, Madison Designs
www.ruthiemadison.com

And I will provide a place for my people Israel and will plant them so that they can have a home of their own and no longer be disturbed. Wicked people will not oppress them anymore, as they did at the beginning and have done ever since the time I appointed leaders over my people Israel. I will also give you rest from all your enemies.

"'The LORD declares to you that the LORD himself will establish a house for you:

2 Samuel 7:10-11

Chapter One

June 1986

Sheriff Jeremiah Wallace was a God-fearing, righteous man with murder on his mind. Watching the movements behind the curtains of the old Victorian house, he felt rabid fear pool in his body. Unable to ignore the clawing sensation in his chest, he concentrated on his breathing. Four counts in, four counts out.

"Sheriff?"

Jeremiah didn't turn his head, didn't even acknowledge his best friend and deputy. His tongue, thick and dry, stuck to the roof of his mouth. His green eyes followed every move of the bulging figure, distorted every now and then by the curtains swaying in the sticky air. Night in Kansas offered little relief from the intense heat of the day, and Jeremiah felt sweat stream down his back. The rancid, sweet-smelling odor emanating off his body reminded him of the anger and fear churning inside.

"Sheriff?" This time the question was accompanied by a brief tap on the shoulder.

Jeremiah jumped and wiped his hand over his mouth. A brief glance at his partner told him what he already knew; it was time to move.

"Let's roll."

Jeremiah looked behind him and noted that his backup was in their positions. He knew his team wouldn't let him down; he just prayed that he wouldn't be the one making a deadly mistake. Or was it too late for that? He knew without a doubt he should have passed this one on.

But no one, not even the devil himself, kidnapped his children without a personal visit.

Shaking the cobwebs from his mind, he crept with the grace and agility of a cat along the weeds bordering the old house. Ignoring the thorns piercing his hands and the noxious odor of stinkweed, Jeremiah steadily moved on until he heard the wails of his children. His gut clenched, and he had to fight to keep from vomiting. Forcing the visions of his two little girls from his mind, he concentrated on every noise, every movement, his every breath. One wrong move and his only reason for living would be destroyed.

With bated breath, Jeremiah checked his gun one more time and risking everything, he lifted himself up just enough to look into the large picture window. Vicious lights danced before his eyes, and Jeremiah knew and accepted it for what it was--cold, blind hatred. His palm itched, and he knew firing his bullets into the soft belly of the man who had kidnapped his daughters was exactly what he wanted to do.

Unwanted and dangerous tears threatened to surface as he studied the two small forms of his daughters huddled on the grimy green couch. He wanted to see their faces, but all he could see was their hair. One red and one black. The dresses they'd been wearing the day they were taken away from him were torn, and his little ones' feet were gritty with dirt.

The only one to see Jeremiah's eyes go cold and blank was the moonless night and God. Inside he locked it all away and stored it for later. *Later. What a stupid concept*, Jeremiah thought. Later never got anybody anywhere. It just stalled it. Later meant that the fat man currently stuffing his gorged mouth with a Hot Pocket would be sitting in a jail cell watching *Days of Our Lives*. Sooner meant that he'd be lying on the green couch with a bullet between his eyes. Fighting for control, Jeremiah breathed through his nose and counted again, this time to ten.

With deft finger motions and hand signals, Jeremiah readied his team, and everyone positioned themselves. The time was right. The time was now.

June 2012

Ugly! Grace McIntyre slipped on her oversized sunglasses and glared at the ugly, dilapidated Victorian house. Panic wrapped its scaly body around her gut and squeezed. Fighting the urge to kick at the red dirt at her feet, she whirled around and glared at the fat, balding man standing next to her. *How dare he be so ugly, too.* Surveying her surroundings, she winced at the sun-scorched pasture in which the old graying house was nestled. *Is everything in this God-forsaken place dying?* She longed for the cool, refreshing mountains she'd fled. Tears pricked her green eyes.

With a silent prayer toward Heaven, she tried to breathe. She needed to breathe, just like her father had taught her: inhale for four counts and exhale for four counts. But breathing didn't come easy with air as clammy as her Aunt Agatha's handkerchief kept safely stashed in her perspiring and ample bosom. Grace shook the cobwebs from her brain and put her game face on. This balding man would soon know that no one messed with Grace McIntyre. She gave the black-haired girl in 80's flashback gear next to her a glance. Nobody messed with Phoebe either, sister by fate, best friend by choice, and Xena, Warrior Princess look-alike. If only Phoebe weren't the biggest wimp in the world! Phoebe met Grace's look, rolled her sapphire eyes, and looked back at the house with noticeable trepidation.

The man standing next to Grace cleared his throat. "This is a lovely house. It just needs some work."

3

"Needs some work?" Grace stared down the realtor with flaming green eyes. "Some work! This house is a mess. Look at it! You specifically stated over the phone that the house was in good condition."

The man mopped his sweaty head with a yellowed hankie and stuffed it back into the left pocket of his knee-length khaki shorts. Nervously, he patted the pocket on the breast of his tight yellow polo shirt. With a sheepish grin he stammered, "Wife keeps stealing my cigarettes." When he received no response, he cleared his throat and pointed to the house. "It's got character."

Grace huffed, stared at the house, and waited. Nothing! No nightmares, not even a twinge of a memory. Whipping her auburn hair into a pony tail, she walked toward the house, critiquing every detail. Once a grand house, it had fallen into disarray from years of neglect. Grace felt a tug of pity for the sagging wraparound porch enfolding the front and two sides of the house. A rounded corner tower peaked over the house, and a bay window on the opposite side balanced out the look. Double hung windows adorned the façade of the house, and the occasional stained glass window glinted in the sweltering, June morning.

Dandelions carpeted the brown lawn surrounding the house. The cheery yellow did nothing to hide the other weeds growing up around the structure. Stinkweed and creeping jenny intertwined with the rickety porch steps and seemed to be the only thing holding up the stairs.

Grace bit her lip. As much as this house needed her, she needed this house. For too long she had wandered, trying to fill the bottomless void. With a quick sniff, she straightened her shoulders. Imagining all the possibilities stretching out in front of her, Grace nodded her head vigorously. "We'll take it! Dad would approve, right, Phoebe?" Grace turned toward Phoebe, her little sister.

Phoebe smiled sadly. "He most certainly would."

Grace faced the sweaty realtor. "We'll take this house. But I swear, if this thing falls on us and kills us, I will come back and haunt you!"

He blanched. "Well...this is a solid house and ..."

"Save it, Mr. Weasel. I was only partially joking." Grace looked at the house and prayed that this would be the home she and Phoebe needed.

The shaking realtor fished out the now sopping wet bandana, wiped his forehead, and took a deep breath. "It's actually Mr. Wisel, and you've got quite a lot of house for the price." At the incredulous stares of the two females, Mr. Wisel backtracked slightly. "Since you seem like such nice young ladies, I'm knocking off a couple of thousand from the price, and I'll give you the name of a really good contractor."

Grace glanced back at the house. She grabbed for Phoebe's perfectly manicured hand and squeezed. Phoebe tucked a stray strand of jet black hair behind her right ear and squeezed her sister's hand in return. Together they could do anything.

Grace released her sister's hand and turned toward Mr. Wisel. "Where do we sign?"

Mr. Wisel beckoned toward his car, and the ladies followed him to his pink Cadillac.

"Nice wheels!" Grace leaned against the hood.

"It's my wife's car." He blushed and dug his shiny shoe into the dirt. "She does the whole Mary Kay thing." He leaned into the car and reached for the papers on the passenger seat. His short arms couldn't make the distance, so he wriggled his ample butt farther into the car and blessed Grace and Phoebe with the sight of a hairy plumber's crack. Mr. Wisel seized the papers and emerged red-faced and panting.

Grace put her arms across her chest. "Would've been easier going to the passenger side."

Mr. Wisel struggled with an armload of papers while attempting to pull his shirt down over his droopy belly. "Suppose it would've, but it don't open. Stupid Cadillac. They don't build them like they used to."

Phoebe smiled over Mr. Wisel's head at Grace, placed her index finger to her forehead and twirled it around in a circle. Grace swallowed a giggle and continued to watch in amazed horror the sickly jig going on in front of her.

After Mr. Wisel arranged himself and his papers, he laid them out on the hood of the Caddy and had Grace and Phoebe sign by the little yellow sticky arrows. As they signed, he rubbed his hands together like a fat fly. "So are you two, you know, 'together'?" He made quote signs in the air.

Grace stifled a laugh and putting her arm around Phoebe, kissed her sister on the cheek. "Together forever!"

Mr. Wisel licked his lips. "I've never met one of your kind before. The guys at the Moose will be so jealous."

Grace studied his khaki shorts, armpit-stained yellow polo, and knee socks. *Shoot.* She'd guessed the Elks, but she was still in the right animal family. "The Moose Lodge? Maybe we could come over and meet all your friends."

Mr. Wisel searched in vain for his cigarettes. "Um...I don't know if my wife would approve."

Grace leaned closer. "What your wife doesn't know won't hurt her."

Phoebe couldn't stifle her giggles anymore. With a snort, Phoebe playfully punched Grace's upper arm. "Leave the poor man alone." Phoebe smiled apologetically at Mr. Wisel. "She's pulling your leg. We're sisters."

"Oh." Grace had never seen a grown man pout before. In a huff, Mr. Wisel handed them the keys to their newly acquired gamble. "There, you two are now the proud owners of a beautiful Victorian home."

Ignoring the glare from Grace and the incredulous gaze of Phoebe, he quickly jotted down the name and number of a carpenter, climbed into the Caddy, mumbled something about being there to help if they needed any, slammed the car into drive, and soared out of the yard.

Phoebe involuntarily shivered. "What a fat little creep!"

Grace nodded in agreement and turned to silently look at the house they had just purchased. "This could be the biggest mistake we've ever made, Pheebs."

"No! The biggest is when we mooned Superintendent Wick."

Grace laughed at the memory. "Yeah, those were the days. Now we're stuck with a house that will make the one from *The Money Pit* look like a five-star hotel." She stuck her hands in her back pockets and rocked back and forth on her heels. "Are you getting any vibes from this place?"

Phoebe pulled a cherry sucker out of her purse. "Yeah, kind of. I'm not scared or anything, but I'm just a little nervous about this being the exact same house. Funny, I don't really recognize it at all." Phoebe studied the house and suddenly whispered, "What if we can't do this, Grace? What if we fail? What if…"

"Phoebe, remember Dad's old saying? Well, this is certainly a time to get back on that darn horse." Grace

7

wrapped an arm around her sister and squeezed. "Let's take a look inside the house, jot down some ideas, and then grab some lunch." Grace bit her lip. "We should have asked Mr. Weasel if he knew of a good place to eat in this town."

As the two women entered through the creaking front door, they failed to notice a black pickup idling on the shoulder of the gravel road parallel to the house. The sweet-smelling cigar smoke drifting from the window never reached them; it exhaled from the dark-tinted windows, the smoke curling wistfully and then disappearing. The man inside was patient. Another curl of smoke emerged from the idling Chevy. As a spider spins a web and awaits his prey, he, too, would lie in wait. With a slow, curling smile, he enjoyed watching them coming down the steps of the ridiculous excuse of a house. Of all the girls' features, he remembered their hair most of all: one flame red, the other coal black. Both reminded him of their father. He ignored the fact that they had grown up to be real beauties. This was business. Unfinished business. He waited as they pulled from the drive and drove down the rutted gravel road. With a flick of his fingers, the cigar flew out the window and lay dying on the side of the road. With gravel crunching, the Chevy obeyed its driver and followed the rusted-out Ford to town.

Grace and Phoebe seated themselves in a neat little diner on the main street of town. Red booths, black table tops, and shiny chrome walls and ceiling made up the color décor. Reed's Diner boasted the best hot beef sandwich in the area and an old-fashioned ice cream fountain.

Grace eyed the ice cream area with something just short of lust.

"You know, your passion for ice cream is just a little creepy." Phoebe dunked a fry in ketchup and waved it at Grace.

"And the fact that you're eating ketchup makes me want to hurl." Grace dunked her fries into a big blob of mustard and stuck them in her mouth. "Mmmmm. That's a good fry right there."

Phoebe glanced down at the notebook in front of her. "From the looks of things, the previous owners at least attempted to remodel the place." She nabbed a fry from Grace's plate and pointed to the paper. "Looking at this drawing we did, I think we should keep the front parlor for our guests to use. We can use the back parlor for our own personal use," she pointed to a large mustard smear, "and where you splattered mustard is where we could place the front desk."

"That was totally an accident! But, yeah, that sounds good, and we should also try to keep it all in the Queen Victorian style as much as possible. We'll have to scope out some antique stores in the area and see what we can find. We want guests thinking that the Queen herself will be dining with them." She bit into her sandwich and chewed slowly. "Dang, that's good!" Grace swallowed and closed her eyes. "Just imagine it, Pheebs, tasseled lamp shades, elegantly carved mahogany furniture, elaborate tapestries will just make our bed and breakfast the most opulent place in Kansas!"

"I don't think that'll be hard to accomplish." Phoebe reached for another napkin and passed it to Grace. "You got a little something on your chin. Looks like beef juice and mustard."

After wiping her chin, Grace continued discussing the plans for their bed and breakfast. "We'll need to renovate the upstairs though. Every room should have its

9

own private bathroom with a sink, toilet, and a stand-up shower."

Phoebe nodded in agreement between bites of her Monday Special, a double bacon cheeseburger on a sourdough bun. "I think we have space to put five rooms upstairs, and the downstairs bedrooms will be ours to use. We'll have to put a bathroom in one of the downstairs rooms, but that's something to consult the contractor about."

Grace took the name and number of the contractor Mr. Wisel had given them out of her back pocket and placed it on the tabletop. "Dominick Carson." She stuck another fry in her mouth and ate around it as she spoke, "I don't know if we can trust someone who was recommended by a weasel."

Phoebe choked on her Diet Coke. "You know better than to make me laugh when I'm drinking." She cleared her throat, took another sip and continued, "We can just meet with him and get an idea of what he's like. Nothing says we have to hire him."

"True." Grace looked outside the diner's window and watched as meager traffic lazily drove past. "This town is small, but I'm sure it boasts more than one carpenter who can do the job."

Waves of heat blasted the women's faces as they made their way out of the diner. They stopped at a bench situated outside the building and sat down. Eating their ice cream sundaes, they watched small-town life pass by. Cars with no particular place to go or in no particular hurry to get there rumbled down Main Street. The people in them politely waved at other drivers and passengers and occasionally honked at pedestrians strolling along the sidewalks. Evenly-spaced out oak trees provided the hot and sweaty civilians of Beacon, Kansas, the comfort of a shaded walk.

Various businesses made their homes next to the shady trees. A bookstore proclaimed itself the "Tiniest Book Store in the West" and the hardware store next to it had a dude named Hank as its mascot. Between the bookstore and hardware store, there was a pet shop with a couple of sad-looking puppies looking out at some potential owners, a bakery, a bar where bikers were welcome, and a lamp and shade store. Other businesses dotted the landscape and Grace knew she'd eventually step into every single one, especially the lamp and shade store. Which woman doesn't need a lamp or an extra shade in the prime of her life?

Eating ice cream always evoked thoughtfulness in Grace, so as she sat next to her sister enjoying cold, creamy spoonfuls of heaven, she took stock of her life. Currently she owned a run-down money pit, a used Buick LeSabre, and a cat named Mrs. Sloucombe. Grace dug into her sundae in despair. *My life sucks*, she thought. Shoveling the vanilla and fudge goo into her mouth, she thought about things that no longer belonged to her: a cheating, slithery husband with a penchant for enjoying blonde bimbos on their dining room table, a house on The Hill, and a membership to the Hill Valley Country Club. She'd miss the country club the most. Even though its members emitted snobbery, the place always had the best little éclairs.

She'd left Hill Valley, Colorado, for the vast open plains of Kansas, hoping that conquering her past and working on a new business adventure would help heal the wounds. With a bank account full of money from her divorce and a house waiting to be reborn, she pondered her future.

Grace snuck a glance at her sister. Phoebe, a wild child and female Desperado, sat licking the inside of the sundae cup. Growing up, Grace had coveted Phoebe's black hair and perpetually sun-kissed skin. Phoebe inherited all the beauty from their mother. Grace, on the other hand, took after their rancher father, with his red hair, green eyes, and whip-like temper.

She saw her father in her mind's eye and smiled as she witnessed Phoebe struggling to reach the gooey goodness at the bottom of the container. Phoebe's tongue couldn't make the distance, so she slicked it up with a finger and stuck the fudge in her mouth. *Regardless,* Grace thought, *of what I do or do not have, I am totally thankful I have her.*

Phoebe snuck a guilty glance at Grace. "Did you see that?"

"Every disturbing moment."

Phoebe glanced nervously around, and seeing no one staring at her, she relaxed. "So, what do you think of this place?" Crunching up her licked clean bowl, she attempted to make a basket. "Crap. Never was any good at basketball, was I?"

"Not if you had to run and dribble at the same time."

"Look who's talking! Didn't you rip your shorts twice in gym class, on the same day?"

"That was a nasty rumor started by Prissy-Crissy-Pees-Her-Pants. She just wanted the attention taken away from her for a while."

"Right." Phoebe folded her hands in her lap and watched as the lazy traffic ambled down the road. "I like it here. It's hotter than H-E-double hockey sticks, but it's a good little place."

Grace nodded. *Yeah, it was.* In order to escape their father's haunting death, both had tried making lives. Both had failed miserably. Combined, they had one failed marriage, a broken-off engagement (courtesy of Phoebe), and a horrible aversion to the only home they'd ever known. Grace tried to erase the image of their father's dead body dangling across the saddle of Scout, his faithful buckskin. The ranch they'd grown up on, the ranch that had made and then killed their father was no longer a home. *This,* Grace sighed, *would have to be it.* Because if it weren't, it meant they'd forever be running from a ghost they couldn't out run.

Grace shrugged. "We'll see. We've only been here for a short while."

Phoebe, intent on being the silver lining to Grace's little black rain cloud, nudged her gently. "They might have shopping malls around here!"

Grace watched as five Ford F-350's roared down Main Street. "Um, I think the feedlot won out on that battle. I'm thinking you'd have to drive into Wichita."

"Oooohh, shopping spree! That'll be fun."

Grace pushed herself up from the bench. "Come on. Let's get to work." At Phoebe's pout, Grace continued, "I'll make a deal with you. If you work really hard for the next week, I promise we'll take a day and go shopping."

Phoebe's face lit up. "Now, that's compromise!"

Not having a reply, Grace chucked her ice cream container into the garbage. "Come on, Phoebe; we've got a phone call to make."

That night, Grace lay awake, body shaking with each boom of thunder. Fat raindrops splattered against the window panes and fell in torrential streams to the red dirt below.   Never a fan of storms, Grace hid under the blankets, careful not to let the hotel comforter touch her face.   Next to thunderstorms, hotel comforters came in second on Grace's phobia list.   With a shudder, she bit off a shriek at the next crash.   Telling herself to grow up, she peeked out of her blanket fort and glanced at Phoebe who was snoozing away.

"Yeesh.   At least she'll be sleeping when we get blown to Oz."   Unable to take the suffocating atmosphere around her, Grace slipped out of bed and shuffled to the bathroom.   Not wanting to be caught with her underwear around her ankles when she met the Wizard, she quickly did her business and quietly washed her hands with the hotel's bar soap.

"They call this soap?"   Grace asked herself in the mirror.   A streak of lightning and a crash of thunder exploded over the hotel.   Windows shook with violence, and Grace swore she heard the Munchkin's theme song.   With determination, she refused to run to her bed.   Instead, she studied herself in the mirror.   For two in the morning, she didn't think she looked too bad.   Then again, she certainly wasn't company-ready, something her mother always strove to instill in her two girls.   With a huff and habitual eye-roll, Grace stuck her tongue out at the image of herself and hoped somewhere her mother knew both she and Phoebe were rebelling against everything she had ever tried to teach her daughters about being the perfect women.   Her mother's ideal men for her two daughters had crashed and burned.   Grace's face burned as the face of Kevin, her ex-husband, flashed in her memory.   Egotistical, neurotic, self-absorbed…Grace staunched the flow of insults.   She was expected to forgive.   That's what God called her to do.

Memories of her father suddenly replaced the visions of Kevin.   For as long as she could remember, she'd

14

followed her father like an adoring lap dog. The barn, the stables, the never-ending expanse of land called to her and fed her soul, just like it did her father's. The familiar ache formed in her chest and expanded like a mushroom cloud. Taking in her green eyes, she saw her father's gazing back at her. Those eyes had once been full of mischief and love. What did they see now? Tears welled up, balanced on her lower lid, and fell freely to the cheap white hotel sink below. In her mind's eye she saw him lovingly petting Scout's neck and cooing in his ear. The pinching sensation in her chest spread as she remembered his laughing eyes and battered Stetson. What was the last thing he'd said? Grace's mouth moved silently, "Keep the home fires burning, Gracie." Grace opened her eyes and whispered, "I will, Daddy, when I find a home."

Grace tried shaking off the suffocating sadness and sent a prayer to Heaven. With a frustrated snort, she crawled back into bed. She often wondered when God would get with the 21st century and participate in email. Facebook might be too much of a shock for Him, but email was pretty tame. She certainly had a lot of questions, and so far, not many answers were coming her way. Willing herself to sleep, she finally fell into a deep sleep where she dreamt of her father's eyes and another set, sinister and watching her every move.

Chapter Two

The next day dawned with vivacious colors of pink and purple streaking across the sky. The pasture behind the Victorian farmhouse, revitalized with last night's rain, sprang to life with yellow and purple wildflowers. Cows lazed in the morning sun, watching their babies frolic. In the tree belt surrounding the house, birds sang and danced from treetop to treetop, serenading Grace and Phoebe as the women yanked and pulled at a weather-beaten window shutter.

"Holy buttersnap!" Grace used her arm to swipe at her brow. She shaded her eyes and glared up into the sky. "Is it always this hot in June? It's not even 8:00 in the morning, and I'm already sweating." Grunting, she gave another futile tug at the shutter. "And this darn thing won't budge!"

Phoebe ran to the rusted out Ford truck they'd rented for the renovation. "I got just the thing," she cried as she dug around in the truck bed. "A-ha!" Phoebe did a booty shake and held up a crowbar as if it were an Olympic gold medal.

Grace reached for it when Phoebe came up beside her again. "Phoebe, you do realize that the 80's are over, right?"

"That's why I'm trying to bring them back." Phoebe smoothed out her hot pink shorty shorts.

Grace rolled her eyes. "You're impossible!" With an evil grin she faced the stubborn shutter. "I would love the pleasure of teaching this shutter who is boss."

"Be my guest."

Grace slammed the crowbar into a tiny crevice between the shutter and the side of the building. "One, two, three!" Grace lunged against the bar, and a loud crackling sound preceded the gaping hole in the side of the house.

Both Phoebe and Grace stared in amazement at the hole in the house and at the shutter that hadn't moved an inch. "You have got to be kidding me! What is this thing made out of?"

Grace slammed the crowbar back into place, counted to three, and pushed her weight against the bar. Another crack. This time, however, the shutter crumpled to the ground in a sad heap of wood and nails the size of railroad spikes.

Phoebe gingerly touched one of the nails. "I take it whoever put this up didn't want it coming down again."

Grace kicked the broken shutter out of the way and started on the other one. "What color is this anyway? Puke green?"

"I think it's a combination of green and yellow with a layer of brown in between."

"Awesome," Grace grunted as she repeated the process of levering another shutter off the house. "I'm trying to think positively about this. I really am. I won't have to work out today."

Phoebe rolled her eyes. "The day you don't work out is the day the sun will turn pink."

"Hey, you've seen my butt when I don't work out. Something's got to keep the fat off my hinder, and its running."

For the rest of the morning Grace tackled the remaining window shutters while Phoebe began scraping the old, peeling paint off the house. Visions of her old life flittered before Grace's eyes. Grace didn't like to think

17

about her life with her ex-husband, Kevin, but the memories kept replaying in her mind. They'd met in college and had married two years later at the urging of her mother. Her father thought she was too young to get married. Six years later, the truth behind that statement glared in her mind like flashing neon signs. She had too easily mistaken the outlandish presents, exotic vacations, and beautiful houses at her disposal as love. They were merely tools of deception which Kevin knew how to use with expert precision.

A day as Kevin's wife had usually consisted of lying by the pool, having Maria occasionally bring her a glass of lemonade, finished up by a pedicure or massage, and then a long wait for Kevin to get home. Usually late and slightly disheveled, his excuse never changed: work was rough; his boss was really riding him. Grace had soon found out that it was actually him riding the boss which explained the nonexistent sex life that had Grace believing he no longer found her desirable. The one time she had confronted Kevin about it he had stated, "I'm too tired after work, sweetie. I'll rock your world this weekend." The weekend had never turned out to be anything spectacular.

Grace wiped away a tear and pushed against the crowbar. "Idiot!" Humiliation haunted her as she remembered what kind of person she'd become as Kevin's wife. Her father hadn't raised her to be a princess. Grace grunted in frustration. For as long as she could remember, her father had instilled in his two girls the importance of good, honest, hard work. To do anything other than that was spitting in the face of God. Grace allowed a small smile. Her father was never one for textbook theology. But she had no doubt that he was feasting and talking horses with Jesus as she was partaking in that good, honest, hard work. Grace made a vow to herself to never become

18

that princess again. She would work for what she got. Grace sighed and leaned her forehead against the rough paint. Glancing down at her naked, left ring finger, Grace felt a certain freedom. She no longer had to be that perfect wife that Kevin had demanded. She was a free woman! So what were these chains that still seemed to bind her heart?

Resigned to finding an answer to that question later, Grace moved on to the last ground floor shutter and watched with pleasure as it bit the dust. The pleasure changed to a grimace as she craned her neck upwards and saw all the nasty, puke-colored shutters waiting for her.

"Problem!" Grace yelled.

Phoebe came running around the corner of the house. "What is it?"

Grace put one hand on her hip and pointed up with the other hand. Phoebe nodded. They both knew that Grace hated ladders. The fact that they'd need a big ladder wasn't lost on them either. They both stood facing the house, looking up, expecting a miracle to happen. Maybe a very tall person, a giant perhaps, would magically appear and take away their worries. And while he was there, they'd have him strip the paint off, too.

Dominick Carson sped out of town, trying to wrangle a cell phone and the little slip of paper with chicken-scratched names scrawled across it. Never one for being late, Dominick checked the truck's green digital clock and cursed. Passing a black Chevy with dark-tinted windows, he turned on to the gravel drive. Dominick glanced at the names again. Grace McIntyre and Phoebe Wallace. *Wonder what they're doing buying that old run down piece of junk?* Dominick wondered as he parked his truck in the front of the house. It'd been a long time since he'd been on the property and time certainly had not been kind. With a low whistle, he grabbed his briefcase and ambled to the front porch. High-pitched voices, seemingly in distress, met his ear, and with quick, smooth movements, Dominick skirted the edge of the house and came to a complete stop at the sight in front of him.

Two rather attractive women, one with ebony hair and dressed like a tame Cindy Lauper, the other with wild auburn hair, ripped Levi's, and a man's white undershirt, were gesticulating wildly between the ladder and the upper floor of the house. Crumpled shutters littered the ground at their feet and the red-head, for emphasis, smashed one with her sneakers. Stifling a bark of laughter, Dominick cleared his throat.

"Ladies?"

Grace and Phoebe, surprised by the pleasant drawl, stood very straight and turned in unison. Grace heard Phoebe swallow at the sight before them. At the saliva that pooled in her own mouth, Grace decided that swallowing wouldn't be a bad idea either. The man before them stood well over six feet and had a body that claimed long, lean muscle. Honey-brown hair framed a rugged and intriguing face. Long eyelashes shaded eyes of melted chocolate and his nose looked as if it'd been broken once or twice. A long thin scar ran from the corner of his left eyebrow to his left ear and a set of full lips curled back into a warm smile, revealing perfectly straight teeth.

"You two must be Grace McIntyre and Phoebe Wallace. I'm Dominick Carson." Dominick Carson held out a calloused hand.

Grace, wiping her hands on her jeans, grasped his hand first. "I'm Grace, and this is my sister, Phoebe." At Grace's nudge, Phoebe held out her hand. Grace could swear she heard a moan escape Phoebe's lips.

Dominick glanced at the house. "This is some building you've got here." He turned to walk back to the front of the house. "My truck's around front. I want to take a look at the inside, and then I can give you an estimate on what it will take to fix this beauty."

The two sisters nodded and followed him around the house. Phoebe nudged Grace and winked. Grace lightly smacked Phoebe's head. "Wipe off the drool, and quit ogling him!"

Phoebe whispered back, "I'm not ogling; I'm enjoying the view."

Grace rolled her eyes. She'd been sucked in by a gorgeous man before, and she certainly wasn't bound to let that happen again. She checked off her first reaction to him as purely hormonal. She'd be sure to keep her hormones in check from now on.

Dominick turned as they reached the front veranda. "I take it Weasel, I mean, Wisel, sold this house to you?" At Grace's nod, Dominick shook his head. "Wisel has been trying to sell this house for the longest time. After the first buyers left in a hurry, no one from the area would buy it. Not a bad house though. From just looking at the outside, the foundation looks to be in good shape. The majority of the outside issues are all cosmetic, except for the hole in the house which looks brand new."

Phoebe bit back a laugh and Grace ducked her head. "We kind of put that there this morning trying to get those stupid shutter thingies off."

"Thingies?" Dominick winked at Grace. "Must be a technical term, huh? Well, that's pretty easy to fix. Just try not to put any more holes in your house."

Dominick headed up the steps to the house and went through the door.

"Oh my goodness!" Phoebe grabbed Grace's arm and yanked on it. "Carpenter Hottie just winked at you!"

Grace slapped away Phoebe's hand. "Stop it; we're not in high school anymore, and he's not the captain of the football team."

"Better watch out, though. I think Carpenter Hottie just might be a little on the dangerous side. You see his scar?"

"Maybe he got it in a bar fight."

Phoebe sighed. "Maybe it was over a damsel in distress."

Grace rolled her eyes. "Dork."

"Ladies, you coming?" Dominick's voiced beckoned from within.

Grace gave Phoebe the "don't-do-anything-stupid" look. "Yup. Right behind you."

"I think my age keeps dropping the longer I'm around this guy. Before I know it, I'll be snapping my gum and twirling my fingers in my hair," Phoebe whispered as they climbed the steps.

"Don't worry; I'll just put you in a convent."

Phoebe looked horrified. "I love God and all, don't get me wrong, but I don't know if I could," she twirled her hand in the air, seeming to find the perfect word, "survive."

With another warning glance for Phoebe to behave, they stepped into the old house and situated themselves where the future front desk would sit.

Using her best professional manner Grace explained to Dominick, "This is the spot where we would like the front desk. Over to the right, we'd like to have a front parlor where our guests can visit or just hang out."

Grace continued through the house, giving Dominick an idea of what they envisioned. "Through this archway we have the dining room. It's pretty big and will probably accommodate our guests just fine. The kitchen needs mainly cosmetic work and new appliances. The size is a little cramped, but we can make do with it for now. The back parlor and small study we would like to use as a private area."

Grace and Phoebe finished showing Dominick the lower two bedrooms. One already had a bathroom attached, so not much work would be needed there. The other room proved smaller and had no bathroom.

Dominick looked around, took out his measuring tape and jotted down some measurements. "From what I can tell, this wall here," he indicated the wall separating the bedroom from the hallway "is a weight-bearing wall, which means it has to stay. We can add on to the outside of the house, making this room a little bigger, allowing me ample space to create a bathroom."

Phoebe nodded. "And how much would that cost?"

"Don't know just yet. As soon as I'm done here, I'll head back to my office and run an itemized estimate for you. That way you'll know exactly what needs to be done and what it's going to cost."

They headed up the grand open staircase to the top floor. The once luxurious bedrooms lay in disarray and decay. Cobwebs hung from the ceiling and dust covered every visible surface. Some of the windows were cracked and one in the far left bedroom was entirely smashed. Water damage around the window had stained the wood floors a swampy-black.

They walked into the smallest of the bedrooms. Here a large fireplace on the west wall dominated the room. Grace swiped her index finger along the top of the marble mantel. The single line, now free of dust, shone white in the sunshine. She wiped the dust on her shirt and walked over to the smashed window. Curtains, tattered and weathered, hung limply off the rod. Grace made a mental note to take them down soon. They were simply too depressing to look at. The wallpaper next to the window seemed loose, so Grace tugged at it. The faded maroon material shredded off the wall, revealing images of faded lambs frolicking in what used to be bright green pastures. Grace unconsciously rested her right hand on her abdomen and traced the baby lambs with her right. She'd always wanted children. Kevin had thought they were a nuisance. With a sad smile, Grace figured God had said "no" for the right reasons. Shaking her head, resigned to the fact she'd die a shriveled, old, spinster prune, she turned at Dominick's chuckle.

When Grace arched an eyebrow, Phoebe explained, "I just told Dominick how you put Mr. Wisel in his place. And the fact that he thought we were lovers."

Grace shrugged nonchalantly. "The man seemed a little bored. A little spice never hurt anybody."

"Spice, huh? I don't think you're going to get much spice in this town, unless you call Bingo night at the VFW spicy. Some of those old ladies can get downright nasty. My grandma, God rest her soul, got her one and only black eye playing Bingo. She thought some 'tramp' was being especially flirty with my grandpa and called this lady out." Dominick shoved a hand through his thick hair. "I guess it was an all-out fight, two little old ladies duking it out over a man who had fake teeth and wore Depends."

Grace found herself laughing. "Sounds like my kind of woman."

Dominick smiled and busied himself with measurements, taking special care to discreetly study Grace who, for the moment, was busy showing Phoebe her nursery lamb discovery. Her auburn hair had worked its

24

way from its ponytail prison. He watched as Grace impatiently confined it again with an elastic hair tie. He could see in the snap and sparkle of her green eyes that her personality just might match her hair. As he measured the length of the room, he studied her face. Grace wasn't as beautiful as her sister, but her high cheekbones adorned by tiny freckles, her full lips, and a graceful nose beckoned to him. Grace suddenly laughed at something Phoebe said, and his attention was again averted to her eyes. The green evoked the presence of kindness, but he was captivated by the specks of fire in them. This woman was no push-over. Yet there was something else there, something deep-rooted and haunting. Dominick felt a tug on his heartstrings. He knew what it was to be haunted. Before he could avert his eyes from her, Grace met his stare. She cocked her head and lifted her right eyebrow.

Caught, Dominick looked away and cleared his throat. "Well, ladies, this is a mess." He walked over to the fireplace. "This will take some time and money. Actually, a lot of time and money. It wouldn't be bad if you didn't need bathrooms put in. That's where it's going to bite you."

Grace and Phoebe nodded that they understood and traipsed downstairs after Dominick. Grace stood in the foyer and nervously played with the waistband of her ripped jeans. She wiped her face with her white t-shirt and only managed to smear dirt and wood debris over her forehead and cheeks.

Phoebe slung an arm around her sister's shoulder. "Don't worry. For as long as I've known you, you've never given up." Phoebe tucked a stray black hair behind her ear. "We can do this."

Grace studied Phoebe for a second. "It's a little difficult taking you seriously with the outfit you have on today."

Phoebe looked down at her hot pink running shorts and white tube top. "What's wrong with what I'm wearing?"

"Nothing. If we were going to a roller rink after this."

Phoebe pouted. "And here I was trying to say something nice to you. You're kind of mean when you're stressed."

"I'm not stressed! I'm just a little…"

"Stressed!" Phoebe stated emphatically. She turned to Dominick for backup.

Leaning up against the wall with his arms crossed loosely over his chest, he looked a little bewildered and amused. "I really don't want to get in the middle of this, but I'm thinking the problem lies in the color paint chip you're sporting. Pink paint chips would go much better than the pukey-green." He turned his gaze to Grace. "And there is nothing wrong with a roller rink."

While Phoebe brushed at herself, wildly trying to abolish the evidence of her scraping, Grace smiled in spite of herself. "True. There are many benefits of roller skating under a disco ball."

Phoebe, failing miserably in trying to clean herself off, gave up and huffed. "That's it. I quit."

Dominick stuck his hands in his pockets and studied the two women before him. Odd. Strange. And slightly neurotic. But, just like his grandma, he liked a little spice in his life. His eyes locked with a pair of green ones. His heart, much to his chagrin and horror, beat faster. Ignoring it, he smiled. "Don't worry, ladies. You're in good hands with me and my crew. We'll have this place open for business in no time."

Grace spoke first, "Thanks. When you're done with the estimate, you can either find us here or at the Super 8 motel."

"High living, huh?"

"Yup. Got to live somewhere, and it sure isn't going to be here until I'm personally assured all ghosts and spiders have vacated the premises."

Dominick smiled. "Good plan." He tipped an imaginary hat. "See you ladies later."

Grace and Phoebe watched Dominick saunter out of the house, get in his truck, and drive down the driveway.

"Hate to see him go, but love to watch him leave."

Grace playfully punched Phoebe's arm. "I thought you swore off men since Brett."

Phoebe picked at the hem of her pink shorts. She turned serious eyes to Grace. "Right after Brett left me at the altar, I swore to myself I'd never trust another man. But my heart is healing. Let's just say I'm keeping my eyes and heart open. You?"

Grace sat wearily on the bottom step and watched as her shoes scraped patterns in the dust on the floor. Was six months enough for the wound to heal? How long must she mourn for a relationship that never fulfilled her? Must she miss a man who sabotaged their efforts to have a child? Must she pine over a man who then deserted her in her time of greatest need when her father died? Grace's head pounded; there were too many questions. "I don't know, Pheebs. Sometimes I wish Dad were here. He'd know what to do."

Phoebe sat down beside Grace and enfolded her in a half hug. "I think you deserve to live life to its fullest.

27

And Dad would tell you that when the horse bucks you off…'"

"…you get right back on." Grace finished the cliché with a small smile. Scrubbing her face with her dirty hands, she sighed and peered in the direction of the front parlor. "That room," she gestured toward the closed French doors which cut the room from view. "I know I should feel something toward it, but I don't. Why not?"

"We were so young, Grace. You were three; I was two." Phoebe held Grace's hand. "I'm not surprised, Grace, about the lack of emotion toward this house or that room." Phoebe shrugged. "Maybe your brain refuses to remember that night?"

Grace stood up and brushed her pants off. "Well, enough of memory lane. Oh, and as for the swearing off men thing, I've realized one thing, Pheebs. Not all men are morons like Kevin and Brett. When the right ones come along, we'll know it."

"Like Carpenter Hottie?" Phoebe smiled and picked up a paint scraper. "Maybe he's 'The One.'"

Grace laughed, but her heart cringed.

Unaware that a pair of eyes watched them from the tree grove, Grace and Phoebe worked viciously till their stomachs yearned for Dairy Queen. Sweaty and gross, they piled into their rust-bucket on wheels and motored off for Blizzards and a sappy chick-flick. The figure in the trees put down the binoculars and reached for his gun. When Grace's head appeared in the crosshairs, he licked his lips and steadied his index finger on the trigger. Knowing he'd have to wait for a better time, he eased his finger off the trigger.

"I'll pop you off later, ladies," he promised.

28

Chapter Three

The alarm went off directly at 6:30 a.m. Grace groaned into her pillow and flailed an arm out to smack the snooze button. After muttering curses into her pillow, Grace flopped onto her back and lay in the darkness, looking up at the blinking red light on the smoke detector. *Huh*, Grace thought, *wonder if it actually works*. Visions of her and Phoebe fried to crisps in their beds didn't appeal to the senses. Shaking her head, Grace swung a leg out of the bed and nearly screamed in agony. Whimpering, she tested the other leg. Just as painful. *What did I do to be so stiff?*

"That's why," Grace whispered to herself. Remembering yesterday's work load of ripping off shutters, pulling the various noxious weeds surrounding the house, and running from a pair of squirrel babies she'd found in the attic, Grace understood why she felt as if she'd been mowed down by a bakery truck. *At least it was a bakery truck*, Grace thought as she slipped her feet into a pair of pink, fuzzy slippers.

The morning sun began creeping through the narrow slit in the faded hotel curtains. Light streamed across Phoebe's face, causing her to grunt, drool, and turn away from the invading sun. Grace shook her head in amusement as she trudged to the bathroom.

"Yikes!" The hair on the left side of her head was plastered down while the other side stuck straight out. Quickly, she whipped her hair back into a manageable ponytail. After a quick brushing of her teeth, Grace pulled on her running clothes, slapped a hat on her head, slipped the room key into her sock, grabbed her iPod, and headed out the door.

Breathing in the fresh morning air, Grace headed out at a fast walk. She caught herself a couple of times singing out loud to the tunes pumping into her ears. "Oops. Doesn't matter," Grace stated to the squirrel who'd stopped fiddling with an acorn to study her, "everyone likes a little 50 Cent." Soon Grace warmed up enough to settle into a medium-paced run.

Grace steadied her breathing, and the rhythm of her legs took her across town, providing her an intimate knowledge of the place she'd hopefully call home.

Moms loaded kids, soccer balls, and lunch coolers into minivans and scooted on to a day's worth of practice. The dads soared off in trucks and cars either in the direction of a paycheck or the golf course.

Dogs barked their hellos as Grace ran by house after house. Some dogs, not attached to a leash or barricaded by fences, thought Grace an irresistible target and brought their welcome a little too close for comfort.

A few people driving by looked at Grace with curiosity; who ran for fun? Grace simply smiled and waved. Passing a mom strolling along with her baby girl who was all decked out in pink lambs brought back visions of the old nursery. As Cee Lo Green sang in her ears about forgetting a girl who didn't think he was good enough, Grace's memory flashed back to the moment her marriage hit rock bottom. She could have lived with the infidelity, but not the emotional betrayal. He'd led her to believe he wanted children, so they started trying. She'd quit taking the pill and started taking prenatal vitamins. When her periods hadn't happened, she had chalked it up to a hormone issue. Unbeknownst to her, Kevin had commandeered the remainder of her birth control pills and had crushed one into her yogurt every morning for months.

Fighting the urge to stop in front of the 7-Eleven and weep, Grace ran harder. As her sneakers pounded the pavement, she questioned God's plans for her life. Was it His idea to hook her up with a no-good loser lying husband? Did He want her to die alone? Why did He allow her father to die? What did He want from her anyway? It certainly felt as though He had stopped listening to her. She'd never felt so far from God before. He needed a phone. Heck, even Morse code would help. Anything. As she neared the hotel, Grace shoved her emotions back into their hidey hole. Eventually she and God would have it out, but today was not the day.

"Where did you run to? Timbuktu?" Phoebe asked as soon as Grace stepped into the hotel room.

"Nope, just through some neighborhoods and down Main Street. That diner we ate at yesterday looks like it has a really good breakfast menu."

"You are absolutely insane, you know that, right?" Phoebe paused and concentrated on applying mascara. "You know you could really lose a toenail."

Grace tore off her shoes and laid spread eagle on the bed. "I sure as heck hope not. My feet are too cute in flip flops." Grace picked her head up and peered at Phoebe. "Why are you putting on makeup?"

Phoebe huffed and rolled her eyes. "Did you see how I looked yesterday when Carpenter Hottie came around? A girl can't look like that when there's a cute guy lurking around every corner!"

Grace rolled her eyes and sighed. "You are beyond all hope. I'm addicted to running, and you're addicted to mascara. Even combined I don't think we'd come close to making a semi-normal person."

31

Phoebe waved her lipstick tube in the air. "Crazy women need to be beautiful," she tossed the tube to Grace, "so load up."

Reed's Diner did indeed have an awe-inspiring breakfast menu. Both Grace and Phoebe ordered the Kansas Sunrise Breakfast Platter and dove in with reckless abandon. Halfway through the double order of hash browns, Grace leaned back, unbuttoned her jeans and then proceeded to finish eating.

Phoebe glanced down at her expanding stomach and gave her green shorts an appreciative pat. "Certainly glad I wore gym shorts and lots of mascara. Any hot guys come around, I won't have a stomach roll, and my eyes will look stunning." She looked at Grace and shook her head, "You, however, are in a world of hurt. Look at you! You got the muffin top even with your top button undone."

"How did you know I undid my top button?"

Phoebe glanced at the barstools filled with old men across from them. "Honey, everyone saw you unbutton your pants."

"Crap! Whatever! Who cares what they think anyway? I like hash browns." Grace slumped farther down in the booth and rubbed her extended tummy. The tight tank top she wore today wouldn't be much help either. "Maybe I like hash browns more than I should."

"I wouldn't worry about it. Maybe Carpenter Hottie likes squishy women."

Grace chucked a rumpled napkin at Phoebe's head. "I don't care what Dominick thinks. We only met him yesterday, remember?" She tapped her temple. "Didn't you get the message? I've given up on men. Especially ones that have nothing better to do than look good all day."

Phoebe reached for the bill. "Actually, my dear sister, you said yesterday that you *hadn't* given up on men! I think the lady doth protest too much!"

"Just for that, you're paying." Grace scooted out from the booth. Passing the pie display with amazing willpower, Grace paused at a bulletin board displaying posters and advertisements. Someone willing to mow lawns all year and a dog breeder selling Puggles took up the most space.

"I've always wanted a Puggle," Phoebe stated from behind Grace.

"They are kind of cute. I'm not sure how Mrs. Sloucombe would like a new pet in my life. She's kind of jealous."

"No offense or anything, but your cat wouldn't care if you up and died."

"Ouch. That hurt." Grace pushed open the door and stepped into the withering heat waves.

"Just stating the obvious. Speaking of your cat, did you just leave her at the old house?"

"Yeah. I didn't think the hotel maid would like being attacked by an obese ball of grey fur."

Phoebe opened the creaky passenger door. "Good plan."

"Excuse me?"

Both women turned toward the voice and studied the man who had hailed them. Leaning against a black Chevy, he took off a black Stetson revealing blonde hair, cut in a military style. Hazel eyes studied them both, and a quick smile had his full lips pulling back to reveal white teeth. Dimples softened his chiseled, square face. "I was wondering if you two lovely ladies were Grace McIntyre and Phoebe Wallace?"

Grace stepped forward. "Yup. That'd be us. What can we do for you?"

The man smiled shyly. "My name's Andrew Carnegie, not at all any relation to the rich ones. Actually, I heard that you were fixing up an old house and could use some help."

Grace studied the man. He was handsome and built like a fighter. Something about him though had her putting on a polite, yet reserved, smile. "We actually just hired a contractor, Dominick Carson. If you're looking to help, he'd be the one to talk to."

The man smiled gratefully. "That'd be great." With a smooth motion he placed his Stetson back on his head and climbed up into his truck. A sweet smoke smell emanated from the vehicle, teasing Grace's nose. Something about it tickled a distant memory. She'd smelled that somewhere, but where? Shaking off the sensation, she waved in return to his friendly salute and watched as he carefully reversed out of the parking spot and into traffic.

"Well, Pheebs, that was…" Grace trailed off as she turned and looked at her sister's face. "Pheebs? Earth to Phoebe." Grace waved her hand in front of Phoebe's face.

"What?" Phoebe jumped. Wiping a hand over her face, Phoebe grinned stupidly. "He was so pretty."

"Yeah. Whatever." Grace felt Phoebe's forehead. "Not warm. Now, I don't want you going off half-cocked for a man you hardly met. Remember what you said yesterday?"

Phoebe only grinned as she opened the passenger door. "When the horse bucks you off…"

With a huff Grace opened the driver's door, hopped in, and slammed the old truck into reverse, forcing the rusted gears into drive. As they soon became part of the lazy morning traffic, Grace wondered about Andrew

Carnegie. *Why does he give me the shivers?* She shook her head. *Must be the lead from the old paint,* she mused. *He's just a handsome cowboy looking for work.*

Forgetting the shy cowboy, Grace guided the old truck down the pothole-ridden highway.

"I take it the county workers are on strike for a longer coffee break," Grace announced as she maneuvered the truck onto the poorly graded gravel road. The truck they'd rented came with unlimited rust and limited shock absorbers, causing Grace and Phoebe to bounce along to their future business.

"Yyyaaa, kknnoooww," Grace tried to speak but the bouncing caused every word to reverberate. "Neeevveerrr mmiinndd."

Phoebe nodded and held on to the seat to compensate for the constant up and down motion. They remained silent for the rest of the short journey and soon came to a gravel-crunching stop in the driveway.

"So, that was fun!"

Phoebe planted herself on un-shaking ground. "What were you trying to tell me earlier?"

"Oh, I was just going to say that eating a large breakfast and then taking a ride in this behemoth probably isn't a good idea."

"You can say that again." Phoebe gingerly felt her crooked eye tooth. "I think my teeth are loose."

Grace laughed and grabbed the toolbox from the bed of the truck. "I'm telling you, between Mr. Weasel and the loser who rented us this truck; I'm starting to think that every business man in this town is a swindler and a crook."

Phoebe nodded. "Except for the owner of Reed's Diner. I like his food. And Dominick. He's hot."

Grace thought of her ex-husband and snorted in disbelief. "Hot guys can be creeps, too."

Phoebe tucked a stray hair behind her ear. "True. But a hot creep is better than an ugly creep."

Grace rolled her eyes, handed Phoebe a paint scraper, grabbed one for herself, and they both set off for the back of the house. "Let's begin this. Let's try to get as high as we can, and then you can get on the ladder and scrape."

"Why me?"

"I thought this was an unspoken agreement between us. You go on the ladders. I supervise and call 911 if needed."

Phoebe rolled her eyes, mumbled under her breath, and started scraping off the old paint with a vengeance.

For two hours, they scraped, swore, and scraped some more. The never-ending peeling paint loomed on and on.

"For the love of Pete!" Grace sat in the shade and wiped her brow with a dirty forearm, consequently placing dust and icky paint chips where the sweat used to be. "This job sucks, and I don't think I want to do this anymore."

Phoebe grunted as she sat next to Grace. "Ditto. You know, there are better things we could be doing, like shoving needles under our nails."

Grace laughed and leaned her head back to rest on a scraped section of wood. "I wish we could just leave this for Dominick and his crew, but there is a very small part of me that refuses to pay for something we can do ourselves."

Phoebe groaned and took a long pull from her water bottle. "Why? With the amount of money you're getting from the divorce, we could have three such houses built." At the glare from Grace, Phoebe pouted. "Fine. You're a hard task master, aren't you?" She pushed herself off the ground with a grunt of protest. "Well, this house isn't going to scrape itself."

Noontime arrived and Grace and Phoebe stopped for lunch. A couple of ham sandwiches and a super-size bag of Doritos chips later, Grace and Phoebe stood in the front parlor area, hands on hips, scoping out the scenery.

"This old wallpaper definitely needs to go, and those cupboards on the back wall could probably be ripped out." Grace walked into the dining room. "This room also has some nasty wallpaper. You can take this room, and I'll start tackling the parlor."

"Sounds like a deal." Phoebe grabbed a chunk of loose, rotting wall covering and yanked. A cloud of dust and goodness knows what else spewed into the air. Phoebe coughed and gagged. "This job sucks, too."

"I don't think there will be a pleasant job to do anywhere in this old thing."

Phoebe fanned the air and frowned at the wallpaper. "I'm afraid you're right."

Grace gave a tiny wave. "Have fun." She walked back to the parlor and closed her eyes, trying to conjure up any memory. Still nothing. The only events that whirled through her head were those she knew from her father telling and retelling the story. Oh, what she wouldn't give to hear his strong, slow voice again. Refusing to cry, Grace forced her eyes open and scowled at the old cupboards filling up the majority of the back wall, swinging loosely from their hinges. Smack dab in the middle of them was the most beautiful picture window Grace had ever seen. Under the grey film of dust, Grace noticed the intricate ivy carvings weaving up and down the oak trimming. Stained glass, done in the same ivy pattern, shimmered dully at the top of the window. Under the fine dust, Grace made out the delicate green ivy, interwoven with purple morning glories on a backdrop of azure blue.

Grace turned a steely eye at the cupboards. The ugly things had to go! With a low growl, Grace stalked toward them, sledgehammer heaved high on her shoulder. Before she could bring it down, though, little flickers of light from the small woods behind the house caught her attention through the window.

Placing the sledgehammer on the floor, Grace moved to the grimy picture window. Having no rag handy, Grace lifted the hem of her shirt and erased months of dust off the glass. Sunlight, uninhibited, poured in. The trees stood as sentinels around the house and a few squirrels played King of the Mountain on a precarious tree branch. Grace absently wondered if they were the parents to the squirrel babies running rampant in the attic. With a shiver at the thought of their tiny squirrel feet, Grace studied the tree grove for the pulsating light. After standing there for several minutes and seeing nothing, Grace shrugged her shoulders and turned her attention back to the doomed cupboards, just in time to miss the odd little pulses of light emanating from the dense trees.

Trying to gauge the strength of the doors, she gingerly touched one of the cupboard doors and shrieked as it tumbled to the floor.

"You okay?" Phoebe asked from the next room.

"Yup, everything's just peachy."

Grace looked at the dead door on the floor and decided taking these apart wouldn't be so bad. With the sledgehammer and a little elbow grease, Grace soon had over half the cupboards disassembled. It was then that she heard it. With a strained whisper, Grace called Phoebe's name. In seconds Phoebe appeared in the doorway and crouched next to her sister when Grace beckoned to her. With a finger to her lips, Grace pointed toward a gaping hole in the back of one of the cupboards.

There was no mistaking it now. Phoebe's flushed face drained of all color, and her eyes slowly rounded to huge spheres. Both of them backed up and stopped only when the exterior wall halted farther retreat.

"What is that noise?" whispered Grace.

Phoebe shrugged her shoulders, bit her lip, and cowered in the corner. She looked expectantly at Grace. "Go check it out."

"What?! You want *me* to check it out? Are you nuts?"

Scraaaaaatchhhhhhh!

"Holy crap, we are going to die!" Phoebe covered her eyes and squealed in terror.

Something was clawing its way between the walls. Every now and then a hiss emanated through the plaster walls, sending chills of horror down Grace's spine. In spite of the strong urge to run for her life, Grace crept closer to the wall. It was approaching the opening.

"It's coming," Grace whispered, glancing back at Phoebe for support. Phoebe shook her head and squealed again. "Sissy!"

Grace stared at the opening, praying that what came out of it wasn't supposed to be dead and wasn't rabid. Suddenly, it tore out of the hole with a demented hiss, and oddly, a meow.

"Mrs. Sloucombe!" Grace grabbed for her cat and got rewarded with a scratch to the face. "Bad kitty! What were you doing in the wall in the first place?"

Mrs. Sloucombe, a ball of raised grey fur, responded with a meow and struggled to free herself.

"Fine, leave! No one wants you around anyway." Grace put the cat on the ground and it sashayed away, fluffy tail in the air.

Grace looked around for Phoebe. "Phoebe? Where are you?"

"Outside waiting to die."

"It was Mrs. Sloucombe. Nothing to be afraid of."

Phoebe tiptoed back into the house and peered anxiously around the corner. "What was your cat doing in the wall in the first place?"

"Beats me. She was probably hunting for mice."

"Yeah, right," Phoebe muttered as she watched the cat curl up on the steps. Grace had hoped Mrs. Sloucombe would become a cat for once in its life and catch mice. So far its victims included an old sock, a piece of yarn, and an old chewing tobacco tin.

Grace wiped her brow and had a strong hankering for a Snickers Blizzard. "Need another trip to town?"

"Does this trip include ice cream and maybe a trip to an antique store?"

"You bet!" The ladies left Mrs. Sloucombe to her own devices and loaded up in the rented truck.

Chapter Four

Leo Muldoon laughed to himself as he inhaled another drag from his cigar. Andrew Carnegie, indeed! A heck of a lot better than the name his mother had given him. Gone was the shy cowboy Grace and Phoebe encountered in front of the diner. The face of a killer now studied them as they pulled in front of an antique store.

"My, my, ladies. What do we have here?" Leo pulled a drag from his cigar and let the smoke swirl in his mouth. Letting it out slowly, he studied his prey. It'd be a pity to kill such beauty, but none of what Jeremiah Wallace brought into this world would survive if Leo had anything to do about it. He chuckled at the memory of Jeremiah's shocked face when he realized death was at his door. And the look of absolute fear in his eyes was priceless when Leo told him his precious daughters were next.

Leo's mouth curved back into a malicious grin. "Yes, ladies, you are next. But not yet; I'm enjoying this little cat and mouse game, and Leo wants to play." He sat back and let loose another stream of smoke.

Oblivious of an audience, Grace and Phoebe parked in front of Annie's AntiCues, conveniently located next to the Seed-n-Feed on the outskirts of town. Annie's AntiCues, with its log cabin façade, looked out of place next to the farm and implement businesses surrounding it. A hitching post ran parallel to the entrance and a wooden sign advised visitors to never squat with spurs on.

"Need a salt block?"

Grace tore her eyes from the spur sign and glanced at the large stack of white salt blocks located outside the Seed-n-Feed store. A sign promised a "Buy One, Get One Free" offer. "Trying to cut back, actually."

Phoebe glanced around to make sure no one was looking, licked her finger, swiped a block of salt, and stuck her finger in her mouth.

Grace gaped at Phoebe. "Could you try to be civilized! What would mother say if she saw you doing that?"

Phoebe swiped more salt off the block. "Which is the very reason I left Colorado, my dear sister. Mmmm. This is actually very good. Are you sure you don't want a swipe?"

Grace rebelliously ran her finger along the salt block and licked off the salty residue. She froze as her cell phone chirped. "She knows!" Grace paled as the caller ID confirmed her worst fears. Swallowing her salty saliva, Grace swiped the keypad. "Mother."

"Grace." Grace cringed. Her mother always said her name as if she were simply pointing out a tree or a rock. "I trust everything is fine with you and Phoebe."

"Yup. We're just peachy, Mother. Never been better."

"I have some news." Grace's heart lurched. Her mother rarely called. This had to be important. But what could possibly be more important than Mother's endless societal engagements? Maybe there was a break in the case of her father's murder? She put the phone on speaker so Phoebe could hear the news. "I'm getting married."

"What!"

"Oh, don't shout, Grace. You know I hate that despicable volume. A lady must never shout." Grace rolled her eyes and pictured her mother with her perfectly

42

manicured hand tapping the crystal glass encasing her mother's best friend--Scotch.

Grace looked to Phoebe for support. Phoebe simply rolled her eyes. Mother would always be Mother. Grace didn't even bother to inquire as to the new fiancé. She knew the man would either be half her mother's age or double her mother's age. "Sorry. I was just taken by surprise."

"I feel it is time to move on. Your father's been dead for over a year, you know. Besides, this ranch house is a little too big for just one person."

Grace fought the rising bile. Anger blinded her, and the temper she'd inherited from her father threatened to lash out. Phoebe's hand on her upper arm stopped her tongue from spewing forth ugly irretrievable words. "Yes, Mother. We've all had to make sacrifices."

"Hmpf! Don't speak of sacrifices like you know them, Grace. You don't know what I suffered. What I still suffer. I'll have you know being stuck on this insufferable ranch is killing me." Her mother inhaled a deep breath. "Which is exactly why I'm selling the place."

Grace caught Phoebe's hand. The look of horror in Phoebe's eyes must have mirrored her own. "You what?!"

"Again with the shouting. It's just a piece of land. I don't know what you're so upset about?"

"Dad's ranch is more than a piece of land. It's a piece of him. Of me." Grace squeezed Phoebe's hand till it turned white. Phoebe never once flinched. "You can't sell it."

"You are too much like your father, Grace. If you knew what was good for you, you'd come back to Colorado and apologize to Kevin."

"Me apologize to Kevin? For what, pray tell?"

"Why leaving him, of course. He's just devastated."

Grace snorted. "I bet." Grace had enough. "Mother, I've got to go. Phoebe's making out with a salt block." Grace ended the call to the sounds of her mother's shriek.

Phoebe stood there shocked. "What the..." She ripped her hand out of Grace's iron grasp. "Why did you have to throw me under the bus? That was not a nice thing to do."

Both women jumped when Phoebe's phone buzzed. Phoebe snatched it out of her purse, paled at the number, and ignored the call.

Grace and Phoebe, still horrified by their mother's news, entered the log cabin. A welcoming blast of cool air greeted the sisters, and the smell of age and leather assailed their senses. Leather products, guns and ammo, china and glassware, dolls and toys, furniture, knick-knacks, and jewelry each dominated a particular part of the store. Each section then was divided by the time period and price.

Grace packed away her anger for another day. She was becoming an expert at storing her emotions into the hidey-holes of her heart. *Sooner or later*, Grace thought as she studied the items in front of her, *I'll be out of places to stuff my feelings. Some will have to come out.* She silently prayed that it wouldn't destroy her.

"Come on, Grace, let's look around!" At Phoebe's urging, Grace started to wander the orderly and efficient little store, looking for items she just had to have. Several "Holy craps", "How cutes", and "You gotta look at this" later, Grace met up with Poebe, who was admiring a walnut buffet and matching china hutch, both in the Victorian style they were looking for. The expensive price tag did nothing to dash their hopes of these two pieces eventually calling their bed and breakfast home.

"Can I help you?"

Grace and Phoebe turned at being addressed and looked down. A plump and cheery-looking looking woman beamed up at them with an endearing smile, showing off slightly discolored but straight teeth. Graying hair framed a face full of wrinkles from sun and smiles. Creases crinkled around her aquamarine eyes and freckles adorned her nose and cheekbones.

Grace instantly liked her and extended her hand. "My name's Grace Macintyre, and this is my sister, Phoebe Wallace. We just bought the old house on the hill two miles east of town."

"My name's Annie, and as you can probably guess, I am the owner and the sole employee." Annie peered up at the two women. "So, you're the two lovely ladies that bought the old Hamlin place. You two do look familiar." The short woman tapped her index finger on her bottom lip. "Your names sound familiar, too. Humpf. Well, must be a sign of old age. I once knew little girls with your names, but that would just be impossible, wouldn't it?" Grace opened her mouth to respond, but Annie had waddled off excitedly. Grace glanced at Phoebe. Phoebe shrugged her shoulders.

Annie soon came back huffing and puffing. "Looky what I have!" She brandished the picture.

Grace and Phoebe looked at the picture and froze. Grace was the first to find her voice. "That's us!" In the faded photograph, a little Grace and Phoebe dressed in what looked like matching brand-new dresses sat in front of a flower garden. Grace had an arm protectively around Phoebe's shoulders. Neither of them was smiling.

"Oh my." Before the girls could react, Annie crushed them both to her. "I can't believe you are standing here right in front of me after all these years! You two were

45

never far from my thoughts or prayers. I often wonder what happened to you two."

"How did you get a picture of us?" Grace asked before Annie could catch her breath and start chattering again.

"Well, after that nasty man was killed in a shootout with your daddy, I volunteered to take you girls in 'til all the bureaucratic red tape was finished. I was a social worker at the time and got to keep you blessed children for two days. Your daddy wouldn't let you out of his sight for long, but he trusted me. I bought you those dresses." Annie brushed a stray tear off her cheek. "Even though I only had you for a short time, you two stole my heart. Such sweet little things. I just still can't believe you're standing right in front of me after all this time!" Annie cocked her head to the side. "Why did you come back?"

"Let's just say we have some skeletons in our closet that need to be cleared away. We figured we'd start at the beginning." Grace, usually not so open in her feelings, felt an instant kinship with Annie. "Our father was murdered a year ago."

Annie's face fell and, for the first time, was struck speechless. "Oh, my dears!" Again she pulled them to her. Phoebe raised an eyebrow at Grace. Grace looked down on the top of Annie's head. It was certainly awkward having this stranger murmur comforting words into their chests.

Finally Annie released them. "I'm so sorry about your father. He was a good man." Annie wiped her eyes. "So, you two are trying to rebuild your lives, yes?" At their nods, Annie smiled. "Well, how can I help you do that?"

"We need to furnish and decorate the house." Phoebe pulled a sucker from her purse. "We'd like to keep it in the Victorian style as much as possible."

46

"Perfect!" Annie beamed. "I'm glad you are looking into that style. The old Hamlin place just wouldn't be the same. Can you believe the other owners, a husband and wife, were going to turn it into a cowboy retreat! 'Lord, have mercy on my soul', I prayed when I found out about it. Almost seems like Providence took over when the husband and the superintendent of the school got to liking each other!" Annie looked lovingly at the china hutch. "This style has always been one of my personal favorites, so I try to keep quite a bit of that style in stock. Right now, however, these are my only two pieces of furniture. If you look at the glassware and plates, though, I do have plenty of those in the style you're looking at."

"Thank you," Grace smiled at Annie, "for your help now and for your help so long ago. I'm sure you were a little ray of sunshine for both Phoebe and me."

"I tried my best, my dear, but you two were the little rays of sunshine for me." Annie reached for their hands. "I'm so glad you are here, now. If you need anything you let me know. Annie will fix you up!"

"We are so glad we found someone here you knows us!" Phoebe exclaimed as she clasped Annie's proffered hand. "But we'd really appreciate it if we could keep our identity a little secret for a while; we don't want…"

Before Phoebe could finish her statement, the sound of a slamming back door and random curses emanated from the back of the store. What sounded like file cabinets being opened and shut with violence peppered the once calm interior of the store.

Annie gave an apologetic shrug and a smile. "That'd be my husband. I don't suppose you'd remember him. He keeps an office in the back of the store." She cringed at an especially crude word. "He tends to get a little excited sometimes."

Grace and Phoebe glanced at one another. They had heard that voice before, but where?

Mr. Wisel yanked open the door leading into the store and peered around it. "Pookey-pants, have you seen my..." His bottom jaw dropped at seeing Grace and Phoebe towering over his wife. "Holy balls and buckshot! How did you find me? You signed the papers. There's no going back on the contract. No refunds!"

For a moment Grace studied Mr. Wisel. His shirt, a faded and worn green polo, barely contained his protruding belly. A perfect outline of his bellybutton and perky man boobs gave evidence of one too many frosted doughnuts. In fact, remnants of powdered sugar clung to his ample bosom. Two fat-creased knees peeked out between the bottom of a pair of khaki shorts and the tops of white knee socks. A pair of dusty black shoes completed the ensemble.

"Looking good Mr. Wisel," Grace stated with a straight face.

Mr. Wisel actually looked down and began preening. "Well, it's not much, but..." he paused abruptly and began feverishly wiping away the powdered sugar.

"It's too late, dear; I've already seen the sugar. You promised me you'd cut back on the doughnuts in the mornings."

Mr. Wisel studied the toes of his shoes. "Well, it was just one..." at a look from his wife he amended his statement, "or two. That's all, I swear. Just two."

Annie sniffed in her husband's general direction. "Dear, have you been smoking again?"

Mr. Wisel studied the dust on his shoes. "No. I had to run into the bar for a...diet Coke...and well...you know...people are smoking in there so..."

Grace wondered at Annie's inability to see the clear outline of a pack of cigarettes bulging from the left front pocket. "Okay, dear, you know I just want you to be around for a long time. Don't be dying on me and leaving me to find a bet...different man."

Grace and Phoebe watched this exchange between man and wife with confusion. Grace leaned over and whispered, "How can this woman put up with that man and not kill him?"

Phoebe shrugged. "Maybe she likes his hairy bellybutton and knee socks."

Annie turned back to Grace and Phoebe. "Richard can sometimes be a little rough around the edges, but he doesn't mean any harm." She turned again to her husband. "Richard, you shouldn't scare these girls so. Do you remember...?" At Grace's loud cough, Annie looked at her and caught the subtle shake of Grace's head. "Nothing, dear. These girls are just potential customers of mine. Be a gentleman."

Grace smiled at Richard. "So, Dick..."

"It's Richard." He scowled, caught his wife's head shake, and forced a smile. "How's the house coming?"

"The house is coming along just fine, thank you. We got Dominick Carson getting us some estimates." Grace glanced at her watch. "Well, we've gotta get going."

Grace and Phoebe shook Annie's hand and promised to come back. With a half-hearted wave to Richard, they nearly ran for the exit. As the door slowly shut behind them, they heard Annie scolding Richard for such poor behavior and asking if he were raised by a pack of wolves. They didn't get Richard's reply, but Grace would've placed money on the possibility that he was.

Phoebe jumped in the truck cab and instantly jumped back out. "Hot!" She gingerly touched the back of her thighs. "Man, that sucked bad!"

Grace, choking on her laughter, leaned over the passenger seat, opened the glove compartment, grabbed a wad of napkins and spread them on the seat. "There, now you won't burn your butt."

Phoebe very carefully sat on the spread out Dairy Queen napkins. "I always knew Dairy Queen would go straight to my hinder."

Grace chuckled. "This really was an enlightening trip. Can you believe Mrs. Dickie Weasel is the lady who watched us? I don't remember her, just as I don't remember anything from those few horrible days, but still…it's pretty cool to meet her. She seems really nice. I like her."

"I don't see how she's married to such a moron. Maybe there's one small redeeming quality. I mean there's got to be something about him because Annie seems to like him, and as you said, she seems normal."

"Key word is *seems*. She's a little flighty. Maybe she stuffs her pets after they die." Grace stopped at the only stoplight in town. "But who am I to judge?"

A black, pimped-out Camaro pulled up next to Grace and Phoebe in the turning lane. Spinner rims spun around, giving the illusion that the wheels were still turning and the silhouette of a naked woman was plastered on each side of the back window. Bass from the invisible speakers tucked away in the trunk caused things, including Grace and Phoebe, to vibrate. Black-tinted windows hid the passengers from view, but Grace guessed that there'd be a pair of fuzzy dice hanging from the rearview mirror and maybe a graduation tassel from four years ago.

The passenger window rolled down, and a boy who was trying very hard to look like a homie from the hood leaned out and shouted. "Hey, baby, wanna be with a man?"

Grace smiled sweetly. "Sure, let me find one first."

Several seconds lapsed before for the insult hit home. The boy scowled and flipped Grace the bird. "Bitch!"

"You kiss your mamma with that mouth or just your other homies?" Grace smiled politely.

Another homeboy with a cowboy hat and a handle bar mustache stuck his head out of the rear passenger window. Before he could say anything, however, the light turned green and the car roared off, causing the young cowboy homie's head to whiplash against the window jam. Grace and Phoebe laughed until tears streamed down their faces.

Grace pulled into the parking lot of the 7-Eleven. Putting the truck in park, she laid her head on the steering wheel and sniffled back tears of laughter. Catching her breath, she leaned her head back against the head rest and glanced at Phoebe who was dabbing her eyes with a napkin. "I haven't laughed that hard in a long time. Did you see Cheech's head when the car took off?" Stifling another giggle, Grace grabbed some cash out of her purse. "Do you want anything?"

"Diet Coke, please."

Bells jingled when Grace entered the gas station. Smells of freshly-made pizza caused Grace's mouth to water. Trying desperately to ignore the pizza, Grace grabbed two Diet Cokes, a Snickers bar, and a package of Mike and Ikes.

"Screw it!" Grace grabbed a personal size extra cheese pizza on her way to the cash register.

"Hungry?"

Grace whirled around, smacked into pectoral muscle, and shrieked. Looking up she stared into the melted chocolate eyes of Dominick. A tiny smile played on his lips as he studied her.

51

Embarrassed, Grace roughly pushed off, planted herself a couple of feet away, and hugged her snack food to her chest. "You shouldn't sneak up on a person. It's rude."

Dominick's tiny smile spread into a wide grin of amusement. "I saw your truck outside and thought I'd drop off the estimate that I did for you." He made a grab for the pizza. "You don't want to eat this, considering who made it."

Grace glanced back to the revolving rack of hot and bubbly pizza. Nothing icky there. Peering past the rack of cheesy, gooey goodness, Grace spotted a boy with hair as greasy as the slick of oil on top of a slab of pepperoni. *Maybe he wears a hat*, Grace thought. And then the boy picked his nose, studied the green object on his finger, and ate it.

Grace fought the urge to throw up and just gagged. Dominick made a grab for the rest of the snack food. "Here, let me hold this for you."

Grace nodded and unwillingly stared at the greasy-haired boy going to town on the endless booger buffet. Finally forcing her eyes away from the debacle, she reached for her snack food. "I can take this now. Thanks for the advice on the pizza purchasing. I don't like boogers with extra cheese."

Dominick grinned and accompanied her to the cash register. He gave a brief head nod to the clerk and asked him to put Grace's purchases on his charge account.

Grace interrupted him. "Oh, no. I can get my own."

"My treat. Besides, you can consider this our first date. A guy always pays on the first date." He picked the paper sack off the counter and walked out the door with Grace directly on his heels.

"Date?" Grace stumbled and caught herself by placing her hands squarely on his butt.

"Whoa now, little missy, I don't usually get to second base on the first date." Dominick turned to face her, seeming to enjoy the blush that crept up her neck and face.

Grace turned five shades of red, glared at Phoebe who could be heard howling with laughter from inside the truck, and then avoided all eye contact with Dominick. "I tripped, you see...and well...I kind of ran into your...your..."

"Butt?"

"Yeah, your butt." Grace licked her lips and forced herself to look directly in his eyes. "It was by accident, and it won't happen again."

The tiny smiled played on his lips. "That's too bad."

Grace huffed, tore the bag out of Dominick's arms, and stomped to the driver's side of the truck. Climbing into the truck, her toe caught on the running board. Blushing again she glared at Dominick, daring him to say a word.

Grace tore out of the parking lot. "Jerk!"

Phoebe dried her eyes and sucked in a shaky breath. "I don't think you think he's a jerk." Phoebe then broke out into a little song to the tune of "La Cucaracha." "I think you like him, I think you want him, you want to date him, you want to squeeze him..."

"Enough!" Grace shook her head. "Where do you come up with this stuff, anyway?"

Phoebe tapped her temple. "It would stun you to know how much is really going on up here. My happy meal isn't missing any fries."

"Yeah, right."

Phoebe fanned herself. "Next time it's my turn; you always get to do the fun things."

Dominick watched the truck round the corner and disappear. With a shake of his head he climbed into his own truck. It had been a long time since any woman made him feel this way. The words of Forrest Gump ran through his head. "Life is like a box of chocolates; you never know what you're going to get." Dominick smiled. Somehow he had the strange feeling that Grace was very much like a box of chocolates. And lucky for him, he loved chocolate.

He turned right off Main and drove down Orchard Avenue. He knew this street like the back of his hand. It had been his home before he'd run away to make something of himself. Whether or not he succeeded was still up for debate. He'd done what he had set out to do, see the world. Maybe he'd seen too much, done too much. With amazing mental will, he locked his ghosts away for the time being. For now, he needed to concentrate on the one good thing he did bring back home.

As he pulled into his driveway, his heart grew lighter at the sight of a little girl with blonde pigtails who came running down the porch steps. With a squeal of delight she threw herself into Dominick's waiting arms. "Daddy!"

Chapter Five

Conversation stopped as the girls bounced over the wash-boarded gravel road to the old house. Grace looked longingly at her box of Mike and Ikes, but knew better than to try to eat and drive at the same time. She tore her eyes off the box of candy and concentrated on driving. The landscape outside her driver's window and windshield bumped along with a jarring rhythm. They passed a pasture where cattle grazed and dozed in the hazy summer heat. Several cows looked up at the old pickup shuddering down the road, but for the most part, they were seemingly oblivious to the world of humans.

"This place reminds me of the ranch, in a way. I wish I had the strength to go back," Phoebe murmured.

Grace studied the road ahead of her. Even after a year, the pain of their father's death still hummed incessantly. Grace ignored the tear tracking down her face. She'd faced her demons before, but the memory of her father's lifeless body flung across Scout's saddle as the wild-eyed horse galloped into the safety of its familiar corral haunted her. "I just don't understand what happened, Pheebs. I mean what coward would shoot a man in the forehead and then go through the trouble of putting him back on Scout, knowing the horse would take him back home to the ranch?"

Phoebe gripped the armrest of the truck. "I talked to Detective Landers before moving here. There were no new leads. The case has gone cold, Grace. It sickens me to think that the person who killed Dad is out there somewhere."

"But who?" Grace's knuckles turned white as she gripped the steering wheel harder.

Phoebe didn't answer, and Grace watched as a tumbleweed twisted and tumbled over the prairie. Her father had often told her that tumbleweeds were the souls of long gone cowboys, still searching for fulfillment and purpose. She smiled a little as she imagined her father's soul riding one of those twisted weeds as if it were a bucking bronco.

The battered truck pulled into the driveway of the old house, and the two women sat for a minute looking at the decrepit building. Grace's eyes were drawn to a dancing tumbleweed, somersaulting across the prairie. Could a tumbleweed be the soul of someone still living yet not living? Grace shook her head at the foolish notion; all she knew is that she felt for the unfortunate weed with no direction of its own; it was simply pushed and driven where the wind willed. Her life was the same: people telling her what to do, when to do it, and who to do it with. Her mother's face and her pointed finger wagging with disdain flashed before Grace's eyes. Nothing she'd ever done had been good enough. Her father had been the only one to truly understand her and her need for freedom. A tear traced down her face and plopped onto her lap. Her heart squeezed at the memory of her father, and she fought the urge to weep. If only her Heavenly Father didn't seem so far away.

"This house is just so sad," Phoebe stated as she opened the door and jumped out. "Because it's day time and ghosts don't wander around during the day, we should take a look in the attic. Maybe we'll find…"

"Squirrel babies."

"Right. Always dangerous." Phoebe slammed the door shut with her foot. "Maybe we can have Carpenter Hottie fetch the squirrel babies for you."

"Are you kidding? I don't want him thinking I'm a loser."

"Too late. Besides, I thought you didn't care what he thought of you."

Grace hopped out and slammed the driver's door shut. "You suck."

"Sticks and stones, my friend, sticks and stones."

Grace huffed and stomped up the porch steps and stopped dead in her tracks. With a strained whisper she called for Phoebe. "Pheebs. Slowly and carefully get over here. Now!"

Phoebe crept up beside Grace and came to a quick halt. "Holy crap!" she whispered, "is that what I think it is?"

A mamma skunk and her little babies lay curled up in the corner of the porch. Snoozing away the late afternoon, the mamma skunk seemed oblivious to the presence of the two shocked women.

With baited breath, Grace and Phoebe slowly backed away. Within several feet of the pickup they broke out in a run and hurled themselves in the pickup. Grace slammed the truck into drive and barreled out of the driveway in the direction of town and safety.

That evening, Grace and Phoebe sat tucked up in their hotel room, munching on chips, drinking Miller Lite, and weeping over the movie *Beaches*.

"That is about the saddest movie ever made," Grace blubbered through a tissue.

Phoebe dabbed her eyes, bunched up the twice-used tissue, and chucked it at the television screen. "Stupid movie."

Grace hiccupped through her tears. "Ow! Great, now I have the hiccups. Today has just been the pinnacle of all days, especially with the addition of the skunk mom and her children. If only every day were this good."

"Hey, I think the babies were kind of cute. It's not their fault they're smelly. Just think of Peter from the fifth grade. He smelled."

"Yeah, like pee after you've eaten asparagus. And he certainly wasn't as cute as those skunk babies." Grace tapped her chin and thought for a second. "Odd, I never saw him eat any asparagus."

"I think we need a vacation," Phoebe suggested as she made her way to the sink. Placing a band of toothpaste on her toothbrush, she proceeded to talk, "I mean we've only been at this for three days and look at us; we're worn out. I don't know how much more of this I can take."

Grace flopped onto her back and studied the estimate Dominick had given her. "According to this, Pheebs, we might be able to afford Dominick and his crew doing the majority of the work. Besides the minor stuff that we're doing anyway, there's not much more we're capable of doing."

Phoebe paused brushing and spoke through the foamy toothpaste in her mouth. "True. How much did Dominick estimate again?"

"One hundred grand. Seems like a lot of money, but look at what we bought the house for and the things that need to be completed, and it's not such a huge number after all."

Phoebe spit, rinsed, and gargled. "You also have to add the benefit of having Carpenter Hottie around."

Grace threw a wadded up tissue at Phoebe. "Enough with the Carpenter Hottie thing! I'm not even interested in him anyway."

"Whatever." Phoebe bounded to bed and snuggled under the covers. Phoebe's smile faded when she glanced at Grace's face. "Something's bothering you. What is it?"

"Andrew Carnegie. There's just something about him." Grace tapped her front tooth with a fingernail. "Dominick called earlier and stated that Andrew had called him."

Phoebe chewed on her bottom lip. "Okay. So? If the guy doesn't work out, just have Dominick fire him, right? No fuss, no muss. Besides, I like him. He's cute."

Grace shuffled to the sink and began getting ready for bed. "Yeah. So were those baby skunks, and I don't see you offering to snuggle with one."

"That's totally different," Phoebe mumbled from under the covers.

Grace snorted and finished brushing her teeth. The mystery nagged at her and no matter what she did, she couldn't get Andrew out of her mind. She raked a brush through her hair and tucked herself into bed. After saying goodnight to Phoebe, Grace rolled over and watched the curtains dance in the cool air from the air conditioning unit. She just needed to think and pray. *Pray?* Grace sighed. When was the last time she'd prayed for real? The day she witnessed her husband lace her yogurt. No matter how much she tried, her prayers seemed forced. Something done out of habit rather than love. Grace punched her pillow into a relatively comfortable shape. It was as if God and she were in a boxing ring. She danced and sparred, boxing left and right, yelling for God to fight, to defend himself. If only he'd take a swing. At least she'd know he wasn't just a figment of her imagination.

Grace brushed away a stray tear. She was tired of crying! With a huff, Grace rolled over and closed her eyes.

She dreamt of her father. She could see it. She tried covering her eyes as a blurred figure put the gun to her father's head and pulled the trigger. A scream tore out of her, and the figure turned toward her. With slow, deliberate paces, he closed the distance. Frozen, Grace watched as the same gun used to murder her beloved father aimed for her head.

With a jolt, Grace's eyes opened and stared at the blinking red light on the smoke detector. Gasping for air, Grace raked a shaky hand through her sweaty hair. *What was that all about?* Grace gripped the sheets around her and fought to erase the insane images from her head. She eased back on her pillows and willed the morning to come soon.

Thursday morning dawned with a vengeance. The sun bore down on the land and waves of heat shivered in the air. Grace and Phoebe melted to the cheap vinyl seats of the old truck the instant they jumped in.

"Son of a baby duck!" Grace slammed the key into the ignition and turned. The old truck roared to life and hot air spewed out of the vents. The temperature lever was already as far in the blue as it could get, and the fan lever was on high blast. "Seriously?" Grace smacked the dashboard.

"Interesting swear word. You still haunted by what Father McNally told you about swearing?" Phoebe pulled down the mirror and checked her makeup.

"Hey, I just don't want God to cry every time I swear. And that makeup is gonna melt right off your face."

"Jeez, what crawled up your butt and died? Besides, don't you remember who's going to be at the house today? Carpenter Hottie and his crew of miscellaneous hotties."

Grace maneuvered the old truck out of the Super 8 parking lot and motored down the highway. "Sorry. I had this awful dream last night, and I can't shake it." Grace turned on to the gravel. "How do you know he has hotties working for him?"

Phoebe simply looked at her as if Grace had just sprouted ten heads.

"Enough said." Grace pulled into the driveway leading to the old house. Even at this distance she could see men mill around the house. "This oughta be fun."

Several heads turned as Grace and Phoebe parked in front of the house. "Sorry to disappoint you, Pheebs, but there doesn't seem to be too many hotties walking around our property."

Phoebe hid her disappointment. "Good, wouldn't want there to be any distractions while I'm working." Phoebe suddenly burst into a silly grin. "Look! It's Andrew."

Grace grabbed Phoebe's hand. "Be careful, please. We only just met him, and I can't shake..."

"I'm not a child, Grace. I am twenty-seven and totally capable of handling myself, thank you very much!"

Grace sighed. "Sorry. I trust your judgment." Resigning herself to leaving Phoebe alone, she dealt with another pressing issue. "You think the skunks are still around, waiting for us to return?"

"I'm assuming the skunk family has vacated the premises beings the men don't seem overly concerned."

"Your mind's a steal trap, isn't it, Pheebs."

"That was an insult, wasn't it?"

Grace rolled her eyes and leaped out of the pickup. She bit her tongue as she watched Phoebe saunter up to Andrew. His smile was nothing but shy and kind. Telling herself to relax, she glanced around. She saw men on the roof, men throwing things out the top story windows and men working on the wraparound porch. Men were everywhere, but the one she wanted to see couldn't be found.

"Looking for me?"

Grace shrieked and jumped. "Dang it! You really need to quit sneaking up on me. Like I said yesterday, it's rude."

"I think I will keep you and name you Spitfire." That irritating yet captivating little smile played on his lips. "You're fun to have around."

Grace ignored his comment. "What's on the agenda for today?"

"We're ripping out all the rotted wood and debris. I've got some men ripping off the old shingles." He glanced at Grace, and she began to fidget under his gaze. He finally broke eye contact and gestured to the home. "You'll have to get me your color choices so we can get shingles that will complement those colors."

"Phoebe and I weren't sure what we wanted for colors on the outside of the house."

Dominick studied the house for a moment and looked around at the landscape. "If it were my house, I'd use a buttercup yellow for the house, red for the new window shutters and white for the rest of the trim. It would complement the green hills and tree grove to the back of the house, and then during the winter it'd feel warm and cozy against the drab landscape."

Grace saw it in her mind and loved it. Hiding her enthusiasm, however, she simply smiled and stated she'd have to consult Phoebe. Phoebe joined the two, and they talked for a few minutes discussing the plans for the day and future needs.

"The first thing you'll want to do, ladies, is put a security and fire alarm system in. There are a couple of hooligans in this town, and we don't want this place vandalized."

Grace's mind instantly rewound to her little run in with the homies in the black Camaro. "Yeah, that might not be a bad idea," Grace stated out load.

"I can have my men get right on that. We'll also hook it up where the alarms, both security and fire, will immediately alert both the police and fire department. Also, I thought that you guys might be a little tired of staying at the hotel, so I put your two bedrooms and the kitchen as top priorities."

Dominick placed his hands in his back pockets and rocked back on forth on his heels studying Grace. "Oh, and by the way, one of my men told me there's some old stuff up in the attic. You might want to take a look through it, see what you want to keep, and throw the rest." He grinned. "He also told me that he found fresh footprints in the dust up there."

Grace blushed and studied the red Kansas dirt on her tennis shoes. "Well, I went up there to check things out, and I didn't look around much because..." Grace faltered and began digging her toe into the dirt. At a prompting hand gesture from Dominick, Grace sucked in a breath. "There were squirrel babies up there."

"I hear that squirrel babies are very vicious this time of year."

"Oooohhhh!" Grace clenched her fists at her sides and stamped her foot.

"Well, ladies, if you need me I'll be around." Dominick tipped his imaginary hat and walked off in the direction of a group of his men. Phoebe watched him leave and grinned at Grace.

Grace rolled her eyes. "It's not that good."

"Yeah, right," Phoebe countered as they made their way to the house and began working again.

"What did Andrew say to you?" Grace asked as they entered the parlor.

"Oh, nothing much. He seems very shy and awkward around girls. I think I even made him blush."

"What did you say?"

"Nothing. I just said it'd be nice to have such a handsome cowboy on the premises." Phoebe snorted and stuck her tongue out. "Don't you feel foolish now? You and your feelings."

Dominick lost himself in his work. Occasionally he heard Grace's laughter float down the old hallway. Last night as he'd tucked his little Lilly into bed and turned on her Tinkerbell nightlight, his mind had turned to Grace. He knew it was ludicrous. He'd only known her for a few days. Now seeing her today did nothing to ease his feelings. As if out of nowhere, the image of his first wife slammed into his mind. Her death still stung his heart. What hurt most was the fact that she'd never see their daughter grow up. Never see her get married. Dominick quickly stemmed the torrential thoughts. They did nobody any good. Knowing he needed to get to work, he powered on the reciprocating saw and allowed the noise and power of the tool to soothe him.

Grace bent her mind to the task at hand: finish ripping apart the parlor. But her eyes were constantly studying the stairs. Tired of pretending to work, Grace glanced tentatively at the staircase, looked to make sure no one saw her, and climbed the wooden staircase. Not knowing what to expect after her initial reaction to the room, Grace hesitantly opened the door to the old nursery.

Nothing had changed. The same old stuffiness and heat poured out at her.

Refusing to dwell on "what ifs," Grace quietly left, closing the door softly after her. She made her way to the attic and ascended into the hot, stale air. Cobwebs clung to the exposed rafters, and the sound of scurrying nearly sent Grace screaming out of the encroached space. Biting her lip, she entered farther and moved carefully, avoiding the low-hanging rafters, toward a cluttered pile of assorted dusty and rotting things.

An old kid's tricycle, some old sports equipment, and some faded and torn children's books were placed to the side. Looking in vain for a clean place to sit, Grace sighed and plopped herself down on the dusty floorboards. A cloud of dust erupted around her. Coughing and waving a hand in front of her face, Grace wriggled her butt to find a comfortable spot. Finding none, she dove into the pile with reigned anticipation.

Old newspapers ranging from the 1940's on up nearly crumbled in her hands, so Grace threw them to the side. Forcing herself to ignore the patter of tiny, claw-tipped feet around her, she carefully placed the body of a porcelain doll with a missing arm to the side. Blonde curly hair covered with the dust of time hung limply around a smudged white cherub face. Blue glass eyes stared unseeing at the world around, and its once pink frilly dress was demoted to a moth-eaten rag. Grace felt a tug of pity for this small doll. Where was the girl it once belonged to? Had she grown up and abandoned it, just as she'd probably abandoned her hair ribbons and imaginary friends?

Grace dug farther in the clutter. An old pipe clattered to the floor. Grace sniffed it. Whatever was smoked last still lingered after all this time. She sat that next to the one-armed doll and continued searching. Some hair pins, empty hat boxes, and moth-eaten clothes later, Grace wiped the sweat from her forehead. Small dark stains spread under her armpits and down her back. The oppressive heat bore down on Grace, and she knew the squirrel babies huddled in some corner, concocting a plan to eat her alive.

Not able to take it anymore, she nearly ran out of the attic and down the steps. Catching her breath and warily looking behind her for any trailing squirrel babies, she began working on the parlor again. After several minutes of ripping and pitching, a pile of wood and boards lay in a dusty pile at Grace's feet. With hands on her hips, Grace studied the mess.

"How's it going?"

Grace wiped a filthy hand across her forehead and turned to face Dominick. "Nothing like a little demolition to make my heart sing."

Dominick grinned and kicked at the old wood. "That's good." He winked. "I like my women dirty."

Grace stammered and cursed the blush she knew had spread across her face. She bristled at the look of triumph on his face and refused to look any lower than his shoulder blades when he turned to leave. Grace scowled at his retreating form.

"I saw that."

"What! How did…?" Grace stared flabbergasted as Dominick turned, gave an exasperating grin, and turned the corner.

Grace muttered to herself and kicked at an innocent piece of wood. "Moron."

"Did you call my name?" Phoebe asked from the dining room.

Grace smiled and shook her head in amusement. She walked in the direction of her sister and found her sitting cross-legged on the floor covered with dust and wallpaper shrapnel. Phoebe looked up and made a face.

Grace sat down next to Phoebe. "You look like poo. Glad you wore mascara now, huh?"

"You don't look any better." At Phoebe's comment, Grace glanced down at herself and realized that Phoebe was correct. Dust and dirt clung to her sweaty legs, and she could only assume that her face looked the same.

"Is my face as bad as I think it is?"

Phoebe bit her lip and looked Grace over. She clucked her tongue as she eyed Grace's askew ponytail, dirty shorts and ripped tank top, and smudges of dirt adorning every visible layer of skin. "You're not looking your best today. Haven't spoken with anyone hot recently, have you?"

"Well, if you consider Dominick hot, then…"

"You're in big trouble, sister. You're going to have to do some serious damage control the next couple of days." Phoebe squinted out of a red eye dripping with mascara runs. "This sucks! It's hotter than hell in this house, I've got mascara dripping everywhere, and my underwear is so wet it feels as if I peed myself."

The ladies turned at a roar of laughter. Several men stood in the threshold, laughing at Phoebe.

Phoebe planted a scowl on her face and scolded, "It's rude to eavesdrop."

The men left with another bark of laughter, and Phoebe groaned with humiliation. "Why me?"

Grace patted her back. "If it makes you feel any better, it is lunch time."

While Grace and Phoebe sat themselves on the front step of the veranda and munched on ham salad sandwiches and pickles, Leo took his own lunch break. He never knew how fun this could be. He obviously couldn't kill them 'til his fun had run out. With a newfound vigor, he bit into his sandwich and munched happily to the plan he'd hatched. Just like a spider, he reminded himself. Reel them in, slowly, almost tenderly, and then, strike. It was almost too much to bear. Phoebe telling him he was a cute cowboy. He couldn't wait to hear what she'd say seconds before he slit her throat like the pig she was.

Grace threw her sandwich baggie into her lunchbox. "I need a walk." She actually needed to get away from people, but saying that would only worry Phoebe.

"All right. Wake me up when you get back. I'm gonna take a ten minute nap."

Grace made her way to the tree belt hugging the back of the property. On a whim, Grace decided to investigate the flickering light she saw the other day. With careful steps, Grace made her way to the spot where she thought she'd seen it. Nothing.

"Who am I kidding?" Grace gesticulated to the rustling leaves. "I wouldn't know what to look for if a herd of elephants tromped through this." After taking a second look, Grace huffed out a breath and made her way back out of the mini-woods. Over the sound of her own feet, she never heard the muffled steps retreating farther into the trees.

Coming out of the trees, she stopped before the clear pond which rested underneath the leaf-laden boughs. Grace closed her eyes and for several minutes imagined a beautiful little sitting area, maybe with a gazebo. It could become her sanctuary. She opened her eyes and sighed; some serious landscaping would have to be done first. Her fingers itched to get started. But for now, she needed some down time, time to think and pray.

Grace sat against an old tree and rested her head against its gnarly and knotted bark. Closing her eyes to painful memories, she heard the distant rumble of farm equipment from the neighbors down the road and the even closer and more invasive slight buzzing of bees. Grace peeked open an eye to see how close the danger was. Not seeing anything, she tried to relax. She told herself she didn't need sleep but her eyes closed, and before she knew it, she was thrown into a nightmare.

Something warm and strong touched Grace's leg. She bolted upright, opened her eyes, and stared into Dominick's face. She could feel the heat of his hand on her leg. Very aware of their closeness and of his touch, Grace's heart pumped and her breathing shallowed. Grace sat up a little bit and tried shaking off her dream.

Dominick studied her face. Her luminous green eyes were filled with terror and sweat beaded on her paled face. "You were thrashing in your sleep and crying out. Are you okay?"

Grace jerked herself up, wiped her face with her hands, and put some distance between them. "I'm fine...I was just..."

Grace paused and pushed a palm to her beating forehead. "I'm fine."

Dominick still looked concerned. "Are you sure?"

Grace simply nodded her head, wishing he'd go away. As if he read her mood, Dominick gave a supporting smile and walked away toward the house, leaving her to compose herself.

Grace leaned against the tree and breathed deeply. The same dream she'd had before ripped through her again. *Dang it all!* Grace exhaled sharply. Why these dreams all of a sudden? With shaky movements, Grace got to her feet and walked back to the house.

"Grace." Phoebe stepped breathlessly out the back door and met her halfway. "I've been trying to find you! Let's run away and never come back. I hear the Bahamas are really lovely this time of year."

"What's wrong?"

Phoebe rolled her eyes and grabbed Grace's arm. "It's the Wisels. I guess Annie's okay. She's quirky, but she brought food...cookies!" Phoebe's eyes glassed over.

"You're beginning to drool."

Phoebe sucked in her excess saliva. "Sorry. I went to my happy place for a bit. Anyhoo, where was I? Oh, yeah. It's Dickie I can't stand. He always stares at my boobs." Phoebe glanced down at her chest. "I know they're pretty and all, but I don't want *him* checking me out."

"Look on the bright side; at least you have boobs worth looking at." Grace looked down at hers and wished upon the same breast star as she'd done since puberty. *Stupid star, it probably didn't exist anyway.* Grace huffed and followed Phoebe in the house.

"Oh my, girls! You look so...so...terrible." Annie cringed and began taking out a handkerchief stuffed securely in her cleavage. Both Grace and Phoebe instantly declined the offer. Annie shoved the handkerchief back in between her boobs. "I told Richard that we should come and check on you girls. Besides, I really wanted to snoop around a bit."

Grace and Phoebe glanced at the picnic basket smelling of chocolate chip cookies placed on the floor. "Feel free to snoop wherever you wish."

Annie, wearing white peddle-pushers and a fuchsia tank top, waddled off, oohing and ahhing. Richard, in his standard khaki shorts, knee-high socks, and stretched polo shirt, gave a curt nod toward the girls with a longer than

70

necessary stare at Phoebe's chest and followed dutifully after his wife.

Grace jumped toward the basket, tore the red checkered cloth off the top, and nabbed a cookie. "Mmmm. This is heaven." She handed Phoebe a cookie and grabbed another for herself.

Phoebe's eyes rolled in ecstasy. With a mouthful of one cookie, Phoebe snatched another and proceeded to stuff the second one in her mouth, all the while trying to express her gratitude for the chef.

Grace finished her third cookie and contemplated having a fourth. She pinched at her miniscule love handles. Yup, she had room. With a furtive glance around, Grace snatched a fourth cookie and shoved it in her mouth.

"I saw that," Phoebe mumbled around mashed cookie. She glared at her sister's slender waist. "I hate you."

Grace rolled her eyes. "Whatever." Catching sight of Dominick, she held up a finger to stop Phoebe from replying with a middle school comeback. "I need to speak with the carpenter about paint selection, so I can't join your pity party right now. I'll take a rain check, however." Grace scooted off in the direction of Dominick and left Phoebe unattended with the basket of cookies.

Phoebe licked her lips and stepped away from the basket. "You can do this, Phoebe Wallace! Just step away from the basket of goodies. You are the cookie. Be the cookie." Phoebe's rousing speech did nothing for her self-control. With a sigh of defeat, she lunged for a cookie. "Ha-ha, my lovely. You are mine. All mine." Phoebe shoved the cookie in her mouth.

"Excuse me, but can you tell me where I could find Annie and Richard?" A slight southern drawl asked from behind Phoebe.

Phoebe gulped down the last of the crumbs and turned around. The man before her peered down at her with blue eyes shaded with light eyelashes. Darker eyebrows were pulled up in either amusement or disbelief. Blondish hair, cut short and spiked with gel, adorned the top of the man's square face. A Romanesque nose, strong cheekbones, a cleft chin, and a friendly smile completed the picture.

Cookie crumbs caught in her throat, and Phoebe tried unsuccessfully to clear it without sounding like a dying bullfrog. "Sorry. Crumbs." She swallowed and looked around for anything wet. Eyeing a bottle of soda on a work bench, Phoebe grabbed it, ignored the gesture of warning from the tall guy, and drank.

"What kind of soda is this?" Phoebe stated, eyeing the soda bottle as if it were poison.

The tall guy grabbed the bottle, turned it a certain way, and showed Phoebe the cigarette butts floating in the bottle. Phoebe stared incredulously at the little white filters bobbing up and down and gagged. The mystery man moved to the side as Phoebe continued gagging and spitting on the floor.

"Sick. Gross. Icky." Phoebe wiped her tongue with her shirt and fought the urge to gag again. "That's it!" Leaving the very confused man in her wake, Phoebe stomped off in search of the culprit.

"Is this yours?" Phoebe approached the first guy she found. Even though the man easily had two hundred pounds on her, he backed up and shook his head vigorously. Phoebe snorted and moved on down the line. After scaring half the construction crew, Phoebe found the vicious cigarette butt offender smoking outside the house. A new Pepsi bottle dangled aimlessly from the fingers of one hand while the other held the cigarette.

"This yours?" Phoebe demanded holding up the atrocious bottle.

A pug-nose man of about thirty-five met her gaze. His brown eyes didn't water with fear, and his bulky form didn't quiver at the sight of her. Maybe she was losing her authority. Phoebe strutted a little more and stuck out her chest a little further. The man clearly wasn't intimidated. He looked pleased. The ugly dude pulled his chapped lips back into an eat-crap-and-die smile. "Yeah. What of it?"

Phoebe gave her sweetest smile. "Oh, just thought I would return the contents of this bottle to its rightful owner." With a quick motion, Phoebe reached over the man's head, tipped the bottle upside down, and dumped the warm, sticky soda plus cigarette butts over the man's head. "There. Now I feel better."

Phoebe left the ugly man sputtering and cursing. Winding her way back to the foyer, Phoebe halted in surprise at the presence of the newcomer. "Oh, I'm so sorry. I thought you'd found them by now."

"Later, I wanted to find out the outcome of your little mission." The smile deepened and a dimple appeared in his right cheek. He glanced at the ugly guy attempting to clean himself off with ice-cold water from a nearby water jug. "Glad I didn't miss the finale."

Phoebe blushed. "Well, he had it coming. What was he thinking, leaving beverages lying around with icky things floating around in them? Disgusting!"

"Yes, I do agree that it is a travesty for a man to leave *his* pop bottle lying around. What is this world coming to?"

Phoebe's eyebrows shot up. "I'm sorry. I don't think I caught your name."

"Noah. Noah Wisel."

Phoebe tapped her lip in concentration. "Wisel. Wisel? The last name seems so familiar." Phoebe gave an apologetic look to the man towering over her. The epiphany finally hit her like a bursting fluorescent light bulb. "Holy…Are you their nephew, because I don't think they could…" Phoebe stopped herself when Noah started laughing.

Noah smiled and shook his head. "I'm their one and only attempt at increasing the human population."

Phoebe did her best to hide her surprise and extended her hand in greeting. "I'm Phoebe Wallace, co-owner of this future business. It's a pleasure to meet you."

Noah gripped her hand with warmth and strength. "The pleasure's all mine." He looked at the room they stood in. "This really is an amazing house. A lot of work though, huh?"

Phoebe nodded and offered him a cookie. "Yeah. Good thing we have Dominick. He's done so much already in such a short amount of time."

Noah accepted the cookie and bit into it with straight teeth. "Mom always did make a good cookie."

"So what do you do?"

"I'm the fire inspector and a member of the volunteer fire department. When I'm not doing that, I'm teaching high school history and coaching the football team." Noah smiled when he witnessed Phoebe's jaw drop. "What? Don't I look like a teacher?"

Phoebe blushed. "No, it just seems like a very busy schedule."

Noah finished off the cookie. "It has its moments." He glanced at his watch. "I've got to speak with Dominick really quick, and then I've got to head out. It was nice meeting you, Phoebe, and I hope to repeat the pleasure often." He smiled and sauntered off in search of Dominick.

Phoebe watched him leave and grabbed for an emergency cookie. Phoebe breathed deeply and made her way to the dining room.

Phoebe wasn't the only one watching him leave. Leo put down the crowbar he'd been using and studied Noah. He and that Dominick guy could certainly cramp his style. Oh, well, he thought as he smashed the crowbar in place. He'd just have to make time in his schedule for them.

Work sounds decreased as men began packing up for the day. Power tools were stored away and toolboxes slammed shut with metal clangs. Men's voices rose and a couple suggestions to go out for a drink echoed through the house.

Dominick stuck his head around the corner and paused. Both Grace and Phoebe were propped against the walls of the future study like Raggedy Ann dolls. His heart lurched as he studied Grace sitting in a pile of rubble with dirt smeared on every visible inch of her. A seed of hope he'd never dared to dream of seemed to land, kerplunk, in his chest. After the death of his wife, he knew he would never love again. Now, because of Grace, he was not too sure.

Dominick cleared his throat. "Grace, I'll go ahead and pick up the paint you wanted and have it here Monday morning. Let me know what you choose for the other rooms as well." He tipped his imaginary hat and smiled. "Have a good evening, ladies. Oh, and some of us are going to Willy's Tavern after this if you'd like to swing by."

Dominick turned to go and felt his heart thud in his chest. What would he do if she actually showed up?

Before the girls could respond, Dominick retreated, and they watched out the window as Dominick spoke to a couple of his men before roaring off in his pickup. Dominick's men soon piled into pickups, cars, and a few minivans and tore out of the gravel driveway on their way to the local watering hole.

Grace and Phoebe made their way through the house and witnessed the changes being made. Most of the old stuff either lay in discarded heaps on the floor or were tossed out the windows. Dust still lingered in the humid air, and the smell of sawdust tickled the women's noses.

With excitement bubbling over, Phoebe danced her happy dance. "This is it, Grace. This is really coming true. We're soon going to be in business."

Grace, excited and frightened at the prospect, smiled calmly. "Yes. This is it."

The two sisters exited the house and looked up at their two-story home. With only five days under their belts, Dominick's men had made a significant dent in the mess. Maybe God knew this is what she needed. She only hoped that this crazy idea came to fruition, and she and Phoebe could finally find closure.

Grace and Phoebe bounced off in the old truck toward town and stopped as Andrew's pickup came in the opposite direction. Grace put her window down as Andrew pulled over to stop next to her.

"Hey. You mind if I go back to the house. I forgot my wallet." Andrew smiled shyly and fiddled with the brim of his Stetson.

Grace bit her lip. "Sorry. The alarms are set. We can go back with you, if you wish."

"Don't be ridiculous, Grace!" Phoebe admonished from the passenger seat. Before Grace could react, Phoebe rattled off the security code. Ignoring the scathing look from Grace, Phoebe smiled at Andrew. "Hope you find it in that mess."

Andrew tipped the brim of his hat. "Thanks." Within seconds his face disappeared behind the tinted window. Looking in his rearview mirror, he watched the battered pickup make its way back to town. With a slow grin he pulled into the drive, waited until the dust settled, and pulled back out. The security code would come in handy, eventually. A bark of laughter echoed in the truck. Phoebe was certainly easy prey. Grace on the other hand, well, she's what made the hunt fun.

Chapter Six

Willy's Tavern was an establishment dedicated to the man himself, although Dominick doubted Willy Nelson ever set foot in it, or knew about it for that matter. Pictures of Willy, his assorted cronies, and tacky Western paraphernalia wallpapered the walls that were discolored by years of grease. Pinball machines, two pool tables, and karaoke were the only entertainment Willy's offered, other than watching friends get fershnickered.

And currently, Dominick was doing just that. "You know, Bobby, if your mother saw you like this, she'd string you up."

Bobby, the youngest of Dominick's crew, grinned stupidly as he started into his second beer. "Never was able to hold my liquor."

Dominick smiled. "I'm expecting you at 7:00 am sharp tomorrow morning. I'd think you better quit after this one."

Bobby lifted his glass in salute and moved on toward one of the pool tables. Dominick continued nursing the beer he didn't want. He didn't know what he wanted. Ever since that confounded woman entered his life, he'd forgot which way was up. He couldn't remember the last time he felt anything. *No,* he thought, as he placed the cold beer bottle to his head; *that was a lie.* He remembered the exact time and place he stopped feeling anything at all. Closing his eyes he saw it all, relived the nightmare that only took seconds to destroy happiness. If only he'd died in her place. Knowing he was sliding into the oily darkness, he clawed his way back up. That's when he heard her.

His heart stammered in his chest, and his blood ran faster. Her laugh barked out followed by Phoebe's unmistakable snort. He chuckled to himself, turned on his barstool, and couldn't help but stare. Gone was the ponytail he'd become accustomed to. In its place hung, shining auburn curls, bouncing around her oval face. The usual ripped jeans or running shorts were replaced with khaki capris and a form-fitting green sleeveless top. Silver hoops hung from her ears, and a silver cross hung around her neck. Grace's green eyes danced with laughter as Phoebe tripped over her own feet; priceless. Dominick lifted an arm and hailed them from across the bar. If he hadn't been looking for it, he would have missed it. Within seconds he watched as Grace's eyes changed. The laughter was still there, but the barrier he'd seen there before erected itself quickly. In that instant he hated whoever or whatever had put that there. Shoving his disappointment and discouragement to the back of his mind, he smiled at her and Phoebe and patted the barstools next to him.

"Ladies!"

Phoebe giggled as she wriggled up on to the barstool. "Why do they make these so high. I mean, people could seriously get hurt."

Grace smiled at Dominick. "She gets hurt just walking in her bedroom."

"For some reason, that does not surprise me." Dominick stood stupidly looking at her for several seconds. Aware he'd been staring, he cleared his throat. "Um...do you want a beer?"

"Actually, I'll take a whiskey diet, please. Oh, and Phoebe has a hankering for some type of foo-foo drink."

If it weren't for Phoebe's excitement over finding "I've Got You Babe" in the karaoke binder, the silence would have been unbearable. "You have to sing with me!

Grace refuses to do it anymore." Phoebe paused long enough to glare at Grace. "Pleeeeaaaase! You know you want to."

"Um...I'm really not that good at singing, and besides..." Dominick's next argument was cut short as he witnessed Phoebe's eyes glass over at the sight of her drink.

"Ooooh. An umbrella!" Phoebe squealed and began sucking with a vengeance on the pink matching straw. "Is this Kool-Aid?"

Dominick simply stared. "Is this your first drink, ever?"

"Oh, goodness, no. I've had..." Phoebe began counting her fingers, "One, two, three..."

"Well, she can count." Grace absently patted Phoebe's head. "Trust me. If Phoebe has more than one fruity drink a night, she turns into a pumpkin." Grace sipped her drink and nodded in approval. "Or at least, she thinks she does. Not a pretty sight."

Before Phoebe could defend herself, a drunken cowboy began belting out Journey's "Oh, Sherri." With a squeal of delight, Phoebe spun around on her barstool, lost control, and landed with a thud on the beer-soaked floor. Every eye in the bar, including the singing cowboy, turned toward Phoebe. Phoebe turned scarlet red, pulled herself off the floor, sat daintily back on the barstool, smoothed her black hair, and straightened her clothing with studied calmness. After several awkward seconds, people returned to their previous activities and the singing cowboy rejoined Steve Perry's stunning vocals.

Dominick studied Phoebe for several seconds. He could tell she was fighting tears. "Are you okay?"

Phoebe just violently shook her head and darted off to the bathroom. At Dominick's look of confusion, Grace explained, "Phoebe has a hard time dealing with public

80

humiliation. She's probably in the bathroom bawling her eyes out as we speak." With a look of relief Dominick found hard to miss, Grace stood up. "In fact, we should probably get going." She paused and shuffled her feet. "Um...thanks...for the drinks." Without another look or word, Grace dashed off toward the bathroom. Dominick watched her leave and spun back toward the bar. With a scowl, he swallowed the rest of his beer. Why of all the towns in the good old U S of A had she picked his?

No longer finding the bar scene to his liking, Dominick headed home. He paid the babysitter and sat beside Lilly's bed, just watching her sleep. Grabbing the portrait of his smiling late wife, Dominick traced the contours of the face he'd known so well. "I remember the first time I saw you; it truly was love at first sight." Dominick smiled at the memory, and then he chuckled. "But I don't think it was the same for you. As I recall, you called me an egotistical, puffed up, buffoon...or something like that. You were right...I was, but somewhere along the way, you changed your mind about me, or did you just learn to love me?" A single tear dropped onto the glass and ran down his wife's face. Gently he brushed it away. "I miss you so much. Why did you have to go and leave me all alone?" Staring at her face, he waited for an answer he knew would never come.

With a sigh he caressed the frame, and then gently, reverently, he placed it back on his daughter's dresser. Turning his attention to his sleeping daughter, he bent down and kissed her on the cheek. "Goodnight, princess." She made a little squeaky sound and squirmed deeper into her little bed. "At least I'm not completely alone," Dominick reminded himself, but he knew it wasn't the same. He looked back at his late wife's smiling face. "I think you'd approve of her, dear. I don't think she likes me very much." He shrugged. "Don't know why, though. You liked me just fine, didn't you? What do you think I should do?" With a sigh, he bent to kiss his daughter's cheek one last time. "Sweet dreams, my little one."

Grace sat up with a jolt. She placed a shaky hand to her throat and swallowed. The blade had felt so real. For a second she was surprised that she was still alive. She swung her legs out of bed and plodded to the motel sink to run the cold tap water. Splashing water on her face, Grace tried to forget the dream, the same dream she'd had over and over again. Only this time, it was a knife slicing her open she wasn't the only one being slaughtered. After turning the water off, she walked back to her bed and sat down. The mattress sagged and squeaked under her, an odd comfort. With a smile of sisterly affection, she watched Phoebe sleep the slumber of the innocent. With a shudder she saw her dream again. Feeling the panic setting in, she closed her eyes and breathed deeply. Sending a prayer to God for peace and freedom from the bondage of dreams, she lay her head back on her pillow and mercifully sank into a deep sleep.

Friday morning's sunbeams crept around the hotel curtains and filtered on Grace's face. Turning away from the attacking sunlight, Grace groaned in her pillow and tried to ignore Phoebe's reminders to get ready. "Go without me," Grace mumbled incoherently from under her pillow. "I don't want to go to work today. I don't want to see him. And I most certainly don't want to look at another paint brush."

Phoebe finished brushing her teeth, swiped mascara on her eyes, checked out her butt in the mirror, and launched herself next to Grace's inert body. "First of all, we don't work. We delegate. Secondly, I don't know who 'him' is. And thirdly, you love to paint." Phoebe studied her fingernails and attacked a cuticle with vengeance. "You know. After all this is done, I'm getting a manicure."

A sudden epiphany had Phoebe jumping up and down on the bed. "Guess what you promised me that you haven't done yet?" After getting no answer, Phoebe lifted one side of the pillow and yelled, "Take me shopping!"

Grace rolled over and peered owlishly at Phoebe. "Now I have a headache, thanks to you. You go ahead and take the Buick. I need some down time. I can always bring the truck." At Phoebe's scowl, Grace smiled. "I'll bring you Dairy Queen."

Grace waited until Phoebe left to break out her scrapbook. In it were the moments, both big and small, that defined her today. Ribbons from showing horses in 4-H, pictures with her father next to his beloved horse, Scout, and only a few snapshots of her with her mother filled the first few pages. Grace bent to pick up the newspaper clipping which fell to the floor. The article delineated in objective words the day Grace's world fell apart. Not a single reporter who had interviewed Grace or Phoebe had captured the horrific nightmare of their father's murder. Allowing the tears to plop on the clipping, she held it in her hand, caressing the picture of her father. She brought the article to her face and kissed the black and white image of the man who was her world. She tried to conjure up his smell of leather and horse and Brut but couldn't. Sighing heavily, she tucked the article safely away and moved on to the next two.

The story of Grace and Phoebe's kidnapping had made the front page news of the Beacon *Town Crier* and their hometown newspaper, the Amsterdam *Gazette*. The same house she and Phoebe bought seemed to stare back at her from the black and white photograph. She didn't need to read the article to know what it said. She'd read it so many times, trying to picture even the slightest image of the man who'd kidnapped them or the house he'd holed up in. Nothing but blackness. She closed her eyes and allowed the information to revolve around in her head. Roy Muldoon, a nasty small-time drug dealer, had decided to take his two year prison sentence out on the man who'd put him there-- Jeremiah Wallace. After kidnapping Grace and Phoebe, Roy had fled east, trying to outrun the cops. It had all come to a head on a sweltering June night in the old mansion outside of Beacon, Kansas. Shots had been fired. Roy Muldoon had died. A young boy had been found in the house. Authorities had presumed the young boy was Roy's son. There had been no way to tell; the boy had refused to speak.

Grace opened her eyes. *I wonder what happened to that boy.* She shook her head. He probably ended up in the foster care system, poor thing. Grace sighed; she couldn't do anything about Roy's son, but she could do something about her future. She would renovate the old mansion, make it beautiful and useful again, and in the process maybe, just maybe, her life could be renovated, too. Grace placed her scrapbook back in her suitcase and left the hotel room with a renewed sense of purpose.

On her way out of town she picked up a burgers, fries, and Blizzards from Dairy Queen and barreled off toward the house. Keeping the old truck from bouncing off the road and keeping the French fries from bouncing out of their box, Grace maneuvered the truck into the driveway and hopped out. Several men hollered their greetings and asked where their food was. Grace replied by smirking and stuffing a salty fried delicacy into her mouth.

"You should be nicer to my men."

Grace turned and faced Dominick. "What in the world happened to you?"

Covered from head to steel-toed boots with a brownish, poo-smelling substance, Dominick cringed. "You really don't want to know."

Grace plugged her nose and stepped back. "You reek! Did you find the cow pies out back a little irresistible or what?"

Dominick smirked and moved a little closer. "There are many things I find irresistible." He backed up a few inches. "Cow pies aren't one of them. There was a mishap with your sewer line this morning. I think you will find Phoebe out back crying and trying to bathe herself out of a Dixie cup."

At Grace's raised eyebrow, Dominick held up his hands in surrender. "Seriously, that's all you pretty much want to know. By the way, I don't think Phoebe will be offering to help me anytime soon, so don't be surprised if I come to you." Dominick walked to the side of the house, turned on the garden hose, and sprayed himself off. He shook himself like a dog and hollered for Phoebe.

Phoebe, muttering under her breath, came trudging around the corner of the house. "I will not help you. No amount of money will convince me otherwise."

Despite a tinge of pity, Grace burst out laughing at the sight before her. A piece of toilet paper clung to Phoebe's right ear, and the only spot that wasn't brown was the left side of Phoebe's face. The Dixie cup must have run out of water. Phoebe, with her arms crossed over her chest, darted a look of death at her sister.

"Looking good, sister."

"Shut up. Just don't even talk to me." Tears welled up in Phoebe's eyes and spilled over, creating white streaks on her right cheek. She looked down at herself, sniffled, and wiped her nose with a brown-colored hand. "I'm covered in someone else's poo."

Wary and cautious, Grace approached Phoebe and tried to pat a poo-free area. Not finding any luck, Grace simply offered a sympathetic smile. "I got you a Blizzard."

Phoebe's eyes lit up. "Really? You're not lying to me are you, because that would be just cruel under these circumstances?"

"Cross my heart and hope to die."

Dominick, an amused witness to this scene, rolled his eyes, turned on the garden hose, and without warning, bombarded Phoebe with the icy blast.

"Cold!" Phoebe repeatedly screamed the word and danced wildly about in the stream of water. By this time the raucous noise drew the presence of the entire construction crew. Roars of laughter soon mingled with Phoebe's yelps.

Dominick turned off the water. "You're welcome."

Phoebe glanced from the crowd to a smiling Dominick. With a haughty shake of her head, she lifted her chin, puffed out her chest, and walked with forced dignity to the old truck.

Grace trotted after her. "Where are you going?"

Without a glance, Phoebe slid into the truck and stated starchly, "I'm going back to the hotel to burn my clothes and shower." Before Phoebe stuck the key into the ignition, a voice heralded her to wait up. "Is it my horrible, evil imagination or did I just hear Noah call my name?"

Grace quickly glanced in the direction of the voice. "It's not your imagination, this time, Sis. It's reality."

Phoebe thumped her head against the steering wheel a couple of times. "Why me?"

"Because you once took the Lord's name in vain?"

"I said 'gall' not 'God'!" Phoebe smacked her hands against her mouth and moaned. "He hates me, doesn't He?"

Grace could only nod. "You make Him cry; what can I say?"

Phoebe watched with trepidation as Noah jogged across the yard. He approached the driver's side window and leaned against the door. "Hey. Are you okay?"

Startled by the genuine concern in Noah's voice, Phoebe stuttered, "Yeah…yeah…um…I'm…"

"She's fine," Grace interjected and nodded supportively at Phoebe.

"I saw the whole thing from the kitchen window."

Phoebe blushed and studied her hands wringing in her lap. "Oh."

"It's nothing to be embarrassed about. I've had similar mishaps, although never with crap." Noah drummed his fingers on the rusted door. "Do you want me to give you a ride to town? I've got an errand to run, and then I've got to come back out and finish inspecting the kitchen."

Phoebe chewed her bottom lip and immediately sputtered, "Crap! I even taste like crap." Another tear squeezed from her eye.

"Pheebs, you're in no condition to drive. Let Noah take you back to town. You'll just come back out when he does." Grace looked Phoebe over. "Seriously, I don't want you behind the wheel, especially in the very spot I'll be sitting later. Oh, wait." Grace handed Phoebe the partially melted Blizzard. "Here, sorry it's a little runny."

Assenting with resignation, Phoebe slumped out of the truck, grabbed her Blizzard, and followed Noah to his car. "I'll get your car dirty."

Noah opened the passenger door. "No worries. Leather cleans up pretty easy." He smiled and shut the door gently. Phoebe cursed at herself and helped herself to a heaping spoonful of Nerds Blizzard.

Grace watched Noah's car pull onto the gravel road, and she immediately went off in search of Dominick. She found him in the kitchen cussing under the kitchen sink. His long legs stuck out from under the sink, and his upper half lay crammed and twisted in order to reach a pipe.

"Problems?"

Dominick's body jerked in surprise, and a sharp curse followed a hollow thump. He struggled out of the tiny space and blinked up at Grace. Rubbing his head, he gave a rueful smile. "You shouldn't sneak up on somebody. It's rude."

Grace didn't return the smile. "You hurt Phoebe's feelings."

Dominick, still sitting on the floor and rubbing his head, looked confused. "What did I do?"

Grace huffed and placed her hands on her hips. "You embarrassed her. Phoebe doesn't deal well with public humiliation."

Dominick got to his feet. "Oh, man. I'm really sorry. I just didn't think. She wanted to get clean, so I cleaned her off the best I knew how."

Grace saw Dominick's genuine remorse and felt her heart soften. A humbled look replaced the over-confident one Dominick usually carried. "Don't worry about it. After a peace offering of a Blizzard and a few doughnuts, Phoebe will be putty in your hands."

Dominick's face crinkled in a smile. "Good to know her weakness. What's yours?"

Grace wagged a finger at him. "Na-ha. Not telling."

Dominick shrugged. "I like a challenge." He sat back down on the floor and shimmied his way under the sink. "You can help me if you wish."

"Will I share the same fate as Phoebe?"

"I sure hope not, beings I'd get the brunt of it again."

Grace crouched next to Dominick's side. "Sure. I've been told I'm an excellent gopher."

Dominick chuckled. "All right, my little rodent sidekick, I need the pipe wrench."

Grace turned and shuffled through the assorted contents of the big tool box. After several panicked moments, Grace swallowed her pride. "And what exactly does a pipe wrench look like?"

Dominick cursed under his breath and a moment of silence suspended in the air. "It's red and big and looks like a wrench on steroids."

Grace rifled through the objects again and with a squeal of excitement pulled out the pipe wrench. "Got it."

"Good. Now can you hand it to me?"

Grace placed the pipe wrench in Dominick's waiting hand and perched expectantly next to his legs. "So, are you from around here?"

Dominick grunted and Grace heard the sound of metal on metal. "Yeah." The pipe slipped and the sound of Dominick's knuckles slamming against the interior of the cupboard caused Grace to cringe in sympathy.

"Need a Band-Aid?"

"Not yet," Dominick grunted and wriggled his body to get a better position. His leg brushed up against Grace's bare one and sparks of heat jumped through her body.

Scooting back, she continued to watch him work. "So, have you always been in the construction business?"

Dominick grunted as he tightened the elbow joint connecting the two pipes. "No."

Grace waited impatiently for the rest of the answer. "And?"

A curse word emanated from under the sink. "Ow. Son of a ..."

Grace quickly interrupted him, "I hope you know that every time you swear, God cries."

"Huh, I always thought a kitten died."

Horrified at the thought, Grace sucked in a breath, "That is just mean." She waited a beat and prompted, "What did you do before becoming a carpenter?"

"Traveled."

"Traveled where?"

"Nowhere and everywhere."

"That doesn't make any sense." Grace huffed and rolled her eyes. Allowing a silence to settle between them, Grace looked about the kitchen. A pot hanger suspended itself over a kitchen island and the appliances were arranged around the room. The sink rested directly below a bay window and the stove sat a counter away to the right. The fridge slumped against the wall across from the sink and stove. Slightly inconvenient.

Grace frowned at the old appliance, hoping it would receive the message and move itself. It did nothing but sit there and buzz. No worries. It'd be gone in a day or two. Grace could hardly contain her excitement for the new stainless steel kitchen appliances.

Fortunately the former owners never wallpapered the kitchen. No need to scrape. Grace envisioned a sage green paint on the wall and white cupboards with glass doors. Grace eyed the ledge above the sink. Small terracotta pots filled with fresh herbs would look great perched on top. A smile lit up Grace's face. There is no way a soufflé would dare flop on her in a kitchen with green walls, glass cupboard doors, and with herbs growing in pots. It just didn't happen.

"Can you hand me a Philips screwdriver? It will be the one with the star-shaped pattern, not the flat head," Dominick interrupted her fantasy world.

"I know that much." Grace pouted a little and retrieved the screwdriver. Handing it to him she asked, "So, where exactly did you travel?"

With a frustrated sigh, Dominick scooted out from under the sink, still clutching the screwdriver, and stared at Grace. "Do you always ask so many questions?"

Grace chewed her bottom lip and thought for a second. "No. Not really."

"Then why are you now?"

"I just thought I'd pass the time by having a conversation. It seems a little one-sided."

Dominick rolled his eyes and burrowed back under the sink. "I like a little peace and quiet when I'm trying to work."

Grace stuck out her tongue. "Okay." The sound of metal against metal, sporadic curses, and manly grunts occasionally emerged from the abyss. Grace drummed her fingers against her legs. After two minutes of sheer boredom and adding a fruit bowl with large, shiny yellow lemons to her imaginary kitchen, Grace began humming. The sound of tinkering stopped and Dominick's voice interrupted her prelude.

"What are you doing?"

"Nothing." Grace continued humming.

"You're humming."

"So."

"It's annoying."

Grace's humming stopped. "I happen to enjoy my humming, thank you very much."

Dominick sighed. "It's not how you're humming; it's what you're humming."

"You don't like "This is the Song That Never Ends"?"

"Does anybody like that song?"

"I do," Grace stated indignantly. "It's a classic."

Dominick re-situated himself with a grunt. "Well, I don't agree. Hum something else if you insist on humming."

"Okay." Grace made a face at his extended legs and began humming "Feed the Birds."

Dominick chuckled and hummed along with her. "Now, that's a classic."

After helping Dominick, Grace sat on the back porch and began sketching ideas for landscaping. Her thoughts never remained on trees or shrubs very long. After several failed attempts at sketching anything, she slammed down her notepad with a huff. What was with that man! She barely knew him, yet it felt as if she'd known him forever.

"Great! Now I'm a walking cliché!" Grace pulled herself to her feet and brushed the dust off her butt. A sound of scampering feet startled Grace. "Oh, gosh! Mrs. S. You scared me to death." With a swift motion, she scooped up her cat and cuddled it to her chest. Mrs. Sloucombe, not one for quality time with humans, wriggled and growled in protest. "Oh, shut up, you poor excuse for a pet. The least you could do after all I've done for you is allow me to hold you."

"I told you she wouldn't care if you died."

"Phoebe!" Grace carefully edged closer and sniffed. "You smell better."

"I'm never talking to the man again! I don't care if he looks like a god that got into a bar fight!" Phoebe stomped her foot. Mrs. Sloucombe eyed her with disdain. "And you cat. One more look from you and I'll skin you and make you into a hat." Mrs. Sloucombe blinked and looked away. Phoebe glared at the back of Mrs. Sloucombe's head. "That cat hates me. You know she has a hidden lair where she plots secret ways to kill me in my sleep."

Grace scratched Mrs. Sloucombe's head. "She loves you. She just doesn't know how to show it." As if in disagreement, the cat glared at Phoebe and wrestled out of Grace's arms. Both women watched as Mrs. Sloucombe sashayed toward the pond.

Grace shook her head. "I think she's taking the divorce hard." Grace ignored Phoebe's snort. "I'm serious! That cat loved Kevin."

"Birds of a feather."

Grace smiled and watched as her cat allowed a mouse to traverse her path. "Kevin was just as lazy, unless it came to chasing skirts." Grace paused for a moment and listened to the sound of improvement. Miter saws whined, nail guns grunted, and sanders whirred. "It's happening, isn't it Pheebs? This is finally coming together. I can't help but think that Dad is looking down on us. I think he's pretty proud."

Phoebe opened her mouth to reply but was cut short when Dominick walked through the door. Dominick gave a prize-winning smile, and Grace visibly saw Phoebe melt in her shoes. *Pushover.* "I was wondering if I could have the pleasure of your company tonight at the diner. It's their all-you-can-eat shrimp buffet tonight. Very popular with the locals. You can mingle with your new neighbors and maybe find ones you've just met a little more appealing."

Grace paused. Something told her to decline. Keep your friends close, your enemies closer, and men who could topple safety walls very, very far away. But before she could give a negative answer, Phoebe grinned from ear to ear and answered for the two of them, "We'd love to go. What time?"

"It's best to get there early. Say sixish?"

Phoebe gave a thumbs up. "Sounds like a plan, Stan."

Dominick shook his head in wonderment and left with an amused look on his face.

"Sounds like a plan, Stan?" Grace mocked her sister. "Where did that come from?"

Phoebe blushed. "I don't know. But that man makes me have the IQ of a cucumber." Phoebe eyed Grace. "What's the huffing and puffing all about? I thought you liked shrimp."

"It's not that." Grace crossed her arms over her chest. "It's the company I'll be in."

"What's wrong with Dominick?" Phoebe tucked another stray hair behind her ear.

"Nothing. That's the problem." Grace kicked at the porch railings. "I'm just not ready for...these feelings."

"I can go tell him I forgot I hated shrimp or something like that and say we can't go."

Grace smiled. "No, thanks though. I'll just suck it up and not let him get to me. That's all. I mean how hard can it be?"

Phoebe smiled. "I wouldn't count on it being easy." Phoebe bounced up and down. "Oh, my gosh! I forgot to tell you about my little drive with Noah."

Grace sat on the bottom step. "Tell all."

"Well. Oh, gosh. I think my heart might explode." Phoebe fanned herself. "So, we're driving, and he starts asking about me and where I grew up and what I do. Just cursory things, but he was so interested in what I said! No one is interested in what I have to say."

"And then what happened?"

"What do you mean what happened? I'm not that kind of girl."

"I didn't mean that! Perv!"

Phoebe toyed with the edge of her shorts. "He offered to punch Dominick's lights out for me."

"How romantic."

"I know! Isn't it though?"

Grace frowned. "You seem a little twitterpated over this guy. Just remember that you just met him. Be careful and take it easy."

Phoebe pouted and sat next to Grace. "I do know him. He's thirty, a teacher, and volunteer firefighter. He's the fire inspector for the county, and he likes rhubarb." Phoebe hung her head. "Doesn't matter anyway. He probably thinks I'm a dork."

"But, sweetie, you are a dork." Grace drew her arm across Phoebe's shoulders and gave a squeeze. "That's what makes you Phoebe."

"I am unique."

Grace started toward the front door. "You can say that again. Well, let's get ourselves ready to rub elbows with the shrimp-loving locals of Beacon, Kansas."

Chapter Seven

The smell of fried shrimp, shrimp scampi, and shrimp Alfredo assailed the women's noses as they entered Reed's Diner.

"Yoo-hoo!" Grace turned her head in the direction of the high-pitched yodel. Annie, the warbler, waved excitedly from a booth to their right. Dickie gave a half-hearted wave and went back to stuffing his face with fried shrimp. Dutifully the girls made their way to the Wisel's booth and stood in the aisle, rocking back and forth awkwardly on their heels.

"So, my girls, I understand you met our son," Annie exclaimed around a mouth of white, mashed Alfredo noodles.

Phoebe tried hard to ignore the see-food. "Yeah. He seems really nice."

Annie glowed. "He makes us so proud. He teaches at the high school you know, and he's the only fire inspector in the county."

Phoebe smiled politely. "I bet you don't get to spend much time with him beings he's so busy."

Annie swallowed a mouthful of noodles and wiped her mouth with a napkin. "I thought with him living here we'd see more of him. But he always seems to have a previous engagement."

Dickie snorted, and Annie shot him a look. The girls made their excuses and moved on to find an empty booth. Grace's stomach grumbled, and the sight of the buffet set her mouth to watering.

"If I don't eat soon, I'm going to start chewing on your arm." Grace studied a fat man heaping shrimp scampi and mashed potatoes on his plate. "He's going to eat it all!"

"Want me to tackle him?"

Grace chuckled at the visual. "No. I wouldn't want him to get hurt."

A warm hand wrapped around Grace's upper arm. "Hey. We've got a table on the other end." Dominick gazed into her face. "You look like you could start gnawing on the furniture."

"If it tastes like shrimp, I'm game."

"Good to know." Dominick led them to a booth situated comfortably in the back. A man with spiky blonde hair sat with their back to them. Phoebe squeezed Grace's arm and whispered a plea for help.

Grace rolled her eyes and patted Phoebe's shoulder. "You'll be fine. Just be yourself."

"That's what I'm worried about."

Noah turned around and beamed a smile at them as they approached the booth. "Hey, ladies." He scooted over toward the window and patted the seat next to him. "Phoebe. Glad to see you aren't too traumatized by the events of this morning."

Phoebe carefully slid in next to him. "Yeah, thanks to Dominick, I'll never go near another pipe ever again."

Noah chuckled and glanced at his friend. "Yeah, he's known for getting his friends and associates in some rather sticky situations."

"Hey now. You aren't telling the whole story. Don't be putting ideas into their heads. I think their imaginations are creative enough."

Grace, caught between the window and Dominick, pushed herself as far as she could to the window. The man, intent on torturing her, wore a pair of faded jeans with a slight rip at the knee and a black polo shirt that stretched nicely across his chest. He oozed sex appeal, and Grace didn't want anything to do with it. She glanced at his smiling profile and shaggy brown hair. Okay. Maybe she did want a little something to do with it. Exasperated with herself and her conflicted feelings, Grace sighed and drank ice water the waitress brought. Needing to look at something besides Dominick, she looked longingly at the beckoning buffet.

"Hungry?" Dominick turned toward her and smiled.

"Starved."

Dominick scooted out, and Grace, Phoebe, and Noah filed to the buffet line to pile their plates high with shrimp and sides.

"So you two went to high school together?" Phoebe asked as they seated themselves again.

"Much to the dismay of many teachers." Noah's dimple winked at Phoebe. "I don't take any of the blame though. I was just the follower. Dominick was the instigator."

"Lies. All lies." Dominick licked scampi juice off his fingers. "Bruce, number three of the musketeers, usually came up with all the hare-brained ideas."

Noah wiped his mouth. "He's getting hitched next weekend. Can't see how his future bride will put up with him."

"I heard she bought a cattle prod." Dominick took a swig from his Sam Adam's bottle. "She'll need it."

Noah swallowed a mouthful of potato salad. "You're the pot calling the kettle black. Any woman stupid enough to marry you will need a little something more than a cattle prod."

Grace watched in fascination as a blush crept over Dominick's face. "Here I thought you were my friend. I see where your loyalties lie. Wave a couple of good-looking women in your face and you turn traitor."

"We all have a breaking point." Noah waved a fried shrimp in Dominick's direction and then plopped it into his mouth. "Mine just happens to be beautiful, mysterious ladies."

Phoebe shot a glance at Grace, who hid a smile behind her water glass. Phoebe laughed nervously and studied Noah using peripheral vision. Grace felt sorry for her sister. She knew her sister well enough to know what was going on in Phoebe's head. The fact that Noah was looking pretty fine in his khaki shorts, a yellow button-up shirt, and leather sandals, was not helping her sister at all. Grace gave Phoebe a supportive smile, but was only rewarded with a nervous grin.

Grace sensed Phoebe's mood and turned her attentions to Noah. "So, I see your parents are here tonight."

"Yup. Good ole' mom and dad." Noah smiled wryly. "Don't get me wrong. I love my parents, but they are possibly the weirdest people on the face of the earth."

"Maybe you're a by-product of the milkman," Dominick suggested as he eased out of the booth. He turned toward Grace. "Did you want some more?"

Grace gauged her full-o-meter; full but not stuffed. "Maybe just a tad bit more."

Grace followed Dominick to the buffet line, smiled politely at Annie and Dickie, and commenced piling her plate full of food. Dominick smiled as she breezed past the salad section without a glance.

"Not big on veggies?"

"Not when there's fried food around. I might eat a carrot or two just to keep up my 20/20 vision, but other than that, raw veggies are for the birds."

"Rabbits," Dominick corrected.

"Whatever." Grace, plate piled high with food, made her way back to the booth. "What have you two been talking about?"

"I was telling him the story about our first week at our new school." Phoebe twirled her finger around a stray piece of hair. "It's a classic"

Grace grimaced. "Yeah, if you're into tragedy."

"What happened?" Dominick scooted in after Grace and sat a little too close for Grace's comfort. Sitting as close to the window as possible, Grace twisted her shoulder so as not to brush his arm.

Phoebe giggled. "We were the new girls during my freshmen and Grace's sophomore year. Grace's bubbly personality and hare-brained schemes awarded her a lot of friends, which was a good thing because I was the shy one. One day during lunch, she convinced us girls that it would be a great idea to moon the superintendent of the school, a man who was a little grumpy due to the fact that his head was as smooth as a baby's butt." Phoebe giggled at the memory and sipped at the ice water in front of her. "Sorry. Anyway, where was I? Oh yes. So us girls lined up in a row and waited for Superintendent Wick to come out of the school. At his approach, we bent over and dropped our pants."

Grace snorted a laugh at the memory. "Oh, my gosh! We were total dweebs, weren't we?" She patted the corner of her eyes. "It was all Phoebe's fault that I got caught, too."

"My fault?" Phoebe exclaimed. "Who can't seem to run and pull up their pants at the same time? Huh?"

"Details, details," Grace mumbled into her drink. "You fell into me first, pulling up your Strawberry Shortcake underwear."

Phoebe sucked in a mortified breath. "We pinky swore that you'd never tell another living soul about those underwear." She shot an embarrassed glance at Noah, who sat red-faced from trying to contain a laugh. "Go ahead. Laugh it up. Phoebe wears Strawberry Shortcake underwear."

"Wears?" Grace asked.

Phoebe blushed and ducked her head. Fighting a losing battle, she exclaimed, "They're cute."

Noah, Dominick, and Grace burst out laughing, and a couple of people surrounding them turned their heads. Phoebe sat, head ducked, face burning with shame. "It's not that bad. They're thongs."

The laughing turned to howling and tears of laughter ran down the cheeks of Phoebe's audience. Phoebe crossed her arms and huffed. That only caused the other three to laugh all the louder.

"All right, guys. It wasn't that funny. Besides, Grace still wears..."

"Don't you dare!" Grace exclaimed. "I wasn't the one who spilled the beans about your *current* character of choice on your underwear. You can't tell."

"No. No." Dominick wiped his eyes and grinned. "Please, Phoebe, continue. I'm strangely intrigued."

Grace speared her sister with a glare, daring her to tattle. An evil smile spread across Phoebe's face. She crooked her finger at the guys, and they leaned forward. She whispered something in their ears. They roared with laughter, and their eyes immediately darted toward Grace red face.

101

Dominick's chocolate brown eyes met Grace's green ones. "The information I just received is strangely hot." He choked on a laugh and croaked, "Could you please tell me what day of the week it is?"

Grace stuck her tongue out at her three companions. "Hardy har har! Next time you're in need of a calendar, you'll be wishing you had me around."

Dominick's eyes searched hers. "I already do."

Grace's heart skipped a beat, and her breath caught. Unable to reply, she sipped her water and cleared her throat. She turned her direction toward Noah. "So, beings man of mystery over here won't tell me about his life before becoming the Ty Pennington of Beacon, Kansas, maybe you can fill me in."

Noah wiped his mouth. "Well, let's see, my pal spent some time in the military. In fact, he was a…"

"I don't think the ladies really want to be told boring stories about me. Besides, it's getting a little late."

Noah received the hint loud and clear. "Dominick's a little shy. Risky past and all."

Grace and Phoebe groaned in disappointment. In spite of her reservations about Dominick, Grace didn't want the night to end. She watched as the waitress laid the bill on the table. She attempted to grab it, but Dominick quickly snatched it.

"No girl pays when she's on a date with me."

Date? Grace swallowed and played with the word in her head. This wasn't a date. She didn't want a date. Or did she? She glanced at Phoebe for help but her sister, lost in a pair of blue eyes, paid no attention.

"You must have a pretty loose interpretation of the word date." Grace fiddled with her torn napkin.

"Date? Oh, yeah. It's just a figure of speech. I wouldn't get your Friday panties all bunched up."

Grace gaped at him. "You're a very incorrigible man. And besides, figures of speech are metaphors and similes."

Dominick plunked down a credit card over the bill. "Don't tell me you're an English teacher or anything like that."

"Would that be a problem?"

Noah barked out a laugh. "Yeah, because every time he'd look at you he'd see Ms. Thorpe, a witchy bat whose knee-high nylons never stayed above her knees."

Grace stuck out her chest and slightly tilted her chin. "Actually, I went to school to become a librarian."

Dominick blinked in surprise, and he looked her over. "Where's the tight bun, glasses, and tweed suit? Aren't those a prerequisite to being a librarian?"

"You don't exactly look like a carpenter either," Grace retorted.

That tiny smile played at the corner of his lips. "Tell me then, Ms. Sherlock, what exactly do I look like?"

Grace tapped a finger to her lip and studied his slightly crooked nose and scar. A five o'clock shadow gave his rugged face a dangerous appeal. And those eyes, haughty yet haunted. She felt her insides go mushy. She cleared her throat and jokingly suggested, "Mercenary."

"Mercenary? You do have an active imagination, don't you?" Dominick's smile didn't quite reach his eyes. Grace's stomach lurched, and her heartbeat quickened. Dominick's eyes, unreadable and suddenly dark, gazed into Grace's. She tore her eyes away from the studying stare and began making excuses why she and Phoebe needed to return to the hotel. Dominick remained quiet and didn't try to persuade her otherwise.

The night humidity hung in the air and soaked through Grace's clothes as she stepped out of the diner.

Her lungs struggled to breathe in the humidity, and her mind raced as she tried to figure out the encrypted information received. She glanced behind her and witnessed Phoebe and the two gentlemen looking at the advertisement for the Puggles. Phoebe must have mentioned her name because both Dominick and Noah glanced in her direction. Noah grinned widely at her, but Dominick, still serious, studied her thoughtfully through the glass doors.

Grace looked away and glanced up in time to see a falling star cascade to the horizon. Grace made a wish and watched the night sky blink and flash in its entire splendor. She remembered a time when her father had taught her most of the constellations. Time had done its thing, however, and Grace struggled to name all but the simple ones. When had she forgotten to look up?

The sound of the door opening ripped Grace from her reverie. She wiped at her eyes, plastered on a smile, and turned toward the three. "It's about time."

"We were just looking at the ad for the Puggles," Phoebe explained. "The guys think they look funny, but I think they'd make a great little pet. It's a Beagle and a Pug combined into one cute package." Turning directly to Dominick, she added, "Who wouldn't want one?"

"Yeah…I guess…if you like small dogs. Look, it's getting late; I gotta get home…I'll see you all later." With that, he nodded and smiled at Phoebe, punched Noah in the arm and walked to his truck; he completely ignored Grace.

Grace fumbled in her purse for her keys and pretended not to have noticed him slighting her. Feeling the familiar stinging behind her eyes, she put on her best smile, said good-bye to Noah, and firmly grasped Phoebe's arm, dragging her toward the Buick LeSabre. With her mind racing, Grace drove back to the motel.

Phoebe hummed in the passenger seat, and a stupid smile plastered itself on her face. "Oh my gosh! That was so fun. We need to do that again."

Grace grunted a response and pulled into the parking lot. The lighted Super 8 sign glowed in the thick darkness and welcomed the girls home. The lady at the front desk nodded a greeting, and Grace followed a skipping Phoebe down the carpeted hallway.

"Is something the matter?" Phoebe asked as Grace unlocked the room door.

Grace flipped on the light switch and threw her purse in the corner. "No."

Phoebe bit her lip and gently locked the door behind them. Giving Grace a wide berth, Phoebe began getting ready for bed.

"Do you have to hum?" Grace demanded.

Phoebe stopped brushing her teeth. "Just because you're not happy, doesn't mean I can't be. I don't know what happened to put you in a bad mood, but don't take it out on me."

Grace sighed and flopped down face first on the bed. "Sorry, Pheebs. I'm just a mess right now." She played with the hem of the pillow. "Did you ever get a present thinking it would be a certain thing and then when you opened it, it was something totally different?"

Phoebe spit out her toothpaste and rinsed her mouth. "Yeah. Why?"

Grace opened her mouth in response and then snapped it shut. She hardly knew how she felt. How was she supposed to explain it out loud? Grace shook her head. "Just wondering. That's all."

Fifteen minutes later, Grace dreamt of death. The unknown assailant stalked her repeatedly through the inky fog. Everywhere she turned ghostly figures herded her back toward the unknown.

Dominick gripped the steering wheel of his truck harder than necessary to navigate the town's quiet streets. "Mercenary!" He shouted out loud, punching the dashboard. "Of all the things she could have said!" Coming up to his street, he ignored his turn and drove right past it. He did not want his daughter to see him in this mood. Knowing he couldn't drive around forever, he took a deep breath and forced himself to release the strangle hold he had on the steering wheel. He chuckled to himself when he pictured the steering wheel turning blue. "Sorry, steering wheel," he gave it a loving pat, "didn't mean to take my frustrations out on you."

Suddenly it hit him so hard that his head reacted as if his jaw had received a right hook. Slamming on his breaks, he pulled the truck to the side of the road and stopped. "Wow! Did I really do that?" He shook his head in disgust at himself. Grace was an innocent girl making an innocent remark, and he had pummeled her. "What kind of a man would do that? A really stupid one!" He raised his fist in the hair to bring it down against the dashboard but stopped mid-air. "No, too many innocent things have suffered for my foolishness." Raking his fingers through his hair, he leaned against the head rest. "Mercenary! Not quite on the mark, but close enough. According to some, my killing for the U.S. government is not quite that different from that of a paid killer."

He smacked himself on the forehead. "Idiot, she didn't know; she meant it as joke. Ha, ha, some joke!" Cupping his head in his hands, he considered the irony.

106

Everyone in town knew about his wife's death, and that it was tragic and unexpected, but only Dominick's two closest friends knew the whole story, and they had sworn not to tell under "pain of death." Now along comes this auburn-headed spitfire of a girl who knows squat about his past, and she dang near nails it. "Remarkable!" Dominick threw his head back again and laughed out loud. When the laugh was spent, so was Dominick's anger. He steered the truck back on the road and headed home.

"Daddy!" Dominick's face lifted, and all traces of his dark mood were erased at the sound of his daughter's voice, accompanied by the pitter-patter of her chubby little feet hitting the kitchen floor. He whipped her up in his arms and squeezed her to him. Closing his eyes, he allowed himself to lose himself in his daughter for a few seconds.

"If Maybella says I was a good girl, can I get a treat?"

Dominick kissed Lilly's cheek. "Were you good, baby girl?"

Before Lilly could think of the correct response, the babysitter appeared from the living room. "Yes, sir. Little Lilly was great, as usual."

"Treat!" Lilly scampered off in the direction of her room. Dominick inwardly sighed. He knew exactly what "treat" meant. He paid Maybella ten bucks, saw her out, and sauntered off for an invitation-only tea party.

As he rounded the corner of Lilly's room, he stopped in his tracks. Lilly had placed her favorite doll across the table from herself and was busy conversing with it. "I'm glad you've come for a visit, Mommy. Daddy says you were really nice and pretty." Lilly pointed a chubby little finger to her nightstand. "See, I have a picture of you. Daddy says it's okay to talk to you. He's says you'd like it." Dominick watched as Lilly poured her "mother" more tea.

"Thank you. I made it myself. Daddy doesn't like tea. I'll make him coffee." Lilly picked at her lip and turned to stare at the picture next to her bed. "Daddy really misses you, Mommy. I hear him cry at night. Daddies aren't supposed to cry."

With practiced stealth, Dominick backed away from the door and slid to the floor. Cradling his head in his hands, Dominick closed his eyes to pray. God, he missed her so...startled he opened his eyes and stared unseeing at the ceiling. Instead of his wife's face, Grace's face had flooded his mind's eye. Was God trying to tell him something? Could his cold heart of stone really love again? He had spent so much time and energy on "never again"; was "again" even possible? As he continued to ponder this, the band around his heart seemed to melt away as a sense of peace wrapped itself around him.

"Daddy? Mommy and I are waiting for you."

Dominick got up from the floor and brushed himself off. He was ready to have tea with his daughter, and he was ready to start a new life for both of them. The only thing left to do was to convince Grace that she wanted to be a part of their new life.

Chapter Eight

Dominick sat outside the Super 8 hotel in his idling pickup and wondered just what in the heck he was doing. The confidence of the night before was paling in the light of the morning sun as he argued with himself. Beside him sat a bribe he knew neither Grace nor Phoebe could resist. He shook his head and drummed his fingers on the steering wheel. All he had to do was put his pickup in drive and motor on down the road, forgetting Grace and the way she invaded his soul. Knowing that was impossible, Dominick grabbed the goodies and strode to the entrance.

The welcome sign could have been beckoning him into another portal for all he knew. What he was about to start would either end at his total destruction or absolute elation. Ignoring the tingle down his spine, he pulled open the door, called out a friendly greeting to the hotel manager, and searched for room 114.

A persistent knocking on the hotel door woke Grace from a deep sleep. She glanced at the clock; seven in the morning! Wiping the drool from her face, she slipped into her pink, fuzzy slippers, smoothed down her hair, and dragged herself to the door.

She peeked through the peephole and saw Dominick standing outside the door carrying a bakery bag and three steaming cups.

"What in the world is he doing here," Grace whispered to herself. She could once again feel the heat creeping up her neck at the memory of last night and how he had shunned and humiliated her, and for what? "I wonder what he's got to say for himself." Her attempt at trying to imagine what he could possibly say to her to forgive him was cut short by another persistent knock on the door.

"Just a minute," she said through the door. Grace ran to the bathroom and studied herself in the mirror. After clumsily pulling a brush through her hair and stealing some of Phoebe's mouthwash, Grace peered at her reflection. *Scary!* "Oh well, just one comment on how I look and I'll..." she swung her fist in the air, "I'll deck him!"

Standing with her legs spread apart in a fighting stance, she opened the door. Dominick swaggered right past her as cool and calm as an ocean breeze filled with the luscious smells of doughnuts, cappuccino, and his cologne.

Grace breathed in deeply but forced herself to respond in as dry and uncaring voice as possible, "Smells yummy."

Grace studied his face and watched as his eyes traveled her body. His eyes stopped at her face and hair, and she forced herself not to preen right in front of him. Within seconds, his eyes lit up. Not with passion, but with something else Grace couldn't quite define. No sooner had the light sparkled into existence, it was quickly extinguished. His chocolate eyes darkened by a few shades, and his cockiness reemerged. "You like my cologne, huh?"

Grace bit her bottom lip and watched as Dominick's eyes twinkled with playfulness. "I was referring to the doughnuts."

"Sure." Dominick sat the bag on the tiny desk in the corner and sat himself on Grace's bed. He looked her over from her shorts to her tiny tank top. "Nice slippers," he drawled.

Grace shot at him with both barrels. "How dare you? How cheap do you think I am? Do you think you can just show up at my door with a couple of buck's worth of treats and all's forgiven?" Grace raised her fist. "Why I outha…"

Dominick did a backwards summersault on the bed, landing on the floor on the other side, putting much needed distance between them. Peeking over the edge of the bed, he held up his hands in surrender. "Grace, please, let me explain."

Grace stood her ground, legs apart, knees slightly bent, and fists up. He did look ridiculously cute with his brown eyes just barely visible over the rumpled bedding. Putting her hands down and placing them squarely on her hips, ready to shoot out at a moment's notice, she gave him permission to speak, "Okay, explain."

After creeping up the side of the bed, he positioned himself as far away from Grace as he could without falling off again. "Grace, I am really sorry for the way I acted last night. I know I hurt you, and I am here this morning to ask your forgiveness. Please can we be friends again?"

Grace's head felt as if it would implode. What was this man all about anyway? Grace ignored her heart racing and forced herself to be immune to Dominick's chocolaty puppy-dog eyes. Grace lifted her chin slightly and haughtily stated, "Usually I kick impertinent men out of my hotel room, but beings you brought sugary goodness, I will allow you to stay."

Grace rooted around in the bakery bag, retrieved a jelly-filled doughnut and bit into it. A large glob of raspberry filling fell directly on her shirt. "Crap!" Taking a finger she slicked it up and stuck it in her mouth.

"I should bring jelly-filled doughnuts every morning." Dominick grinned and jumped back on the bed.

111

He patted the spot right next to him, all pretense of humility gone; he was the same incorrigible Dominick again. "Come here for a second."

"No." Not knowing all the rules to the game they seemed to be playing, Grace glanced furtively at Phoebe who was still snug as a bug in her bed. *Can she sleep through everything,* Grace wondered as she watched a little trickle of drool fall off the edge of Phoebe's face and splat on the white pillow case.

Dominick laughed. "Don't worry; I'm not going to take advantage of you," he paused and gave a devilish grin, "yet."

Grace gulped and walked over to Phoebe's bed. "Wake up, Phoebe. There is a strange man in our hotel room, and he comes bearing gifts."

Phoebe snorted, stuck her butt up in the hair, and flopped on her side. Cracking open one eye, she fixed her gaze on Dominick and gave a little finger wave. She turned her attention to Grace. "I smell something really good."

Grace showed her the half-eaten jelly doughnut. "Doughnut?"

"Nu-huh."

"Cappuccino?"

"Nope. Not it, either."

"Me?" Dominick smiled from Grace's bed.

Phoebe sniffed in his general direction. "Yup." A silly smile exploded over her face. "But I bet you're not as tasty as a jelly-filled doughnut."

"Pheebs!" Grace blushed for her sister.

Phoebe swung her legs out of bed and shuffled to the bathroom. "Just preaching the truth, sister."

The bathroom door shut, and Grace and Dominick were left alone. Grace shuffled her feet, not knowing where to sit. Sitting next to Dominick seemed like a very

112

dangerous idea, especially with his wolf-in-sheep's-clothing grin. Sitting on the chair in the corner seemed rude, so she sat down on Phoebe's bed across from him.

"So, what brings you to our room at such an unholy hour on a Saturday?"

Dominick snagged a chocolate-covered doughnut and sank his teeth into it. "I came to invite you girls on an outing today. It slipped my mind yesterday, or I would have invited you last night." He gave Grace a sheepish grin. "Some friends and I are going down to the lake this afternoon, and I thought you ladies might want to come with," he scanned the sparse contents of their hotel room, "or, you could just stay in here all day and wilt."

Grace chewed on her bottom lip. It was true that Phoebe and she were at a loss as to what to do today. They certainly didn't want to work on the house, and sitting in this room didn't have any appeal either.

Grace looked Dominick over. Faded Levi's with a slit in one knee, a University of Kansas T-shirt, and untied tennis shoes completed his outfit. Grace bit her lip. The prospect of a day at the lake excited Grace, but the idea that she'd be in Dominick's presence caused her resident butterflies to flutter. The mystery surrounding him both attracted and repelled her. Last night she'd been given a small glimpse into a man she hardly knew, and what she had learned did not set her heart at ease. What she did know was that Dominick was dangerous to a girl who needed to get and keep the upper hand in a relationship. Grace felt weak around him; she couldn't afford to be weak, ever again.

"I don't have a swimsuit."

"Who said you needed one?"

Grace sucked in a breath and choked on her own saliva. Dominick jumped up and slapped her on the back.

113

Grace held up a hand. "Stop. I'm fine." Clearing her throat, she reached for a steaming cup and carefully sipped the hot liquid.

Dominick sat down beside her. "I meant you can wear shorts and a shirt." That tiny smiled played on his lips. "Of course, I'm not going to be the man to stop you if you want to go skinny dipping."

Grace hid behind her cup. "You are an incorrigible man. Has anyone ever told you that?"

"Many times, Spitfire."

Grace rolled her eyes and moved off the bed. She knocked on the bathroom door. "Phoebe, did you fall asleep in there, again?"

A sound of a crash and an exclamation of pain filtered through the door. Phoebe's voice mumbled, "Yeah. I think my leg fell asleep."

"Need help?"

"No. I'll be okay in a bit."

Grace shuffled back to where Dominick sat shaking with laughter. "You two are the oddest women I've ever met."

"Maybe you should get out more."

The sound of the bathroom door opening stopped Dominick's reply. Phoebe came around the corner, snagged a doughnut, and bit into it. "Mmmmm....yummy."

"Pheebs, Dominick has asked if we would be interested in joining him and his friends at the lake today."

"Who all will be there?"

"Just a couple of buddies." Dominick paused and grinned as Phoebe stuffed a huge piece of doughnut in her mouth. "Noah will be there."

"Oh. Really? That's nice," Phoebe stated as nonchalantly as possible around a mouthful of squished doughnut.

114

Dominick grinned at Phoebe and shook his head. He nabbed a second doughnut and a cup, and headed toward the door. "I'll be by to pick you up around 11:00. We'll grill out for lunch, ride around in the speed boat, and just hang out for the rest of the day." He opened the door and paused. Turning to Grace, he winked. "Remember, no swimsuit required."

Grace threw a pillow at his retreating form. "Frustrating, presumptuous moron!"

"What was that all about?" Phoebe asked.

"Nothing. That man just rubs me the wrong way."

Phoebe's hand paused, doughnut halfway to her mouth. "Hmm...now that's a thought."

Grace groaned and retreated to the bathroom. She stepped into the shower and let the hot spray beat her body numb. What was with that man, anyway? Grace vigorously shampooed her hair and mumbled to herself. In her mind she created a pros and cons list: extremely good-looking, nice smile, excellent derriere, charming, funny, and gentle. Grace rinsed her hair and thought about the things that annoyed her. A guy that good-looking couldn't be up to something good, the nice smile often turned into a smart-ass grin, and there was a mysterious side to him. Shivers of excitement traveled Grace's body. She stamped her foot and cursed herself. She needed to be careful; his charm would eventually break down her guard, and she'd be putty in his hands.

"This is ridiculous!" Grace said out loud as she stepped out of the shower and dried herself off.

"What did you say?" Phoebe asked from the other side of the door.

"Nothing. I was just talking to myself. I swear I'm going crazy."

"You're only crazy when you start answering yourself. Remember Aunt Cloe? When she started doing that, they stuck her in an institution."

"I thought they stuck her in the loony bin because she kept trying to stick her cats in various appliances. Didn't she also start eating puzzle pieces?"

"That's beside the point. Anyway, she did try to stuff her cat, Cletus, in the microwave."

Grace laughed as she wrapped her hair in a towel. Slipping her pajamas back on, she walked out of the bathroom and finished her beauty routine. A little make-up, hair pulled back into a messy bun, and sunscreen completed the regimen.

Grace heard rustling from the bedroom area. "What are you doing in there?"

Phoebe came around the corner holding up two bathing suits, a green two piece and a pink one piece. "What do you think? Should I wear the bikini or the one piece?"

Grace put a hand to one hip and tapped her lip with a finger. "Good question. Depends on which one you feel more comfortable in."

Phoebe walked over to the mirror and lifted her shirt to reveal her abdomen. "Oh, that's scary! I've had way too much fast food and calorie-soaked food. Look at this!" Phoebe squeezed a roll on her belly. "This is absolutely disgusting."

Phoebe pulled her shirt down and vaulted herself on the bed, face down in her pillow. "I'm not going! Noah's going to think I'm fat!"

Grace sat down beside her over sister. "Pheebs, you look great. No one's going to notice that small, miniscule love handle."

Phoebe wailed into her pillow. Grace bit her lip; *probably not the best thing to say.* Grace regrouped and dared to speak, "I read in a magazine somewhere that ninety-five percent of guys like girls with some meat on their bones."

The wailing stopped and Phoebe mumbled into her pillow, "Really?"

"Of course, would I lie to you?"

Phoebe turned her head to the side and peered at Grace through one eye. "Yes, you would."

"Okay, so maybe I would, but not this time."

Phoebe rolled over on to her back and stared at the smoke detector. "Do you think that thing works? I mean I don't want to be fried to crisps in our beds."

Grace chuckled. "Yeah, I wondered the same thing. Now get out of bed, get ready for the day, and just wear the one piece."

Phoebe shuffled to the bathroom. "Okay, that means you can have the bikini."

Grace groaned and sank onto her bed. Great, now she was stuck with the stupid two piece. What person in his or her right mind even created it in the first place? *Probably a man*, thought Grace as she studied the bikini from a distance.

Grace repeated Phoebe's actions in the mirror and didn't die with despair. Maybe the bikini would work. She slipped it on and was surprisingly pleased with the result. *The running is paying off*, she thought as she slipped on a pair of black shorts and a yellow tank top over it.

Dominick pulled up into the parking lot of the Super 8 hotel in a shiny black Ford F-350 with subtle silver pin-stripping and window decals advertising "Carson Contracting". Dominick had spent most of the morning in prayer, double-checking God's decision, not that he had trouble accepting God's endorsement. Grace was beginning to chip at his very soul; he couldn't resist her anymore; he wasn't sure he wanted to. As if on cue, the ghost of his past reared up and threw his hopes onto the rocks of despair. "And what do you think she'd do if she knew?" the ghostly whispers screamed at him.

He watched as Grace and Phoebe walked toward the truck. Even though his heart thudded like a thoroughbred's hooves on the racetrack, he knew he had to at least try. "I don't know what she'd do, but for now she doesn't know, so just shut up!" Mentally he gave the ghost a swift kick in the rear.

"Nice ride," Phoebe commented as she hopped in the backseat.

Dominick smiled. "Thanks." He turned toward Grace who was still standing outside the passenger door. "Coming?"

Grace glanced at Phoebe perched happily in the backseat. "I think I'll sit in back with Pheebs."

Here it goes. This was going to be a difficult battle to win. Ignoring the butterflies in his stomach, Dominick flashed his most innocent smile. "I don't usually bite, unless I'm asked."

Grace's blood ran warm. Breathing deeply, she settled herself in the front passenger seat as close as possible to the door. Dominick and Phoebe made most of the conversation on the trip. Grace sat looking out the window, watching the prairie fly by, trying to figure out the emotions that Dominick evoked in her.

Grace inwardly sighed; she didn't want this. The hurt and humiliation from her first marriage still haunted her every move, squashing any ray of hope or budding attraction. She furtively glanced at Dominick's profile. His

118

long eyelashes, strong and slightly crooked nose, and full lips pulled back in a boyish smile over something Phoebe had just said, enchanted her. He had changed into a pair of blue Hawaiian-style Bermuda shorts and flip flops. A plain white undershirt covered his torso. In spite of herself, the pit of Grace's middle warmed at the sight before her eyes.

Dominick must have sensed being studied. He quickly turned his head and locked eyes with Grace. Grace blushed and turned again to look out the window. What was she going to do? Grace watched as the trees thickened and the prairie vanished. They continued driving through the small wooded area until they came to a clearing where a large lake shimmered in the sunshine.

"Well, here we are ladies." Dominick put the truck into park and hopped out. He pushed the driver's seat forward and assisted Phoebe out of the back seat. "My lady."

Phoebe giggled. "You're something, aren't you."

Grace mumbled, "I have another word."

"Excuse me?" Dominick leaned his long body over the seat, his hand dangerously close to Grace's bare leg.

Grace escaped out the passenger side door and turned to look at the lake. A group of people were already seated on picnic tables, and the smell of grilling chicken and hamburgers wafted in the air. Her stomach rumbled in anticipation.

"I'm a little nervous to meet these people," Phoebe stated over Grace's shoulder.

"Me, too."

Dominick passed them carrying a large blue Igloo cooler. "Coming, ladies?"

The two sisters followed closely behind him, chattering nervously.

Dominick placed the cooler next to the other ones and started the round of introductions. "Ladies, this man right here with the Mohawk is the infamous Bruce. Ignore the hair; he lost a bet to me." Bruce bobbed his mohawked head in a greeting. "The woman next to him is his fiancée, Lauren. She hates his hair and wants to kill me. You see, the wedding is next week."

Lauren's white teeth flashed in a smile. She flicked her long blonde hair behind her and patted Dominick's arm. "I hope you haven't become too attached to Dominick, because I really do plan on killing him."

"Hey!" Noah came trotting over from the grill. He smiled at Phoebe and Grace. "It's good you two could come. I was hoping you'd show up." He motioned toward Bruce. "I see you've met the instigator of all our high school adventures."

Bruce's sun-burned face crinkled as he smiled. "Were you telling lies about me again?"

"Nothing but the truth, brother." Noah slapped Bruce's shoulder and situated himself close to Phoebe.

Dominick shook his head. "Anyway," he pointed to a flaming red-headed woman with freckles dotting her entire body, "this is Lucy, my cousin." Next to her sat a ferrety-looking man with no neck. "And this is her boyfriend, Kyle." Lucy smiled politely and extended a hand. Kyle, despite looking like a rodent, burst forth with a huge grin and enveloped the women's hands in his own warm, strong hands.

"It is great meeting you. Noah talked of nothing else this morning," Lucy exclaimed with a wink toward Phoebe. Her thick southern accent fell pleasingly on the ear, and Phoebe watched as Noah ducked his head and blushed.

Kyle chuckled and looked affectionately at Lucy. "Reign it in. You'll scare these Yankee ladies." Both Grace

120

and Phoebe blinked in surprise at the deep tone of his rich southern accent.

"Where are you two from?" Grace asked.

"Alabama. We're just up for a visit." Lucy grinned at Dominick. "I need to check up on this guy every now and then."

Dominick rolled his eyes and continued the introductions, "The rest of these people are troublemakers, and you need to stay as far away from them as possible." He pointed to the four men standing around in Bermuda shorts and flip-flops, drinking beer. "Tyler, Cole, Emmitt, and Brad."

Grace and Phoebe smiled and waved. The men smiled in return and went back to drinking their beer. Everyone found comfortable seats and Phoebe sat across from Noah. Grace looked around her and breathed deeply. She jumped slightly as Dominick bent down and whispered in her ear, "They don't bite."

Grace chewed on her lip. She could feel his warm breath on her neck and smell his Doublemint gum. This was going to be a long day.

She cleared her throat and plastered on her best smile. "Thanks. I think I'll be okay. They seem pretty nice."

"Yeah, they're pretty good people, especially Bruce and Lauren. They've been my best friends since high school. I'm actually the best man in their wedding, if I live long enough."

Grace laughed. "I think Lauren was serious when she said she'd kill you. I'd get police protection or something."

Again Dominick leaned close and whispered, "I hope you have become attached enough to me to care if she does murder me in my sleep."

121

Grace felt tingles travel the length of her body. Not knowing what to say, Grace blushed and fiddled with the ties on her black shorts.

Dominick straightened himself. "Would you like a beer?"

Grace nodded. As soon as Dominick walked away, Grace sat down next to Phoebe and pinched her leg under the table.

"Ow!" Phoebe exclaimed. Heads turned in her direction, and she smiled bashfully. "Something bit me." Turning to Grace she whispered, "What?"

"I think I'm going to hyperventilate."

Phoebe glanced over at the grill and spotted the reason for Grace's panic attack. "I can see why." Phoebe turned back to Grace and whispered, "Why are you fighting this, anyway?"

"I don't know." Grace chewed her bottom lip and watched as Dominick flipped a burger on the grill.

Phoebe squeezed Grace's arm with sisterly support and turned her attention back to Noah. Grace sat there for a moment, watching the exchange between the two. She watched as a blush worked its way up Phoebe's neck and spread across her face. Noah's hand reached out for Phoebe's, and soon the two of them were walking hand-in-hand down the beach. Easing herself out of the picnic bench, she pulled up a lawn chair next to Lauren.

"May I join you?"

Lauren turned herself around on the bench. "Of course. I'm getting tired of looking at Mohawk boy anyway."

"It brings out his eyes."

Lauren laughed, and her blue eyes shone with humor. "Yeah, it's no wonder his eyes are brown, the color of you-know-what. He's constantly getting into it, especially with his sidekick, Dominick. Those two were a pair in high school and especially college. From the way they acted you'd think they were long lost twins." Lauren glanced to the figure approaching. "Speak of the devil."

Dominick handed Grace a beer. "Talking about me?"

Lauren smacked at him. "No. We wouldn't waste our time on such a trivial thing."

"Ouch. That cut deep." Dominick winked at Grace and sauntered off to flip more burgers.

Grace watched him leave. He'd taken off his shirt, and his shorts hung low on his hips. Grace swallowed and tore her eyes back to Lauren.

Lauren sat there watching Grace. "He's a good guy, you know. He's a little cocky sometimes, but deep down inside he's got a good heart."

Grace blushed and sipped her beer. "He seems pretty nice."

Lauren smiled and rolled her eyes. "Nice? Honey, the way you look at the man I'm thinking that you think he's a little more than just nice."

Grace sat shocked. Not knowing what to say, she finished off her beer. If this kept up, she'd be drunk in an hour.

Lauren chuckled. "Sorry. I tend to speak my mind." She took a drink. "So, you've hired Dominick to renovate the old mansion, huh?"

"Yeah. Let's just say the house needs a little TLC."

"Ah, so I see you had an honest realtor in this whole business?" Lauren sighed and checked the area to see if Noah had returned with Phoebe. Seeing the two of them skipping rocks down at the beach, Lauren continued, "Dickie is something else, isn't he? Everyone calls him Dickie because we all know he hates it. Actually, when we were in high school, he was the driver's ed. teacher. We all hated him so much that the boys, including Dominick and Bruce, were constantly tormenting that man. I especially remember one incident. The boys got word that Dickie hated lime Jell-O. So one day they bought some and dumped the powder in the defrost vents of the driver's ed. car. We all thought Dickie was going to burst a blood vessel when he turned the car on and out came green, lime-scented Jell-O powder!"

Grace laughed at the mental picture. "Clever. What else did they do?"

Lauren tapped her chin and thought for a bit. She beckoned to Dominick and Bruce. When the men arrived, a cold beer and hot dog in their hands, she asked, "Hey, what else did you do to our pal, Dickie, in high school?"

Bruce sat next to Lauren and draped an arm around her. Dominick pulled up a lawn chair and sat next to Grace. He bumped her knee with his and grinned. For several minutes, Dominick, Bruce, and Lauren entertained Grace with comical stories of Dickie, the driver's ed. teacher. They regaled Grace with stories of Dickie getting himself locked *inside* the car, driving through the car wash with the back windows open, and not setting the emergency brake and watching the car drive itself into the lake.

Grace put up a hand in surrender. Her side ached from laughing and her head pounded. "Stop, please!" Before she knew what she was doing, she placed a hand on Dominick's thigh and leaned over to whisper in his ear, "Did all this really happen?"

Dominick turned his head quickly. Grace, caught unaware, didn't move back fast enough, and their noses touched. There they sat for a second, not breathing, staring directly in each other's eyes. Grace pulled away first.

That irritating smile played on Dominick's lips. "It's all true. And, they were usually of my doing."

Grace's world rocked beneath her feet. She was saved from her mental earthquake by Emmitt announcing that the food was done. Hopping up, Grace got in line next to a blushing Phoebe who had just walked back up the beach with Noah. Grace loaded her plate with a hamburger, chips, and a variety of salads. She seated herself next to Lauren and dug into her chips with gusto. She felt a presence next to her and groaned. *Dang it!* Couldn't he just let her alone for two seconds!

"Mind if I join you?"

Grace bit her lip. *Yes!* "No, have a seat."

Dominick slid in next to her. "Ready for the speedboat after this?"

Grace swallowed a bite of potato salad. "I've actually never been on one before, and I don't swim in water where I can't see the bottom."

"Really?"

"Yeah. I'm kind of a sissy that way."

Dominick grinned. "What else are you a sissy about?"

"Do you have all day?"

"For you, yeah."

Grace ducked her head and concentrated on putting mustard on her hamburger bun. She took a bite and moaned. "That is the best hamburger I've ever tasted. Which cook do I need to kiss?"

"Me."

Grace cleared her throat. "Oh. I...um..." At a loss for words Grace looked down at her plate again. This guy was causing her to become a major loser. She sensed that Dominick went back to eating, and she quickly finished her meal.

125

"Come with me," Phoebe said from behind Grace.

"Where?"

"In the water."

Grace stared at the water. Visions of slimy fish just waiting to take a nibble on her big toe sent shivers down her spine.

When she shook her head, Phoebe yanked on her arm. "Come on, Grace. It will be fun. We won't go far, and then we can go take a ride on the speedboat."

Grace glared at Phoebe. "I swear, if anything slimy, nasty, or gooey touches my leg, I will beat you with it. Clear?"

"Crystal."

Grace self-consciously peeled off her shorts and tank top, very aware of Dominick's eyes on her. Refusing to meet his glance, she walked to the water with Phoebe. Grace dipped a toe in the water. "Oh! That's cold!"

"Come on. The quicker you get in, the faster you'll warm up."

Grace slowly walked in the water, teeth chattering with the cold. "That is the stupidest thing I've ever heard."

Phoebe merely shrugged her shoulders and swam off, long arms and legs taking her farther out into the lake. Grace stood, waist deep in the murky water, sending silent curses in Phoebe's direction.

Phoebe stopped and treaded water. "Come on, Grace. I know you can swim. The Loch Ness monster lives in Scotland, not in the middle of this lake in Kansas."

Grace wanted to ask her how she could be sure, but she was perfectly aware of her audience on the sandy beach behind her. Sucking in a shaky breath, Grace started swimming toward Phoebe. The water wasn't as cold anymore, and for a blissful moment Grace forgot about the beasts lurking in the shadows of the deep.

Suddenly, something wrapped around her leg, and she felt a slight nibble on her big toe. A scream ripped from Grace, and she started flailing around. Her head submerged under the surface and water poured into her lungs. Coughing and spitting, her head broke the surface. In an instant, a pair of strong arms surrounded her.

"Just hold on to me," Dominick's voice commanded.

Grace fought him. She didn't want or need his help. Struggling to catch her breath, she pushed Dominick away. "What are you doing?"

"Rescuing you, what does it look like I'm doing?"

Grace coughed up more water and snot poured from her nose. "I don't need rescuing."

Dominick refused to let go and wrapped his arms around her tighter. "I disagree. I think you need a lot of rescuing, and I intend to be the man to do it."

Grace stared stunned at him for a millisecond. "Impertinent, presumptuous ignoramus! Unhand me now."

"No," Dominick stated matter-of-factly.

Grace glanced at the sandy beach and noticed that their audience had grown. This needed to end. Drawing back her foot she aimed for his shins and missed. She made contact with something slightly more vulnerable. He sucked in a gasp of pain and instantly let go of her. Grace swam as fast as she could for the shore.

Lauren and Phoebe met her on the beach. Grace glared at Phoebe. "Thanks for all that help out there."

"It looked as if Dominick had it all taken care of."

Lauren wrapped a towel around Grace. "You okay? We all thought you were drowning. Before any of us could react, Dominick jumped in the water. I've never seen him swim so fast."

Grace felt a stab of guilt. She turned around and watched Dominick, stooped over in pain, limp to shore. She saw him wave off help and sit down on one of the lawn chairs. She wanted to apologize but couldn't bring herself to do it. *Why do I care anyway,* she thought. He was just the carpenter she hired to do a job. How dare he assume to be anything more? Anger replaced any remorse she had felt.

Soon the speedboat was ready and everybody piled in the boat. Brad took the wheel and sped around the lake. Grace hung on for dear life, squealing in delight. Her auburn hair, escaped from the confines of the messy bun, flew behind her in waves of liquid red gold. Phoebe grabbed Grace's arm and squeezed. Talking was impossible, but Phoebe's smile told everything. Next to Phoebe sat Noah, and it was impossible to ignore a tanned arm snaking around Phoebe's shoulders. Grace grinned at her sister and gave a small thumbs-up sign.

Unaware of being studied, Grace searched the horizon with piercing green eyes. Not sure what she was looking for, she turned around and met Dominick's stare. He quickly looked away. At that moment, Grace felt a loneliness she hadn't felt since signing the divorce papers six months ago. It didn't make sense; she disliked him, so why did she care if she had burned the bridge to his heart?

Chapter Nine

Dominick sucked in a breath. There she was. Well, he couldn't run now. He was already halfway up the church's center aisle. Leaving now would certainly get tongues wagging. Gripping Lilly's hand in his, he slid into a pew.

"Daddy? This isn't our pew." Lilly tugged on Dominick's hand. He looked into her confused face. How does a man explain his own cowardice over a woman to a girl barely five years old?

With a forced gaiety he didn't feel, Dominick smiled. "Think of this as an adventure. We're simply trying out a new pew today. Maybe the angels can hear you better from here." He winked and felt utter relief when Lilly seemed to take his explanation as Biblical truth.

His attention was diverted from his daughter when the organist began the beginning chords of the opening hymn. Hoping churchy thinking would keep his mind off Grace, Dominick forced himself to pay attention to the service. His eyes, however, kept wandering to stare at Grace's beautiful auburn hair sweeping down her back. Between trying to ignore Grace and making sure Lilly behaved herself, he caught the pastor's words only in snippets and fragments. Something about love; something about Jacob and Rachel; something about a sacrifice. Finally the torturous service was over. If Grace kept coming to this church, he'd seriously have to think about switching. Hoping to get out of there before Grace saw him, he hurried out of the pew and ran smack dab into Annie.

"Well, hello, little darlin'!" Annie bent down and gave Lilly a kiss on the cheek. "I see you tried a new pew out today; did the angels hear you better?"

The fact that Mrs. Wisel knew about the angels, too, caused little Lilly to grin from ear to ear. "I hope so; I sang 'specially loud."

"I know, dear; Annie heard you, and trust me, so did those angels." After giving Lilly a sucker, Annie straightened herself to her full height. With a look of caring curiosity, she studied Dominick. Getting twitchy under her gaze, he started to think of an excuse to go. But Annie saved him from another lie.

"I hear you had some trouble at the lake."

Dominick felt a blush creep up his neck. He hated small towns sometimes. "Nope. No trouble, Mrs. Wisel."

Annie waved a dismissive hand in the air. "Don't you go telling lies, Dominick Carson. I think you have w-o-m-a-n troubles on your hands, don't you?"

"Did a woman get into trouble, Daddy?" Lilly quit licking her sucker long enough to prove that spelling words no longer worked around her.

"No, sweetheart, Mrs. Wisel is just talking about a friend of hers, that's all."

"And here she is," Annie squeaked and waved excitedly for Grace and Phoebe to join their little posse. With an internal groan, Dominick forced a smile on his face and turned to welcome Grace to church. He forced himself to look her in the eyes. He didn't like what he saw. Cursing himself for his stupid hero antics yesterday, Dominick realized from looking into her eyes that he'd screwed up. Her eyes, however, went from quietly resigned to enchanted as she saw the little girl by his side.

"Well, aren't you a pretty little angel." Grace got down on one knee and shook Lilly's hand. "I told my sister, Phoebe, we'd see one today!" Dominick watched as Lilly came to life and began chattering with Grace. By the end of their discussion, Lilly had a new best friend and a guest to tea, a very big deal. *A very big problem*, Dominick sighed as he watched Grace and Phoebe head out to the church parking lot.

"Daddy, do you think Mommy will be mad that I invited Grace to my tea party?"

Dominick stooped down and brushed a wisp of blonde hair behind Lilly's ear. "I think Mommy would be very glad that you've found a new friend."

"Good, because I like her; she's pretty."

Me, too! Dominick shook his head. *It probably didn't matter anymore, though. She probably doesn't want anything to do with me after yesterday.* He held on to Lilly's hand and walked out of the church and into the sunshine. *And yes*, he thought as he watched Grace drive off, *she was pretty*.

Grace stared up at the ceiling at the blinking red light. She dreaded going to the house today. Dominick would be there. Yesterday proved that it'd be difficult to cohabitate the same space. She wished she could give it all up and go home, wherever that was? Grace groaned and rolled over, planting her face deep into her pillow. Why couldn't she have just let him be the hero? Why was it so hard for her to admit the fact that she had overreacted? Dominick really had believed she was drowning. His desire to rescue her had been legit, so why had she fought him off instead of welcome his assistance? After all, if Noah or one of the other men had tried to help her, she would have accepted it gratefully. Instead she had acted like a lunatic. Grace wanted to punch herself. With a grunt of resignation and humiliation, Grace slithered out of bed and dressed for an early morning run.

131

Ignoring the Tuesday morning traffic, Grace sprinted down Main Street. The smell of Reed's Diner tickled her nose. Ignoring the impulse to stop and order a platter of biscuits and gravy, Grace plowed on back to the hotel.

Phoebe jumped at the sound of the door slamming. "What in the world?" With a face plastered in a cucumber masque, Phoebe approached Grace. "Did you break the world record?"

Grace bent over and hugged her knees. Her chest heaved, and her legs ached. "Not quite," Grace panted. She held up a hand to stem another question and commenced stretching.

Phoebe experimentally touched the drying masque. Phoebe grinned, and the green dried goop crackled around her mouth. "Ding. I think I'm done!" Phoebe skipped off to the sink and proceeded to peel off the masque. Grace rolled her eyes and skidded into the bathroom for a quick shower. Once finished and topped off with a slight touch of makeup, Grace sat on the edge of the bed, tapping her foot impatiently.

Phoebe paused with the mascara wand hanging in mid-air. "That will only make me go slower, you know."

Grace huffed and tried to steady her bouncing feet. "It's only going to melt off your face."

Phoebe ignored her and applied lipstick, smacked her lips together, spritzed on perfume, and presented herself in front of her sister. "How do I look?"

Grace refused to answer and shoved Phoebe's purse into Phoebe's arms. With a last look in the mirror, Grace tucked a stray hair behind her ear and stalked out of the room.

Phoebe followed with quick steps. "I suggest that you remove whatever crawled up your butt and died. It's making your attitude really stink."

Grace stopped and blew out a frustrated breath. "I'm sorry. I'm taking my frustration out on you, and that is not fair." Grace continued walking down the hallway. "I'm confused about Dominick, okay. He's an egotistical...oooohhh....whatever! I can't stop thinking about him. And his little girl is so precious. According to Annie, he dotes on her; she is his universe. That says a lot about a man. Why, Kevin did all he could to *not* have children."

Phoebe squeezed Grace's arm. "Not every man is Kevin, Grace. When are you going to understand that? Besides, everything will work out. Remember that verse from 1 Corinthians? The one about God not tempting us beyond what we can handle? Yeah, don't forget the last part about Him saying that He'll make sure He gives you what you need to endure it."

Grace unlocked the truck and scooted in. "Yeah, I suppose you're right. I just wish I wasn't in this crap to begin with."

Grace drove through the Dairy Queen drive-thru and ordered food for them and Dominick. A little peace offering might get him talking to her again. His behavior after the church service on Sunday sure hadn't encouraged her, and yesterday he had only grunted answers at her questions. The playful banter and flirting were gone. It had been all business--water pipes, potential plumbing issues, and more squirrel babies in the attic.

Grace began munching on her meal as she maneuvered the old truck down the highway and onto the gravel road.

Phoebe eyed the third Blizzard. "So, can I have it if Dominick doesn't want it?"

"No!" Grace stuffed a hot, salty fry in her mouth and chewed vigorously. Seeing Phoebe's fallen face she added, "Don't you know a Snicker's Blizzard fixes everything." She glanced at herself in the rear view mirror. Her pale skin and the dark circles under her eyes belied two restless nights and the constant roller coaster of emotion she'd been riding.

"I still can't believe you kicked him in the you-know-where! It's certainly a Blizzard offense." Phoebe snatched a fry from Dominick's bag. "He doesn't need the extra calories."

"I think that man has the metabolism of a teenage boy. Certainly still acts like one."

Phoebe checked her lipstick as the truck approached the driveway. "Someone's got it bad for Carpenter Hottie."

"Enough. You're delirious again." Grace parked in front of the house, slid out of the truck, and slammed the door.

Phoebe grabbed her bag and Nerds Blizzard and with a quick wave ambled off to the back of the house. Grace breathed a silent prayer of thanks for her sister. There is no way she'd be able to do this by herself. With an amused shake of her head, Grace took the two remaining bags and Blizzards and began her search for Dominick. After several inquiries and misleading clues, she found him perched on a ladder fixing the wiring in what would become her room. "Hey."

Dominick looked down at her. "Hey."

She held out a bag and Blizzard. "I got you a burger and fries and a Snickers Blizzard."

"No thanks. I've already eaten."

134

Grace looked over at a cooler sitting in the corner of the room. She stomped over to it and yanked open the cover. In it lay an uneaten lunch.

"What the heck?" Grace demanded.

Dominick stopped fiddling with the different colored wires and studied her for a moment. He had let this woman into his heart, and now she had consumed him; he couldn't get her out of his mind. He dreamed of her; he smelled her perfume no matter where he was. Something inside of him snapped; he just had to know. "Tell me this. Why do you care?"

Grace stared stunned. At a loss for words, she slammed the lid of his cooler, threw his food and Blizzard out the window, and started to walk out. Dominick jumped off the ladder and caught her arm before she made the doorway.

"Let go of me," Grace demanded through clenched teeth.

"Haven't we already been through this? No." Dominick only tightened his grip on her arm.

"Ow! You're hurting me."

Dominick moved quickly and pinned her against the wall with his body. His leg rested comfortably between hers and he could feel heat radiating off her. His breathing was ragged and his breath fell hot on her cheek. "Is that better?"

Grace felt as though she would faint. His chest pressed hard against hers, and she could swear she felt his heart race. Grace turned her face away from his and concentrated on looking out the window. Maybe help would come soon. *No, it wouldn't*, she thought with a mixture of despair and excitement. Phoebe was having a

135

moment with her Nerds Blizzard, and the rest of the men were taking a siesta in any available shade.

Grace struggled to free herself but only succeeded in rubbing her body against his. Fear and desire licked at her insides. She needed to escape before he breached the walls she had worked so hard to build. Bringing back her leg, she prepared to kick.

"I'd rethink that move," Dominick whispered in her ear. "I won't be held responsible for my actions if you choose to kick me again."

"Let me go," Grace breathed.

Dominick slowly released Grace and stood before her. His eyes, the color of dark chocolate, smoldered with emotion. Without a word, he turned his back to her, climbed the ladder, and began working again. For a moment, Grace just leaned against the wall, unable to move a muscle.

Humiliated, Grace snatched her Blizzard and food and dashed from the room right into the arms of Dickie.

Grace shrieked and jumped back a couple of feet.

"I usually don't get that reaction from the ladies, you know. I usually need to beat them off with a stick." Dickie smoothed the wrinkled over-stretched material of his sunny yellow polo shirt.

Humiliation times two! Flustered beyond reply, Grace tried to squeeze past him in the narrow hallway. Just when she thought she was free to run, a meaty hand grabbed her arm.

"Wait a minute; I got something I gotta ask you." Dickie's grinned at her, his face only inches from her own. "My wife wanted me to come by and see if you'd be interested in going on a trip to an auction this Friday. She wanted me to relay the message that there will be 'oodles and oodles' of whatever it is you're looking for."

Forcing her mind to register this information, it took Grace a second or two to realize that she needed to respond to this man before she could be rid of him. "Yeah, sure, that'll be great." Glancing down at her arm which was still being held hostage by his clammy hand, she yanked it away, and without another word, strode away. Dickie looked after her and shrugged his shoulders.

Grace didn't know it, but her run in with Dickie was the best thing that could have happened at that moment. Her spunk was back along with her determination not to let Dominick, or any other man, get the best of her. What she needed now was to find Phoebe; some comic relief would make her feel her old self again. She found Phoebe on the back porch just wrapping up an intimate date with her Nerds Blizzard. Grace smiled. *Yup, it worked!*

"And you think my infatuation with ice cream is creepy." Grace plopped herself down beside her sister and counted her blessings.

Phoebe grinned at her. "I want to marry the person who thought of combining Nerds and a Blizzard."

Grace gave Phoebe a quick squeeze. "You'd probably end up marrying some snot-nosed high school booger-eater in need of a sugar fix."

Phoebe chewed on her spoon and contemplated the idea. "Worth it."

Grace rolled her eyes and rested her head on one of the porch railings. "We've been invited to go on a treasure hunt with Annie. I ran into Dickie, literally, just now."

Phoebe shivered. "That man gives me the creeps. Is he coming with on this little hunt?"

Grace shivered at the idea. "I don't think so; he really didn't say."

"Good. Then I'm pumped to go."

Grace and Phoebe sat in mutual silence for several minutes watching the trees sway in the gentle breeze. Insects surfed on the air waves, constantly buzzing their glee. Mrs. Sloucombe came up to Grace and rubbed against her leg, purring for attention. Absentmindedly, she stroked her fluffy fur and tried to understand what had just happened between her and Dominick. It didn't make sense; the fear of failure had her retreating before she even took the first step.

With a sigh of resignation, Grace pushed herself to her feet. "Come on, Pheebs. Just a couple of more hours and we can quit for the day. We've pretty much done everything we can do in the parlor and the dining room. The back parlor is too big of a mess right now for us to handle. I think we should start upstairs. I'll take the nursery. and you can start on the library." Grace pointed to the small pond. "Dominick's men will start digging next week so the gazebo can get built. For some reason they have to level the ground so something can do something else and yadda yadda yadda."

"I didn't think you were on speaking terms with him?"

"I'm not. I simply talked to the next guy in charge." Grace studied the landscape before her. After the shrubs and roses were planted, the gazebo would be the highlight of the place. Enjoying the visions dancing in her head, Grace patted Phoebe's arm. "Time to get to work!"

"Okey dokey, artichokey."

Dominick slammed his truck door with a little more force than necessary. But it felt good. That infernal woman was making him crazy! He checked his watch; the day was almost over, and with any luck, he could avoid her until quitting time. With needed tool in hand, he marched back into the house and ran smack dab into Grace. At her little gasp of surprise, it took all his willpower not to kiss her senseless right in the middle of the foyer, right in front of his men. Forcing himself to look into her eyes, he lost himself in the immense sea of green.

"Sorry." Her mumbled apology snapped him back into reality.

"No, it was my fault." Dominick opened his mouth to say more and then snapped it shut again. After a few more moments of resembling a dying salmon, Dominick stuttered, "Look, I...I...well, I just wanted to say sorry... for what happened earlier." Not willing to wait for a reply, he stalked off in the direction of a pesky piece of sheetrock. At least that didn't make him want to break out sporadically in song one minute and punch himself in the face the next.

Chapter Ten

Grace pulled into the driveway, and the old truck lumbered up to the house. The men were busy at work and didn't even acknowledge the backfire from the tailpipe when Grace turned the truck off.

"You know, I'm getting a little attached to this old thing," Grace stated with a smile as she jumped out.

Phoebe kicked the door shut. "Yeah, I especially love the lack of shock absorbers and the air conditioning that doesn't work."

"It's all part of the experience."

Phoebe snorted a laugh, and they made their way into the house. They stood in stunned silence. Was this the same house they'd bought only two weeks ago? The entire first floor, gutted and cleaned, looked larger and very promising. They ran to their respective bedrooms and both gasped with delight.

"Holy crap, Grace! Come look at this," Phoebe called excitedly from her bedroom.

Across the hall, Grace gaped in stunned silence at her new room. "Yeah, I'll be there in a minute." Walls of grayish blue and gleaming woodwork enveloped the room. The bay window boasted a window seat, complete with an antique vase bursting with blue bachelor buttons. Grace tore her eyes from the bouquet and stared at the shiny hardwood floors glistening with polyurethane. A crow's feet pattern marked the pristine white ceiling and crown molding stained to match the rest of the woodwork in the room elegantly separated the ceiling and walls. Two doors were placed on one wall. One door led to a small bathroom with bronze fixtures. The other door opened up to a small walk-in closet complete with shelves.

"Grace, you need to come see this," Phoebe called again from her bedroom.

"Coming." In a dreamlike trance, Grace pulled herself away from her bedroom.

"Excuse me, ma'am?"

Grace, startled, placed a hand over her heart. Facing the voice, she encountered an acne victim no more than sixteen.

"I didn't mean to scare you, ma'am; it's just that I was wondering if you've seen the boss around."

The boss? Oh, yeah. "No, I haven't seen Dominick for quite some time now." Ever since she'd run into him in the foyer earlier.

"Oh, okay." The boy, looking awkward and uncomfortable, studied his shoes. He kept opening his mouth to talk but kept closing it again. He reminded Grace of a guppie. "Well...I was wondering...since...well...do you like your room?"

All that for such a simple question? Grace looked at the boy with pity. He must get his lunch money taken by the school bully. Grace smiled brightly. "Yes! I love it. Did you work on it?"

The boy ducked his head and watched in fascination as his toe drew imaginary circles in the floorboards. "Well...I...we weren't allowed to be in here."

"What do you mean?"

"Well...the boss told us that this room was...special. He didn't want any screw ups. I heard he was even out here during the evenings when everyone else had gone home."

Grace's mouth went bone dry. She managed to thank the boy and made her way into Phoebe's bedroom.

141

A soft pink met her eye. The ceiling bore the same crow's feet design, and Phoebe's room also housed a bathroom and small walk-in closet.

Phoebe turned to her with a beaming smile. "Isn't this just peachy?" Phoebe danced around the room, skipping and hopping. "It's pink! Just what I wanted! Did you see my bathroom? Isn't it great?"

Grace nodded and smiled at her sister. Phoebe's room, nearly identical except for the bay window, lacked one thing--Dominick's special touch.

Leo Muldoon sat outside the Super 8 motel and watched a set of certain curtains blowing in the night breeze. *How simple it would be to creep up to the window and...*Leo's thoughts were interrupted when his iPhone chirped.

With a scowl he reached for it, but upon seeing the caller ID, his lips writhed into a cruel smile. *My, my, my, little fly. How nice of you to fly back to my little trap.*

Leo tapped the green phone icon on his screen. "Hello, my dear." Gone was the hard and surly voice of Leo. Instead, the voice of Andrew Carnegie drawled softly, "I've missed you."

"Well, you were supposed to call last night, and you didn't! That's not very fair, making me wait up all night. I was worried about you."

Leo lit up a cigar. *What a witch. Maybe I did old Jeremiah a favor by putting a bullet in his head.* He knew she'd have her hand wrapped around a freshly-poured glass of Scotch. He was also aware of what she'd be wearing. Too bad he was in the truck. Their Skype session would have to be postponed. But, some sacrifices had to be made for his revenge to be complete. And Mrs. Wallace was certainly the final corner piece.

"Now, honey, I'm so sorry. I had to work late last night for these two nasty women, and well, I didn't want to interrupt your sweet dreams." Leo exhaled the cigar smoke. "I dreamt of you last night."

The soft cooings of Jeremiah's wife made Leo want to gag. Her cooings soon turned to suggestions. He flicked his half-smoked cigar out of the heavily-tinted truck window, shut it, and roared his truck to the hotel room he'd rented. It was time for the much anticipated Skype session with the heavily intoxicated and very scantily clad Mrs. Jeremiah Wallace.

Chapter Eleven

"There's no place like home. There's no place like home." *Home?* Grace watched as Dorothy clicked the heels of her ruby shoes together. She tore her eyes from the television screen and gazed around the hotel room she shared with her sister. Suitcases stacked neatly against the wall, a pizza box from last night leaking grease onto the little table under it, and Phoebe's dirty socks sticking out from under the bed met her gaze.

Where is my home? Grace chewed her bottom lip and thought about her blue room at the old house. It was perfect, but could it be a home to her? Grace shook her head and tried not to think about the man who created it for her. After all, he was just a man she had hired to do a job. At the end of the project, he'll walk out of her life and into another one.

But this time she would walk first. She stalked to the bathroom and readied herself for a day of antique hunting. As she shaved her legs in the shower, she resolved to leave Dominick behind and continue the new life she'd started for herself.

"Can I come in?" Phoebe called urgently through the door.

"Why?"

"I've got to pee like a race horse!"

Grace huffed, "Yeah, I suppose."

The door slammed open, and Grace could hear Phoebe dance around trying to undo her pajama ties. "Dang it! I can't undo my ties. Ooohhh, I'm so going to pee my pants!"

"Cut them."

Phoebe sucked in a sharp breath. "I can't do that! These are my favorite pajamas."

Grace rolled her eyes and chuckled. "You'll just have to pee your pants then."

Silence. Grace stopped washing her hair. "Phoebe?"

A half cry and half giggle emanated through the shower curtain. Grace poked her head out of the shower curtain and stared. There Phoebe sat on the bathroom floor, hyperventilating with laughter and tears. Her pajama bottoms were wet.

"Holy crap!" Grace exclaimed. "Did you really just pee your pants."

Phoebe, still gasping for breath, nodded her head and then exploded into hysterics. Concerned, Grace quickly rinsed the soap from her hair, snatched a towel from the towel rack, and stepped out from behind the curtain. Careful to avoid the puddle of yellow, Grace perched atop the toilet and patted Phoebe's head. Phoebe, still trying to control herself, snorted a laugh and descended down the spiral of hysterics again. Grace thought about slapping her like people do to the hysterical woman in disaster movies but thought better of it.

"Pheebs, you need to calm down now."

Sniffle, sniffle, snort, burp. Phoebe giggled and pressed a hand over her mouth. With tear-filled eyes, Phoebe looked at her sister. "I peed my pants. I'm a loser."

"No, dear, you're not a loser. You're a dork. There's a big difference."

Phoebe exploded into tears and pressed her face into her hands and mumbled something that sounded strangely like, "Men don't like sporks who peedle themselves."

145

"Did you just call yourself a spork?"

Phoebe giggled into her hands. After a few minutes of composing herself, she lifted her head and stared at her wet bottoms. "I was trying to say dorks but I drooled a little."

Grace rolled her eyes, bent over, and planted a kiss on the top of Phoebe's head. "You are special." Grace sniffed. "You need a shower; you smell like pee."

Grace and Phoebe were about to walk out of the hotel room when Lauren, the bride to be, knocked on their door.

"Hey, ladies." Lauren bounded into the room. "You know that my wedding is tomorrow, right?"

Grace and Phoebe nodded.

"Well, Bruce and I would like you to come to the reception. It's at the VFW."

"Thanks." Grace forced a smile. The last place she wanted to be was in Dominick's presence, willingly.

Lauren peered closely at Grace. "I really would like you to come." With a smile, Lauren headed for the door. "Got to go. Lots of last minute things to do today. Don't forget, tomorrow, VFW, 6:00 p.m." With that, Lauren was gone, leaving Grace and Phoebe in the wake of a bride's fevered excitement.

Phoebe beamed at Grace. "I love going to weddings!"

Grace grimaced. "Yeah, me, too."

The girls met Annie at her store and loaded up in Annie's truck. Annie, her plump little self, looked remarkably silly behind the wheel of the Dodge Ram pickup. A pair of pink fuzzy dice dangled on the rearview mirror, and a pair of bull's nuts dangled off the rear hitch.

Grace smiled to herself. No truck is complete without a pair of gonads and fuzzy dice.

"I've been waiting for this all week," Annie chirped from the driver's seat as she ran the only red light in town.

Grace watched in fascinated terror as a lumbering grain truck slammed on its brakes to avoid T-boning the shiny grey pickup with hot pink pin striping. Sadly, Grace's life never flashed before her eyes. That either meant that seeing that flash was indeed a myth, or she didn't have a life worth a flash.

Shaking her head and breathing deeply, Grace agreed with Annie, "Phoebe and I can't wait to see what they have at the auction. How do these things usually work?"

"Oh, my dear, it's like a jungle. Everyone turns into a rabid hungry beast!" Annie sounded a little too thrilled. "Fights break out, and people sometimes leave with black eyes."

Phoebe squealed in excitement from the backseat, "Awesome. I love watching people duke it out." Phoebe fisted and unfisted her hand. "I'm prepared to kick some butt."

Grace turned around in her seat. "You can't even kill a fly on the off chance it will come back to life and kill you in your sleep."

Phoebe pouted. "So? Anyway, humans are different than flies. They stay dead." Phoebe licked her lips and whispered, "They do, don't they?"

Annie roared with laughter and the truck lurched toward the ditch. "Oh goodness, my dears, you two are a breath of fresh air."

Phoebe grinned stupidly from the backseat. "Thanks."

The majority of the two-hour journey included a few near-death accidents, a couple of motorists sending them rude hand gestures, and a few pit stops because Grace and Phoebe had to pee.

"Well, here we are, dears, fit as fiddles and ready for bloodshed."

Grace and Phoebe untangled themselves from the pickup and bounded into the arena. The sight before them caused them to gape. Booths selling everything from leather products to slushies dotted the outside of the giant oval. In the middle, people of every size, shape, and color milled excitedly and noisily around, studying objects and making wish lists on pads of paper. Smells of dough products baked by little old ladies, leather products made from little old dead animals, and just plain old things mixed into an odd-smelling stew.

Grace crinkled her nose against the onslaught of odors. "Stinky."

"Really?" Phoebe inhaled. "I think it smells good. I'm hungry."

Grace rolled her eyes, grabbed Phoebe's arm, and followed Annie, who forcefully made her way through the thick crowd.

Annie huffed and puffed from the front of the pack. "I told you it was a jungle in here."

Grace and Phoebe grinned at each other and rolled their eyes. A few minutes brought them to the area they'd been looking for. An entire section dedicated to the Queen Victorian style stood before them in all its glory. Grace and Phoebe immediately began browsing.

"Look at this." Phoebe grabbed Grace's arm and tugged.

Grace stared in amazement at the walnut bedstead before her. "Beautiful." The elegantly curved headboard sported intricate carvings and the footboard, with its plain yet graceful lines, begged for a home at the Hamlin house. Grace peered at the recommended selling price and gulped. The price for one bed didn't bother her; it was the price of five of them that had Grace doing quick calculations in her head.

"Here's the deal, Pheebs, we could purchase this bed and put it in the master suite. We were going to charge a little more for that room anyway. We'll have to be careful in purchasing items for the other rooms. We want the furniture to be authentic, but I don't want to be in the poor house either."

Phoebe nodded in agreement. Grace wrote down the item number and began searching again. At the end of two hours, sweat trickled down the girls' backs, and their stomachs rumbled. Glancing down at their wish list, Grace grimaced. Too many wants, too little funds.

Over hot dogs, chips, and funnel cakes, Grace and Phoebe studied the list and sadly crossed many things off.

"Maybe, my dears, the price won't go as high as the recommended selling price. You never know with these animals," Annie chirped around a mouthful of sauerkraut.

Grace wiped her mouth with a napkin and nodded, "I hope that you are right." The sound of feedback from a microphone signaled the auction's start. Grace watched as a chunky man who'd squeezed himself into a very tight pair of Wranglers made his way stiffly up the steps and onto the platform in the middle of the arena. With a large white Stetson hat planted firmly on his head, the auctioneer welcomed all the "antique hunters" to the "greatest auction in the tri-state area."

The auctioneer started out at a fast ramble. Paintings, from some artist Grace had never heard of, were auctioned off at lightning speed. Being sucked in by the auctioneer's hypnotic rhythm, Grace found herself almost raising her hand to buy a painting of a cow and calf grazing by a gurgling brook.

"Next up, folks, we've got a lovely Queen Victorian bedstead made from solid walnut with one-of-a-kind carvings." The auctioneer began his rhythmic and hypnotic chanting. Grace stuck her number in the air. The auctioneer's assistants pointed her out. A few other people as well stuck their numbers in the air, and Grace immediately hated them. The price continued to climb and sweat beaded on Grace's forehead. She could feel sweat running down her armpits, and she wished she'd applied the clinical strength stuff.

Soon, Grace and a little grey-haired old lady with the tightest perm Grace had ever seen were the only ones left standing. Grace studied her opponent. No more than five feet tall, the old lady wore a yellow calico polyester dress that hit just below saggy, wrinkly knees. Thigh high nylons sagged around the woman's varicose-vein infested ankles, and white orthopedic tennis shoes completed the ensemble. Grace shrugged nonchalantly; she could take this little old lady down. No problem. Just then the little old lady turned and sent death rays out of her eyes.

Grace gasped and turned in fear to Phoebe. "If looks could kill, I'd be dead by now!" She tilted her head toward the woman. "Do you see her? She's freaky."

Phoebe studied her sister's enemy. "Sorry, can't help you. She looks like she might be like a fly and not stay dead."

Grace gulped with nervousness and met the old lady's steely glare with a glare of her own. Just like the old Westerns, Grace thought. All they needed were some six-shooters and some chaps. With lightning speed the old lady raised her number in the air. Grace shot her number up in the air as well. There was no way this old bat was going to sleep in that bed.

The old lady mouthed the word "hussy" as she shot her number up in the air again. Grace gasped in shock at the dirty-mouthed, old hag. Grace thought about giving her some Orbit gum but she only had one piece left. With a slight growl of determination Grace popped her arm up and heard something go "pop." Sucking in a gasp of pain, Grace quickly switched hands. Sacrifice your body for the game, Grace told herself.

Phoebe patted Grace's back. "Go get 'em, tiger." Phoebe squealed with excitement, "Annie was right. This is a jungle, and these people are crazy!"

Grace nodded and concentrated on the auctioneer's prices. Keeping a wary gaze on the yellow-clad crazy lady, Grace hoped that her hip would give out. No, she'd still be able to raise her arm. *Maybe a small break in both arms?* Grace shook her head. Not good. There would be witnesses and she was far too pretty to go to jail.

The price called out sent Grace into a tizzy. This was the price at which she and Phoebe had agreed to stop. Staring at the old lady, she prayed that she wouldn't see that creepy, claw-like hand paw at the air. The old lady cussed and spat on the floor. With a derogatory name thrown in Grace's direction, the old lady stomped off in her orthopedics, looking for another enemy.

"Holy crap! That lady scared me." Phoebe quit hiding behind Grace and peeked around Grace's bad shoulder.

"Thanks for all the love and support. I couldn't have done it without you."

"Ya know, sarcasm doesn't look good on you; it clashes with your eyes."

Annie bustled up to Grace, huffing and puffing with excitement. "Oh, my dear, that was just like one of the Rocky movies I've seen. I think it was the one with the Russian. He was hot. Anyway, where was I? Oh, yeah. She had you in the corner, but you just kept going and going like the Energizer Bunny."

Grace rapidly blinked and tried to compute everything said to her. "Annie, I'm not sure, but I think that's the first time anyone has compared me to Rocky and the Energizer Bunny in the same sentence."

"Did I offend you?" Annie patted Grace's bad shoulder, causing Grace to suck in a breath. "Oh, my dear, those are total compliments. They're superheroes."

Phoebe leaned over and whispered in Grace's ear. "She's a loon."

Grace waited until Annie had walked off in the direction of the slushie stand. "That's what happens when you marry a Dick."

The hot pink pin striped Dodge Ram groaned under the weight of numerous antique items ranging from dinnerware to furniture. Grace and Phoebe held on for dear life as Annie lurched into oncoming traffic.

"Um, Annie, do you mind if I drive? I've always wanted to drive such a big truck."

Annie gave a toothy grin. "Sure. Why don't we swing through McDonald's and then we can switch over.

"Can we swing into the mall first? Phoebe and I need to find dresses for Lauren and Bruce's wedding."

"Oooohhhh! I love shopping." Annie clapped her hands with glee and jumped up and down. Grace furtively checked for a puddle under Annie and was glad to see that Annie hadn't wet herself.

Two hours later, the three women, armed with new dresses, chocolate milk shakes, Big Macs, and fries, started making their way back to Beacon.

"I've never had this much fun," Annie mumbled over a bite of Big Mac.

Grace thought about the day and couldn't help but agree. "Yeah, it was pretty fun. And you were right about the whole jungle thing. I think I saw two old men in suspenders having a fist fight over the last hot dog."

Phoebe piped up from the back. "I saw some skinny woman punch out a rather large lady with a rose tattoo on her shoulder. But I think that was because the skinny lady caught her husband doing the fat lady in the bathroom."

Grace choked on a half-swallowed fry. Annie assisted by slapping her on the back. Grace held up one hand. "Stop!" Taking a drink of Diet Coke, Grace cleared her throat.

"I don't know why I'm asking this, but how do you know?"

"I was unfortunate enough to be in the stall next to fat lady and cheating husband."

"And you say I have all the fun."

It was after six before the three women pulled into the long gravel drive. Grace's heart stopped. Parked in front of their house were two cop cars with their emergency lights reflecting off the newly-painted house. Her eyes darted over to Dominick's truck and her heart stopped. What if something had happened to him? Not seeing an ambulance, her heart slowed, slightly. With quick movements, Grace slammed the truck in park and jumped out. Phoebe caught up with her and clutched Grace's hand.

"Whoa there, ma'am." Grace whirled on a red-faced young cop. His nervous eyes darted from her face to the entrance of the house. "You can't go in there."

"I'm Grace McIntyre and this is my sister, Phoebe. We own this place." Taking a deep breath and willing herself to hear the worst, she forced herself to ask the question, "What's going on here?"

"Someone broke into your house, ma'am, and well...they did a lot of damage. There's a lot of blood..." Grace stared in fascination as the officer's complexion drained of all color.

"Blood?" Grace nearly threw up on Officer Newbie's shoes. Phoebe simply squeaked.

"Oh, yeah, the perpetrators thought they'd leave you a welcome present of a few disemboweled squirrels."

Grace threw up right on the officer's shiny shoes. The next thing she knew, a pair of familiar strong arms was leading her to the front porch steps. Too exhausted to fight the supportive embrace, she allowed herself a moment of weakness. Just a minute. *Who would do this, and why? My house and those poor little squirrels.* Grace's eyes snapped open and her body sprang to life. "I gotta see it!"

"Shhh." Dominick wrapped his arms tighter around her. "It's okay. I've got it all taken care of. You don't have to worry about a thing." He gently turned her face toward his and studied her.

Her terrified eyes stared back at him. Grace watched him warily as he studied her face. She knew he was taking in the dark circles under her eyes. She saw his hand reach for a lock of her hair, and she quickly jerked away from his hold. Grace stood shakily to her feet. "Where's Phoebe?"

Dominick nodded toward the cop car. Sitting on the hood, Phoebe was leaning against Annie's shoulder and

154

breathing into a paper bag. Dominick got up, careful to keep a small distance between them. "We all left around five. I had just gotten back to my house when I realized I forgot my cell phone. When I got back here, the window was busted so I called the cops." Dominick threaded his fingers through his hair.

"What am I supposed to do?" Grace struggled to regain control. When Dominick gently grabbed her bad arm to pull her toward him, she wrenched it away and yelped in pain.

Concern was etched across his face. "I'm so sorry. I didn't mean to hurt you."

"No, I over extended it today." Grace put distance between her and Dominick. With all that was going on, she certainly did not need man problems. Facing her house she straightened her shoulders. She wasn't about to let some squirrel killers keep her from her dream.

With purposeful strides, she ascended the steps, entered the foyer, and burst into fresh tears. On every wall in the main room were slashes of blood. Ten squirrel carcasses hung from the ceiling by nails driven in to furry little tails. Rage replaced fear. When she found the person responsible for this she'd…she'd…Grace didn't know what she'd do, but she knew without a doubt it'd be painful and long-lasting.

She turned at the sound of Dominick's footsteps behind her. "Whatever you do, do not let Phoebe in here."

Dominick nodded and gestured to the gory mess. "It looks like someone is trying to scare you."

Grace simply stared at him. "Really? What gave you the first clue?

Dominick quickly squelched the hot retort she deserved. He noticed her fighting stance and clenched fists.

If he wasn't careful, he'd get himself into a load of trouble, but maybe that's just what he needed. Every fiber in his body told him not to, but, dang it, she looked so beautiful when she was angry. Without thinking, Dominick grabbed her around the waist, ignored her yelp of surprise, and kissed her. His heart hammered in his chest, and he wasn't sure if he was still breathing; he really didn't care. What mattered was having her body pressed up against his and her warm full lips unmoving under...Dominick stopped. With his lips still on hers, he cautiously opened his eyes. Green eyes, full of anger times rage slammed into him. *Jerk!* Dominick reprimanded himself. Slowly, he released his hold on her. He tried to think of something to say. Anything, really. But nothing came. Knowing that he had just made a complete horse's ass out of himself, he cleared his throat, mumbled something unintelligible, and stalked out of the house.

Grace watched him stomp down the steps, say a few words to the police officers, pat Phoebe on the head, and roar off in his truck. Grace had never fainted in her life, but standing here in the middle of dead squirrels with her lips still tingling from Dominick's kiss, she thought she just might. Instead she gently traced her lips with her tongue. *Dang! Wintergreen! My favorite!* Coming to her senses, she wiped her mouth off on her shirt sleeve. *Ogre! Who kisses a woman in her darkest hour?* Dominick did, and as Grace headed to check out her room, she knew why she was so mad. She had liked it, a lot.

Fumbling for the light switch, she cursed herself. What made him different than Kevin? What made him a man she could trust? Light illuminated Grace's room at the flick of the switch. She sucked in a gasp. Dominick had been at work. Along one of the walls sat a walnut writing

156

desk with a matching chair scooted up to it. On the floor lay a beautiful Oriental rug embellished with peacock blue and forest green swirls. A small lump caught in Grace's throat. That man was slowly breaking down her walls. Defiantly, she chose to put another layer of bricks up as she flicked off the light, leaving her new room in darkness.

Leaving the house, Grace spoke again with the officer in charge, and being reassured there was nothing left for her to do, she gathered up the still weeping Phoebe and loaded her into Annie's awaiting truck.

As they drove down the driveway, the two sisters were unaware of a hunched figure in the tree grove watching the tail lights with fever-pitched hilarity. In silence the man watched the police finish up their business and leave. *Idiot police.* The man chuckled. They wouldn't know a criminal if he wiggled butt-naked on their faces! Knowing he was finally alone again, he straightened up and walked back to his truck. His "romance" with Delilah Wallace was budding just as he'd planned. She'd be the last victim. But first, he had unfinished business with the offspring of the man who'd killed his father. With a wolf-like grin spreading across his face, he knew the time was nearing for the ultimate conquest. Throwing back his head, he howled at the moon.

Chapter Twelve

Humid June air penetrated the house, making Grace's job much more detestable. One of Dominick's men had already removed the tiny squirrel carcasses from the foyer. However, Grace couldn't get the image of the baby squirrels dangling lifelessly out of her head as she scrubbed the blood from the walls and the floor. Those poor things. Grace wiped at the sweat and tears pouring down her face. Her shirt, smudged with red, stuck to her body. Wiping her running nose on the damp sleeve, Grace welcomed the anger. It seemed to be her only company of late. Grace slammed the now pink rag into the bucket. Pink bubbles burst and erupted.

"Need help?"

Grace dipped her head. *Great.* All she needed was him around. The memory of his kiss the night before cascaded down her spine and swam in the pit of her stomach. She snatched the rag from the water and began scrubbing the last of the blood from the floor. "No thanks. I'm just finishing up."

Dominick walked around and knelt in front of her. He laid his hand on top of hers, stopping her furious scrubbing. He studied her tired eyes. "You didn't sleep, did you?"

Grace shrugged and tried to ignore the look of concern in his eyes. "I slept just fine."

Dominick grunted. He released her hand and watched as she finished. "Where's Phoebe?"

"Oh, Noah stole her away for a day. Let's just say he didn't have to twist her arm too hard." Grace scowled.

"What's the matter with Noah?"

Grace grabbed the bucket of dirty water and walked to the front porch and down the steps. She dumped the contents onto the gravel and watched as the ground sucked up the soapy moisture. "Nothing's the matter with Noah. It's just that Phoebe is…" Grace stopped herself. Shaking her head, she headed back into the house.

"Phoebe is…?" Dominick followed closely as she made her way to the kitchen. Opening the fridge, Grace grabbed a Diet Coke, offered one to Dominick, and took a cool swig from the bottle.

Grace sighed. "It's really none of your business, but Phoebe's the type of girl who falls in love hard and fast. She's been really hurt before by men who take advantage of her free spirit and open heart." Grace held the cold bottle to her forehead, hoping the cooling sensation would demolish her sudden headache. "I'm just worried that Phoebe will fall hard and fast for your friend only to have her heart broken again."

"Isn't that her problem, though? It seems if Phoebe's willing to take the risk of loving again, you should let her." Grace watched as Dominick's eyes transformed from regular old chocolate to the yummy stuff buried deep within dark chocolate truffles. Before she could register the movement and escape, Dominick reached out and gently smoothed a stray auburn tendril behind her ear. "Why do you take so much on your shoulders, Grace?"

Jerking back, Grace bit out, "She's my little sister!" Guilt flooded Grace. She shrugged her shoulders. "I just don't want her to get hurt again. That's all."

Dominick put his hands up in surrender. "Okay! I didn't mean to pry." A smile lit up Dominick's face, causing his scar to crinkle. Grace suddenly wondered what it would feel like if she traced her index finger over it. She

159

mentally slapped her itchy right hand as if it were going for the forbidden cookie jar. She forced her mind back to Dominick who was looking at her as if she'd suddenly lost her mind. *Crap! How long have I been staring at his scar?* Grace cleared her throat. "Sorry, lost my train of thought there for a minute."

Dominick self-consciously rubbed his scar. "I...well...that is if you don't mind...I..." Dominick massaged the back of his neck and blew out a deep breath. "I actually came to whisk you away as well." He ignored Grace's raised eyebrow. "You can't argue, or I'll quit." Dominick winked.

"Who said I'd argue?" It was Dominick's eyebrow this time which quirked. Grace smiled sheepishly. "Right, I won't argue. I need you too much." Grace instantly regretted her choice of words. Dominick's eyes darkened and she stammered, "I mean for the construction project."

Dominick's eyes never strayed from hers. "Be ready in ten minutes. Wear jeans and tennis shoes." Grace stuck her tongue out at his retreating form. *Smug man. With an incredibly nice backside.* Grace smacked a hand over her mouth. *Where did that come from?* Grace chucked her empty pop bottle in the garbage and made her way to acquiesce to his demands.

It was the smell that first captured her attention. Memories of her father slammed into her head. His tall form. His intelligent green eyes. His black hair matted and sweaty from wearing his Stetson all day. His strong arms hugging her and Phoebe after a long day on the ranch. Grace closed her eyes to the pain the images created. It had been forever since she'd smelled the comforting smell of horse. The day after the last bit of dirt covered her beloved father's coffin, Grace had left the ranch for good. With

Jeremiah Wallace no longer there to comfort and guide his daughter, there was no point in going home. Grace inhaled deeply as she opened her eyes to take in the horse stables Dominick had parked right in front of.

Grace turned a questioning gaze to Dominick. He beamed at her. "I heard from a very reliable source that you loved horses." He spread his hands toward the red and white stables. "I thought you could use a little cheering up with what happened yesterday."

Grace blinked. Her head attempted to compute what was happening, and her heart did an Olympic-worthy back flip. This man lived by her father's motto. For the amount of times she'd bucked him off, he had every right to take her out to the pasture and shoot her. "Thank you, but you don't have to take time to do this for me. I'm fine."

"You're a terrible liar, Grace. Don't make a habit out of it. Besides," Dominick opened his door, "I need a little vacation as well. Your house is in good hands today." Grace watched as he sauntered around the front of the truck and came around to the passenger side window. Dominick opened the door. "Do you need help unlatching your seatbelt, or should I assist you?"

Grace immediately hit the little red button and hopped out. "This place is amazing." Grace stood stunned for several minutes and relished the sights and smells. Five stables all painted in red and white dotted the vast property. White fences closed off several different exercise areas each with different equine customers enjoying a run in the sunshine. The main house, done in the same color scheme as the stables, sat squarely in the middle with its towering three stories and wraparound porch adorned with white wicker rocking chairs and assorted sizes of terracotta pots filled with red geraniums.

Dominick watched as Grace studied her surroundings. Through surreptitious snooping, he'd found out from Annie that Grace had grown up on a ranch. Well, around here, this was as close as he could get. Panic rose in his chest as tears streaked down her face. Now he'd gone and done it. Dominick attempted to rewind the day. What had he said? What had he done? Did she hate horses? There was only one way to find out.

"Grace?" He tentatively touched Grace's arm.

She dashed away the tears and turned to face him. "I'm okay. It's just some memories." Grace smiled through her tears. "It was very nice of you to bring me here. It's been awhile."

Relief flooded through him. But why the tears? Resolve to find out cemented itself in his mind. Sooner or later, he'd find out what haunted the green-eyed Spitfire in front of him. "We don't have to stay. I don't want this to be a painful experience."

"No. I don't think you understand how much I need this."

Emboldened by Grace's reassurance and smile, Dominick started walking to the house. "I called the other day and made appointments. The owner is a friend of mine. We have all day." Dominick paused and dug the toe of his work boots in the dirt. "I ordered us a picnic as well. I, um, hope you don't mind."

"That sounds wonderful." Grace's smile caused Dominick's heart to flutter. He'd expected a negative answer, but got just the opposite. Dominick took his baseball cap off and scratched his head. He'd never met a more confusing woman in his life, and he looked forward to figuring her out.

The wind was all she heard. Grace lost herself in the magic of the moment. The thundering hooves of her palomino, Velvet, echoed in the depths of her soul, reigniting a passion she thought she'd lost forever. Her eyes soaked in the rolling hills and treeless landscape. June's heat had all but decimated a few wildflowers, which still clung to life. Their small yellow faces staring challengingly into the sun reminded Grace of her promise to herself. Never let the horse buck you off. She lifted her face toward the Heavens and smiled. *See, Dad,* Grace thought, *I got back on the stupid horse! Now what?* Not expecting an answer to boom from the sky, Grace slowed Velvet down to a walk.

"Something wrong?" Dominick brought his grey-dappled gelding, Spackle, next to hers. His sunglasses hid his eyes, but she knew she'd find compassion there and that knowledge had her squirming in her saddle.

"No. I was…" *What? Talking to my dead father? Yeah,* Grace considered; *that wouldn't scare him off at all.* Grace shrugged. "Just thinking. That's all."

Dominick seemed to take her lie in stride. He probably didn't believe her, but he didn't question her either. To hide her guilt over lying, again, Grace concentrated on untangling a knot in Velvet's mane.

"Well," Dominick grinned, "In that case…race ya'!" He spurred his horse into action and within seconds was barreling down the prairie.

Grace yelped in injustice, "You didn't say 'go'!" She urged Velvet into a sprint and took off after Dominick and Spackle. Once more, she was transported back to her childhood home and her first race with her father back to the ranch from the far pasture. She'd had a suspicion he'd let her win, but he'd never contested the final finish. Grace's tears streamed into the wind as Velvet picked up speed. How Grace missed her father. She gritted her teeth.

If she ever found out who killed her father, they were going to wish the Devil were after them instead.

The need to win exploded inside Grace. Leaning forward in the saddle, she spoke to her horse. Velvet seemed to understand, and maybe because male horses were sometimes a little like male humans, Velvet soon passed Spackle. The look of shock on Dominick's face turned quickly into a look of pure pleasure, turning Grace's insides into the consistency of jelly. Maybe she should have worn something besides her tank top and best butt-accentuating jeans. Well, too late for a wardrobe change. Grace lightly kicked her mount's side, and they ran off, leaving Spackle and Dominick in their dust.

By the time Dominick and his stallion reached the picnic spot, Grace had already watered and tethered Velvet to a tree branch.

"What took you so long?" Grace hefted the saddlebags off the saddle.

"I think using rocket fuel while horse racing is considered illegal in all fifty states." Dominick grunted in pain as he slid to the ground. "Whoa! It's been a long time since I've been in the saddle."

Grace stifled a giggle as Dominick sauntered down to the small pond in the center of a tiny oasis in the middle of the dry prairie. Spackle meekly followed after, his grey speckled head hung in defeat. *Poor horse.* Grace laughed out loud and waved her finger at Dominick when he turned to scowl.

After unpacking the provided lunch, Grace sat on the red-checkered blanket and leaned against one of the gnarly oak trees, probably as old and Adam and Eve, that stood in a small circle towering over the brown grassland. Underneath their shady boughs, however, green grass flourished. Small purple and orange wildflowers sprung up

164

in the sunnier spots and honeybees drank thirstily from their depths. Never a fan of bees, Grace pressed her body closer to the tree trunk behind her. Grabbing a plastic bottle filled with pink lemonade, Grace leaned her head back and watched the sunrays ricocheting off the leaves. Shadow and light played for supremacy on the topmost leaves, leaving Grace hypnotized by the swirling motions and movements.

It was only the skittering of little feet above her that slammed her back to reality. Little squirrel feet. *Oh.* Grace ducked her head. *Little squirrels.* The anger she'd packed away reared its head. Knowing anger wasn't going to solve anything, Grace silently beseeched her Heavenly Father to grant her the grace to not go postal and end up tacking the squirrel killer (when she found him) by his little tail to her ceiling. Trying hard not to find some kind of enjoyment in that mental picture, she opened up her eyes to find Dominick looking down at her. He'd removed his sunglasses. She wished he would put them back on. She didn't want to see what was swimming in them.

"You're doing a lot of thinking lately."

Grace offered him the other pink lemonade bottle and began setting out the provided picnic. There were ham sandwiches, potato chips, pickles, and little Hostess cakes as the finale. "Yeah. It's not really doing me a whole lot of good anyway," Grace stated ruefully. "I should quit while I'm ahead."

Dominick grabbed for a ham sandwich and began removing it from its plastic bag, "What are you thinking about?" Dominick ignored her scowl. "Hey, talking things through helps a lot of people. Use me as your sounding board. Maybe it will help."

Grace eyed him. His brown eyes studied her right back. *Well*, Grace figured, *what's the worst that could happen?*

165

Her mind told her she didn't want him to like her anyway. Her heart told her mind to shut up. Throwing her hands up in defeat, Grace grabbed for a sandwich. "I'm thinking about my father a lot."

"Where is he?"

"Heaven."

Dominick choked on his sandwich. "I'm so sorry, Grace." He reached for her hand but didn't seem daunted when she pulled it out of his reach.

"He...ah..." Grace felt the sting of tears pricking her eyes. "He was murdered three years ago." Grace's voice hitched, and she viciously dashed away the unwelcome tears.

Dominick never reached for her hand, but he didn't need to. She could feel his sympathy pouring out to her and filling her. "I'm truly sorry. I can't imagine the pain that caused you and your family."

Dominick didn't press for further information. He simply sat beside her and silently ate while she picked at her food. How he wanted to fold her in his arms and take away all the pain. The strength of that temptation floored him. He glanced at her face. Her freckles, stark under the paleness of her skin, showed her feminine softness. Her green eyes, watery and red, stormed with an emotion he knew personally. Anger. Injustice. Hopelessness. She didn't need his arms or kisses right now, although he certainly wouldn't stop her if she suddenly wanted them. She needed time and his prayers. And in the midst of eating a pickle, Dominick did just that.

Grace snuck a peak at Dominick. Licking pickle juice off his fingers, he looked as harmless as a kitten. She had a strange feeling, though, that the minute she let him in, she'd have a heck of a time getting rid of him. But she needed another ally, someone other than Phoebe in her corner. So she barreled ahead.

"My father was a good man, a little rough around the edges to some, but to those that truly knew him, he was just a big ole' teddy bear. Before Phoebe and I were born, he was the sheriff." Grace cleared her throat. "He, uh, put a guy named Roy Muldoon away for drug dealing and several illegal weapons charges. When Roy got out of prison, he took revenge on my father by kidnapping us." Grace plowed on through Dominick's shocked gasp. "We were so little; it wasn't hard for Roy to manhandle us into the van. I don't remember any of it, to be honest with you. Part of me wishes I did, but I can't conjure up any images. Phoebe says it's because our brains are trying to protect us." Grace shrugged, "Maybe she's right. I don't know."

"He didn't hurt you, did he?"

"Not if you count the rope burns. No. He never hurt us physically or...well...you know. I don't know what his plans for us were, but thank God he never got a chance. My father and a team of law enforcement officials finally tracked him down." Grace paused and looked Dominick squarely in the face. "Here."

Dominick's mouth unhinged. "Here? What do you mean here?"

"Beacon, Kansas."

Realization dawned in his eyes. "Where specifically in Beacon?"

"The old house you are currently working on."

Dominick ignored Grace's slight retreat at his advancing hand. He grabbed it anyway. "Why are you here, Grace? What made you come back to a house that holds nothing but nightmares for you?"

Grace smiled weakly and allowed her hand to stay firmly grasped in his. "If the horse bucks you off…"

Dominick cocked his head. "So you're hoping that coming back to this place will what?"

Grace balked a little. "Well…I…well…I mean…Phoebe and I…" Grace couldn't hold his gaze any longer. She tugged her hand out of his and ripped open a little Hostess cake. "I want closure. I want something to make sense. And there is a spot deep inside me that knows my father's murder was payback for what happened in that house."

Dominick grabbed his own little cake. "What happened in that house, Grace?"

"Don't you know? It was in every paper around the area?"

"I was only five at the time."

Grace began to pack up the garbage. She needed to do something with her hands. "My father, in an attempt to rescue Phoebe and me, killed Roy. It was a righteous kill, nothing vigilante about it. Roy pulled a gun on my father." Grace tightened her ponytail. "My father was just faster pulling the trigger."

Dominick rubbed his temples. "I can't believe you had to go through that." Dominick stopped Grace's frantic cleaning up. "Stop! Just stop."

Grace turned on him. "No!"

Her sharp retort took Dominick by surprise. He let her hand go and backed up a few steps. "I'm sorry. I just wanted you to know it's going to be okay."

"How do you know? Have you lost your father or mother?" Grace's voice sounded foreign to her. *Since when have I become a screeching owl?*

Dominick shook his head. "No. I haven't lost my parents, but I still know what it's like to lose someone you love very much." He dipped his head and studied his hands.

Knowing the picnic was over, Dominick helped Grace stow away the supplies and in uncomfortable silence they rode Velvet and Spackle back to the stables. Dominick scrubbed a hand over his face. This day certainly hadn't gone how it was supposed to. Any sane man would let well enough alone, but no one ever accused Dominick of being a sane man.

Chapter Thirteen

Grace sat, chin resting in her palm, watching the wedding party enter the VFW. Phoebe sat next to her, neck extended as far as possible to ogle the bridesmaid dresses.

"Don't they look cute, especially Noah? He's like a life-sized Ken doll. My Ken doll always lacked a head. I don't know why. I'm just happy that Noah has a head." Phoebe sipped on her Sex on the Beach. "This drink is good."

"Yeah, and it's also your second. You realize that if you keep drinking like this, I'll have to roll you back to the hotel room."

Phoebe smiled happily at the thought, continued slurping and ooed and awed over the dresses and Noah.

Grace sighed and made her way over to the bar. "Whiskey diet, please." The bartender nodded acknowledgement. Grace turned around and watched the bride and groom and the rest of the wedding party seat themselves on the dais.

She licked her lips and remembered his kiss. It seemed to haunt her. Closing her eyes she saw him, standing there head dipping down toward her to capture her lips…Grace opened up her eyes. The memory of her behavior during the picnic smacked away his molten chocolate eyes and luscious lips. Why did she turn into a raging moron when he was around? Maybe it was for the best. She didn't need relationship complications now anyway. She'd just get him out of her mind. That's all. But he wasn't making matters better tonight, looking all James Bondish in his black tuxedo. The urge to trace his scar with her fingertip caused Grace's middle to get all warm and fuzzy. Cursing herself, she grabbed her drink, slapped some money on the bar, and waded through the crowd.

Grace found Phoebe sipping on her second drink and flirting shamelessly with a long-haired hippy. *Oh, boy. No more drinks for Pheebs,* Grace thought as she seated herself next to her slightly buzzed sister.

"Hey there, Pheebs. What'y doing?"

Phoebe finished her drink. "Talking with this nice young man."

Grace studied the "nice young man." Long, greasy hair hung like rat tails over the guy's scrawny shoulders. He looked like a young man going on fifty, and he smelled oddly like weed. "I smelled the oddest thing as I was walking by the door," Grace paused, "coulda swore I smelled marijuana."

With that, he got up and dashed out the door.

"Ah, that sucks. You meet a nice man and puff...I mean...poof! He's gone."

Grace patted Phoebe's shoulder. "Yeah, it happens to the best of us. Besides, I don't think Noah would approve." Grace glanced at Phoebe's empty glass. "Oh, and by the way, no more girly drinks for at least another hour."

"How 'bout if I have one of them there manly drinks like you?"

"No."

Dinner was served; Grace overate and drank another whiskey diet to drown her guilt. Successful evening so far. The whole time, Grace refused to look at Dominick again. Just the knowledge he was in the same room, looking like the hottest James Bond ever was enough to send her into a tizzy.

An hour later, Phoebe, allowed to have a third drink, perched happily on her chair and watched as tables were cleared to make room on the dance floor.

"I love to dance."

"I know." Grace remembered an infamous high school dance where Phoebe had attempted the Running Man and had sprained both ankles. "You're so graceful, too."

A little too tipsy to recognize sarcasm, Phoebe beamed with pride. "I know."

Grace shook her head and chuckled. "Pheebs, you are one of a kind. What would I do without you?"

"Be bored."

"This is true." Grace turned her attention to the dance floor where Lauren and Bruce, now man and wife, danced their first wedding dance together. In spite of Bruce's Mohawk, Lauren gazed up at him with perfect love. Grace swallowed a lump in her throat. She, too, had looked at Kevin like that once. Grace soothed her hurt memories with more alcohol.

Following the bride and groom dance, Lauren danced with her father and Bruce danced with his mother, who oddly enough sported a mullet. Wonder if she lost a bet also, Grace thought.

The wedding party danced the next dance and, in spite of her iron-clad agreement with herself, Grace couldn't tear her eyes away from Dominick and his partner. The maid of honor, a blonde-haired skinny skank, laughed up at Dominick and wrapped her arms seductively around Dominick's tanned neck. Grace squeezed the edge of the table. The fire engine red dress did nothing to hide the sumptuous body writhing against Dominick's. Her boobs nearly spilled out of the V-cut top and her tanned thigh kept playing peek-a-boo through the slit in the leg.

"Can I kill her?" Grace asked Phoebe.

"Who?"

Grace pointed to Dominick's dance partner. Phoebe stared at the woman for a few seconds, "Why? She's pretty." At a look from Grace, the proverbial light bulb went off over Phoebe's head. "Oh. I see. I think it's generally frowned upon to kill the maid of honor at a wedding."

"I thought you'd say that. I could jump her after the wedding."

"You could, but I think you're too pretty to go to prison."

"I'm not as pretty as Miss-Look-At-Me-I'm-A-Skank."

Phoebe looked Grace over. Grace's hair hung loose in red gold ringlets and silver hoops hung elegantly from her ears. Grace's green dress clung to her curves and her cleavage poked modestly out from a V-neck cut. Black strappy heels completed the outfit.

"Nope. Skanky Maid is nowhere near your caliber. You are looking fine, sis." Phoebe slurped at her drink. "Can I have another?"

"No."

"Ah, man. But they're so good."

Grace watched as the wedding party filtered off the dance floor. The DJ flipped songs and the room soon pumped with Bon Jovi. Allowing her head to bob with the beat, Grace spied on Dominick and the Skanky Maid. Angry with herself, she forced her eyes away from the debacle. She had no right to be jealous.

"Dance with me!" Phoebe yanked on her arm.

"I don't feel like dancing."

Phoebe pouted. "Pretty please! I promise I won't embarrass you."

Yeah, right. Grace looked at Phoebe. Dressed in a spaghetti-strapped pink dress, her black hair swept back into a messy bun with diamond earrings sparkling at her ears, Phoebe looked the perfect princess. Grace snorted. With a defeated shrug, Grace assented.

Phoebe beamed at her and dragged her to the dance floor. "You Shook Me All Night Long" reverberated through the speakers and the dance floor filled up. Grace and Phoebe shook their booties to the pumping music and continued dancing through the next five songs. After "Pour Some Sugar on Me" poured out from the speakers, Grace held up a hand and signaled to Phoebe she needed to sit. Phoebe gave her a thumbs-up, found Noah, and began jamming out to the next song. Grace noticed Noah's eyes light up. Someone was very twitterpated.

Grace made her way to the bar and ordered another whiskey diet.

"Thirsty?"

Grace didn't jump this time. She knew who it was. "Nope, just trying to get drunk."

Dominick didn't smile. He'd removed the tux jacket and had rolled up his shirt sleeves. The sexy casual look definitely agreed with him. Grace looked away and waited impatiently for her drink. She could feel his eyes studying her. Trying not to fidget under his gaze, she watched Phoebe dance with Noah. At least someone was having fun.

"Having fun?" Dominick studied Grace over his bottle of beer.

Grace gave a tight smile. "Sure." The bartender handed her the drink; Grace plunked down money and walked away.

Dominick followed close after her. "In polite society people usually don't walk away from a conversation."

Grace fought the urge to punch him. She calmly sat down and took a sip of her drink. Dominick sat down beside her and opened his mouth to speak.

"There you are. I was worried you'd left me." Grace looked over her drink at Skanky Maid who leaned over the table, squishing her amble bosom together. Grace absently wondered if they were real.

Dominick blushed. "I was just getting a drink and stopped to talk to a friend."

Friend? Grace snorted into her drink. Skanky Maid shot her a glance and then ignored her. She batted her eyelashes and wiggled her breasts. "Come on, Dominick. You promised me the first slow song. I requested our song. The DJ said he'd play it next."

Grace sat in horrified silence. She watched the ice bob up and down in her drink and wished they'd go away.

"Okay, I'll be right there." At Skanky Maid's pause, Dominick reassured her. She sauntered away, swaying her hips to the music.

Dominick cleared his throat and finished his beer. Setting down the bottle he began, "That is Molly O'Shannessy. She is…"

"Looks like Molly needs you on the dance floor," Grace interjected. Before Dominick could explain his relationship with Molly, Grace stood up and made her way on the dance floor. Much to her embarrassment the song quickly turned to Kaci and JoJo's love song, "All My Life." Standing all alone on the dance floor, Grace felt conspicuous and started toward her chair again. Weaving through the couples, Grace's face burned bright red.

She just wanted to go home, wherever that was. Before she reached the edge of the dance floor, she felt her right arm captured and held tightly by a hand she knew all too well.

"You need to stop walking away from people. It's rude." Dominick's breath fell hot on her cheek.

Grace tried tugging her arm free. "Why can't you just leave me alone?"

"I wish I could." Dominick's eyes flickered in the strobing lights.

Grace's breath hitched. Feeling strangely light-headed, she yanked free from his grasp. "Please, I need to sit down."

"Just hold on to me." Dominick clasped Grace's hand and pressed her to his hard body. His arms wrapped around her and his large hands rested possessively on the small of her back. Dominick swayed gently to the music, causing his body to rub up against her stationary one.

"You better start moving or some little old ladies are going to see something they didn't bargain for." His voice, hoarse and soft, whispered in her hair.

Desire simmered through her body. Any minute she knew she'd boil over. Needing to escape, she wriggled from his grasp. "I don't feel like dancing."

Dominick's eyes darkened. "What *do* you feel like doing?"

Grace tried to breathe. "Drinking; I need a drink!" Staggering to her chair, she placed the cool glass on her forehead and closed her eyes. She gulped down her drink and searched for a sighting of Phoebe on the dance floor. Nothing. She did catch sight of a very ticked off Molly scolding an equally angry Dominick. Lover's spat. Grace tried not to feel jealous and continued looking for Phoebe. Finally she spotted her pink-clad sister slow dancing with

Noah. Maneuvering through the swaying couples, she seized her sister's arm.

"Hey! I'm dancing here."

"I know, and I'm so very sorry. I'm not feeling well, so I'm going to head out. Can you get a ride from Noah?"

Phoebe smiled. "I'm looking so fine, my friend, that I could make him do anything."

"How many drinks have you had?"

Phoebe giggled and hiccupped. She held up two fingers, stared at them, giggled, and held up two more. "Five, I think...or was it six..."shrugging her shoulders, she gave Grace a tiny finger wave, and swayed back to Noah.

With a huff, Grace made her way out of the VFW. The June summer night hugged around her and breathed humid sultry air in her face. Breathing deeply, Grace decided to walk; it was better to get a nasty blister from her black strappy heels than to get a DUI.

Her mind replayed the events of the evening. She couldn't believe she'd even entertained the idea of liking him. Egotistical fool! How dare he kiss up to Skanky Maid.

Grace watched her feet hit the pavement. Every click of her heels seemed to say his name, "D-o-m-n-i-c-k!"

"Oh, shut-up!" she cursed at her shoes. Trying to ignore their chant, she looked up into the night sky. "So what are you going to do about him?" The stars seemed to twinkle to her in Morse code. "This would be the perfect time, God, for a text message...a messenger pigeon?" Grace called up to the sky. When her phone didn't beep and she heard no flap of wings, Grace snorted. "I will take that as a 'no'?"

The sound of a pickup rumbled behind her. Knowing who it was, Grace ignored it and continued walking along. The truck pulled up next to her, and the passenger window silently slid down. Dominick leaned across the seat and called out to her.

Grace ignored him, held her head up high, and continued walking.

Dominick swore. "Would you please stop?"

Grace stopped. Turning sharply on her high heels, she planted her hands on her hips. "Did you just swear at me?"

"Yes. Sorry. I just need to talk to you!"

Grace spread her stance and braced herself. "Okay. Talk."

"Can I give you a drive back to your hotel?"

"Talk or I start walking again."

Dominick cursed under his breath. "Anybody tell you you're a stubborn woman?"

"Several times." Grace started walking. Much to her dismay and excitement she heard a truck door slam shut. An arm snaked around her and pressed her against the front of the pickup. This was starting to be familiar ground. Her breathing shallowed and her heart raced. She could feel Dominick's blood pulse through his body as he pressed harder against her. In the glow of the street lights, Dominick's chocolate eyes burned with desire and passion. For a frightening yet delicious moment Grace thought he'd kiss her again.

"You're shaking." Dominick curled a piece of her hair around his finger. He released the curl and slowly trailed his finger along her exposed collar bone.

Lightheaded and dizzy, Grace struggled to keep to her feet. Fear and desire licked at her insides. "I…um…" Grace's mind went blank. Panic. Grace pushed hard against Dominick. Caught off guard, Dominick landed hard on the pavement, his head crunching against the curb.

Going with the momentum of her push, Grace stepped over Dominick's horizontal body and stomped off, almost spraining her ankle when her heel caught on a crack in the pavement. Suddenly a low groan stopped her, and she looked back just in time to see Dominick try and raise his head only to have it smack back down. *Now I've gone and killed him,* she thought as she hastened back.

"Oh my gosh, are you okay?" Grace quickly bent down next to him and started checking for broken bones.

Dominick groaned again, opened one eye, and peered up at her. "If you keep checking me for injuries, I can't be held liable for what I'll do."

Her hands stopped mid-thigh. Slowly, never taking her eyes off his, she lifted her hands and placed them in her lap. "I'm sorry I pushed you. I panicked."

Dominick sat up and rubbed his head. "I'll probably have a good-sized lump and a mother of a headache tomorrow." Sighing, Dominick slouched against the curb. "What's going on between us?"

Grace lowered her head and fiddled with the rings on her fingers. "Nothing."

"Really? You call this nothing?" With a quick hand, Dominick captured Grace's chin and gently forced her to look at him. "I see something in your eyes, and I certainly feel something when I'm around you."

Grace slapped his hand away and stood up. Thinking and pacing, Grace tried to formulate an argument in her head. She glanced down at him and silently cursed. His hair, mussed and bed-head looking, fell casually over his forehead. He'd lost his vest and tie somewhere throughout the night, and he wore the shirt half open with the sleeves still rolled up. Sitting on the side of the road, leaning against the curve, wearing a serious expression, he looked as if he belonged in a Calvin Klein shoot. Unable to concentrate while looking at him, Grace continued her pacing. The sharp tapping of her heels echoed through the empty street.

"I don't know you," Grace blurted. Unable to stop herself, she continued rambling, "You're just a guy I hired to do a job. This wasn't supposed to get complicated. You should be nothing to me. I need you to be nothing to me. You walk around thinking you're all that and a bag a Doritos chips. Maybe you are; I don't know. Molly certainly thinks so." She held up a hand to stop Dominick from interrupting her.

"You don't know me either. You know I'm scared of slimy fish and like the color blue. You know I'm slightly crazy and am related to a woman crazier than I. You know I'm haunted by my past. But guess what?" Grace flung her arms out in frustration. "There's a lot more you don't know, all right. You might not like what you don't know, and I'm not willing to take that risk." Grace paused to catch a breath and looked down at Dominick.

He sat there watching her with amazement. That irritatingly sexy smile played on his lips. It broke out into a full grin at Grace's glare. "I think you must have me confused with the model boy of the community. I am far from it."

Grace started to roll her eyes but stopped at the serious expression on his face. Grace gulped and began pacing. "Doesn't matter, this isn't happening."

"What are you afraid of?"

You! Grace wanted to scream. "Myself. I just can't…"

Dominick quickly got to his feet and grabbed her hands. His thumbs caressed the back of her hands. Dominick's eyes held hers and the emotion shining out of them held her in a trance. "I want to be there for you,

Grace. I want to help you through this. I want to help rebuild your life. But I'll respect your decision. Tell me right now that you want me out of your life, and I'll never bother you again."

Grace licked her lips. Emotions and her several whiskey diets clouded her judgment, and she found it hard to formulate a single thought. Memories of her ex-husband and his betrayal exploded in her mind. She couldn't get involved with Dominick. She came with too much baggage.

With tears in her eyes, Grace looked down at his shiny black dress shoes. "I want you out of my life."

She didn't need to look at him to see the rejection slap him in his face. His hands jerked, and he slowly released hers. Without another word, Dominick entered his truck and drove off down the deserted road. Grace stood in the middle of the road looking after his taillights, tears mingled with mascara cascading down her face.

Dominick punched the steering wheel. Refusing to look in his rearview mirror, he turned the volume up and allowed a little Metallica to drown his hurting heart. "What the heck, God?" Dominick raged over *Enter Sandman*. "Why are You making this so difficult?" He calmed himself down as he approached his driveway. He fought the urge to slam the truck door and entered his house silently.

After paying and dismissing the babysitter, Dominick tip-toed into Lilly's room and sat next to her bed. Her blonde curls lay askew on her pink pillow and her little mouth twitched into a small smile. Under her closed eyelids, Dominick knew the color blue that lay behind them. Cornflower blue so pure and innocent, they seemed to mirror the skies of Heaven.

Watching his little girl sleep was the best time of his day. Sometimes he sat there for hours, drinking in her innocent features. Surprised by a sudden wetness on his hand, he put a hand to his face and realized he was crying. Ducking his head, memories he tried to keep on a tight leash broke free and ran rampant in his head. No longer fighting, he allowed the tears to come, allowed himself to remember:

"Hold your fire!" Dominick raised his hand in a closed fist. This mission was going south *and fast.* The small, thatched house in the middle of nowhere Brazil seemed more of a fortress than a hut made of grass and sticks. He was the Big Bad Wolf for goodness sakes. But he knew who was inside. An insane man, marked by the U.S. government, who knew he held the upper hand. He had Dominick's wife and child.

Sweat beaded and ran rivers down Dominick's body. Wiping sweat from his eyes, Dominick studied the structure. Getting Carlos was not the problem. Getting Carlos without losing his wife and child was a whole other animal. A sudden barrage of gunfire erupted from the hut. A searing pain cut across Dominick's upper arm. Sucking in a quick breath, he checked his wound. Not fatal. Looking through the dark jungle, he spotted his men and gave the sign. As one united front, they slithered on their bellies, using their night vision goggles to guide them. They were now within a couple of feet from the building when all Hell broke loose.

The door to the thatched hut burst open and Carlos stepped out--with a hostage. Dominick's heart imploded. Holding a three-month-old Lilly in front of him for protection, Carlos pointed his gun into the dark forest. "I want a helicopter. Now!"

Dominick knew the orders. Do not negotiate with terrorists. Ever. He fought the nausea churning in his stomach. Black hatred filtered over his heart like a dense fog. Knowing Carlos would kill Carmen if his demands weren't fulfilled; Dominick looked into his scope for the kill shot. Not seeing a clear shot, Dominick's soul screamed out to God.

Suddenly, through his goggles, Dominick noticed a figure slowly approaching Carlos from behind. Dread stabbed Dominick's heart as his mouth opened in a silent scream. NO! In a green haze, he saw Carmen raise a knife over her head and bring it down in between Carlos' scapulas. With a scream of pain and surprise, Carlos dropped Lilly and turned around to encounter his attacker. Through the screams of Lilly and the cries of Carmen, Dominick locked in on Carlos' back and pulled the trigger. Simultaneously Carlos pointed his gun at Carmen and shot. The two gun shots intertwined in the thick jungle air and exploded. Dominick dashed to his baby girl and swept her up in his arms, snuggling her against his uniform. Kicking Carlos' dead body away, Dominick grabbed his wife and crushed her limp body to his. Still alive, Carmen touched Dominick's cheek. Tears pooled in her eyes as she heard Lilly cry.

Dominick laid Lilly in Carmen's arms for the last time. Dominick held on fiercely to the two most precious things in his life. Not until he heard a gurgling gasp did he let go. With an animal-like cry, he lowered his wife to the ground. He kissed her still-warm lips and gently shut her eyes. He'd never look into them again.

"Daddy?" Dominick's head jerked up and looked right into his wife's eyes. No, his daughter's eyes. "Why are you crying, Daddy?"

Dominick snatched his baby girl from her bed and held her tight. Lilly was his life, his rock. "Oh, baby girl, I'm just remembering your mamma."

Lilly's pudgy little hands touched his cheek. "Mamma's in Heaven, right?"

Dominick peered into her blue eyes and saw Heaven. "Yes, baby girl."

Lilly wriggled loose from Dominick's tight grasp. "I'm not a baby anymore, Daddy; I'm a big girl."

Dominick smiled. "No matter how old you get, sweetheart, you'll always be my baby girl." With a quick movement, he whisked her up into his arms, spun her around the room, and laid her gently back down on her bed. "Goodnight, my sweet princess."

Lilly kissed his cheek and snuggled down under her Tinkerbell sheets. "Love you, Daddy."

"Love you more." Dominick walked out and gently shut Lilly's door. With hesitant steps, Dominick made his way to his room. Before stripping down to his skivvies and pouring himself into his bed, he studied the emptiness of it. For a quick second he allowed himself to remember back when his bed wasn't so empty. Fighting the sadness and loneliness, he crawled into bed and prayed for no dreams. Not tonight. God had other plans. He dreamt of Grace.

Chapter Fourteen

The week, filled with continued renovations and additions, sped by quickly. Grace and Phoebe showed up every day to find more and more things fixed and complete. The furniture shipment arrived, and they spent the majority of time organizing and decorating their respective bedrooms. Dominick had essentially ignored her. Grace reminded herself she didn't care. It's what she wanted in the first place.

Needing a break from the monotonous sounds of saws and nail guns, Grace spent an hour gathering what was left of the summer wildflowers from the pasture behind the house. On her way back to her house she caught sight of the man she'd been trying hard to avoid. Her fear of being approached was needless. He barely even glanced in her direction. Too afraid to examine her feelings of loneliness over his reaction, Grace cloistered herself in her room and spent the entire afternoon pressing the purple and yellow flowers. After they were done, she'd display them in wooden frames she had already made from wood from the old corral behind the house. Soon they'd adorn the blue walls of her sanctuary.

Finished with that task, Grace hung up white curtains embroidered with a delicate pattern of cornflowers and sunflowers. The June breeze, breathing through the open windows, gently played with the curtains. Grace watched for a few seconds and then moved toward the bed she'd just set up that morning. She sank down onto the soft white comforter embroidered with the same cornflower and sunflower design of the curtains. She hugged a pillow covered with a matching sham to her chest and watched her new curtains sway in the breeze. A familiar sense of loneliness crept around Grace's middle and squeezed.

Shutting her eyes to the nausea and pain, Grace risked an analysis of her life. She still owned a cat that really wouldn't care if she bit the dust, she still owned a used Buick LeSabre that had been temporarily replaced by a dilapidated rusty pickup truck, and she still owned this house. What had she gained? Grace winced at the answer. Nothing. Looking at the losses column, Grace began to cry. Husband, father, trust, hope, and the ability to emotionally give herself freely to another person were gone. Grace wept into her pillow. How long could she keep living her life in the red?

"Can you believe it's been a month since we bought this old thing?" Phoebe asked as she lugged her suitcase up the front steps of the wraparound porch.

Grace hefted her suitcase up the stairs after Phoebe. "I can't. This is absolutely crazy."

Work still progressed on the house, but Grace's and Phoebe's bedrooms were completely finished and decorated, and the kitchen, completed yesterday evening, was ready to prepare meals in. The girls did a happy dance outside the threshold of the resurrected house and grinned at each other. Even though the sounds of power tools, hammering, and cursing filled the air, the girls felt at home.

"I wish I had a hat."

"Why?"

Phoebe smiled. "I now have a place to hang it."

Grace chuckled and motioned for Phoebe to go through the door first. Phoebe grinned and wheeled her suitcase into the house. After several trips, the ladies and their possessions were securely settled in their new digs.

Phoebe perched herself on her soft pink comforter. "This is the best day ever! I can't wait to put my clothes away and set up my pictures." Phoebe paused for breath and both girls fell into silence. Grace fiddled with the ruffle on one of the pillow shams. "Pheebs?"

"Yeah?"

"When do you think it is okay for me to...you know...start...dating again?" Grace dipped her head and studied a minute speck of nothing on the pillow she was holding.

"I don't know. I think it all depends on how you feel. I wouldn't rush things, but then again I wouldn't wait for years and years either. You deserve to be happy and you deserve a good man."

"I'm just not sure. Kevin made me feel so undesirable. He never touched me." Grace fought the tears. "I don't think I can trust anybody ever again. I gave Kevin all of me and what did he do to it? He crapped on it. I don't think I can do that again."

Phoebe looked thoughtfully at her sister. "But part of you wants to, doesn't it?"

Grace nodded her head. "Yeah. I'm just so scared. Scared of trust and scared that I might have ruined it with the only man I think I could've trusted."

"Dominick?"

"Yes. No. I don't know! I'm so confused about him. I barely know him! What am I supposed to do with that? What am I supposed to do with him?"

"I have a strange feeling that Dominick is a very patient man. He looks like a man not afraid of waiting and a man worth waiting for." Phoebe peered at her sister. "And just how do you think you ruined your chances with him?"

Tears welled up in Grace's eyes. "At Lauren and Bruce's wedding he promised to leave me alone if I wanted nothing to do with him…" Grace stared out the window.

"And?"

"I told him I didn't want him." Grace burst into tears. "Tell me what I need to do to make this right with him."

Matching tears filled Phoebe's eyes as she pulled Grace into a hug. "How do you feel about him? Tell the truth."

Grace took a deep breath. "I honestly don't know. I have all these feelings fighting inside me. One minute I want him; the next minute I'm so frustrated with myself that I'd like to throw him out a window. Sometimes I think I could love him, and then my brain takes over and tells me I couldn't possibly love a man I hardly know."

"It's going to be okay, you know that, right? I don't know what you need to do to make it right. I wish I did. Just be yourself and let time do its thing."

Grace dried her eyes and gave a shaky smile. "I'm such a flippin' dweeb."

"Yes, you are. But that's why I love you."

"Thanks."

Phoebe tapped her lip. "I have an idea."

"Uh-oh."

"You say you don't know anything about Dominick? Well, you can tell a lot about a person from the house they live in. Why don't we Google his house, find it, and do some innocent creeping?"

"Absolutely not!" Grace gaped at her sister.

Phoebe, undeterred, continued, "Oh, yeah! I'll bake some cookies, and we'll take it over to his house around seven. No man can resist cookies. This way we gain access to the Hottie's inner sanctum!" Phoebe ignored Grace's eye

188

roll. "Come on, when else do you foresee yourself in Dominick's house?"

Grace ignored the picture of her and Dominick alone in his house. "No!"

At seven o'clock sharp, Grace and Phoebe pulled up to the curb opposite Dominick's house. The white stucco house looked neat and quaint nestled in the middle of a white picket fence. Red and yellow roses crawled their way up the fence and the white walls of his house. This little house inspired Grace more than Kevin's three elaborate mansions. A sudden vision of Dominick, her, and Lilly playing in the front yard smacked her across the brain.

"Phoebe, this is a very stupid idea. If you want to give the man cookies, you can go ring the doorbell yourself."

"Oh, come on." Phoebe began wiggling in her seat. "I've got to pee."

"You always have to pee."

"Fine. I'll just hold it."

"Yeah, because that worked well last time."

Phoebe pouted. "You swore you'd never bring that up again."

"Oops." Grace took pity on her wiggling sister, "Oh, all right." With a huff, Grace pushed the door open. "Let's give the man some cookies."

Grace pushed open the fence and walked to the front door. Feeling her stomach come up to her throat, Grace nearly bolted. Phoebe reached around her and pushed the doorbell. "I hate you," Grace whispered hoarsely.

"Hey, you're never going to give the man your cookies willingly." Phoebe nudged Grace. "I'm simply assisting you."

Several seconds passed. Phoebe began to dance around. "Ohhhhh, I've got to really pee!" She stabbed the doorbell with her finger and continued to wiggle. "Come on! My teeth are beginning to float." After waiting a couple more seconds, Phoebe grabbed the door handle. "That's it; I'm going in."

"You can't just enter someone's house uninvited!"

Phoebe ignored her sister and turned the door handle experimentally. "Sweet! It's open." She turned to Grace. "Are you coming?"

Grace crossed her arms over her chest and glared at Phoebe.

"Fine." Phoebe dashed into his house. "Hey, it smells like freshly-baked pie! It you don't want him, I'll take him!" Phoebe hollered as she searched frantically for the bathroom.

Grace shrugged bad-temperedly and mumbled under her breath, "His mom probably made it." Grace glanced down the block and felt conspicuous just hanging out on Dominick's front porch. Realizing the gossip mills would find this situation worthy of the calling tree, Grace slipped inside the house, determined to go no further. Grace tapped her foot, chewed on her fingernails, and tried to ignore the apple pie sitting on the counter. Curiosity finally got the best of her, and Grace moved through the kitchen. Chrome appliances sat snugly in the kitchen. A window overlooked the sink and a pot of herbs perched atop the windowsill. The fridge, covered with crayon drawings, hummed with cooling energy and somewhere under the oven a cricket chirped. She peeked into the fridge.

"Creeper!"

Grace jumped and clutched at her chest. "Phoebe! You scared a year off my life." Grace eyed her sister

190

suspiciously. "What took you so long in the bathroom, and why do you smell like Dominick?"

Phoebe plastered an innocent look on her face and peeked over Grace's shoulder. "He keeps his little girl fed well. I appreciate that quality in a man, so in gratitude I will drink to his amazing man-ness." Phoebe snatched a beer, cracked it open, and chugged it.

"What are you doing?" Grace whispered hoarsely. "You don't drink beer."

Phoebe made a gagging sound and stared suspiciously at the can. "And there is a very good reason apparently. This is disgusting stuff. But all this breaking and entering is making me nervous. I needed a drink."

"This was your idea! Besides, we didn't break anything. We just entered."

"I know. Starting to regret it, though."

Grace growled, shut the fridge door, and started for the front door.

"What are you doing, Grace?"

"I'm leaving before the two little bears come back and catch the two Goldilocks."

"Oh, come on! Let's take this opportunity to look around. Who knows, we might find Dominick's secret diary where he's written all his secret fantasies about you."

Grace grudgingly assented and they moved to the dining room. They tiptoed around the colonial style table and chairs. Arranged on top of the table, bills and a warm soda sat waiting patiently for the return of their owner. Phoebe snatched the bills off the table and leafed through them quickly.

"He pays his bills on time. One credit card here and it seems as if he pays off the balance every month." Phoebe replaced the bills, and the girls moved off in the direction of the living room.

A leather couch and two matching recliners faced a large, flat screen plasma television suspended on the wall. Landscape paintings and several pictures of Lilly dotted the earth-tone walls. Wood carvings of various animals were arranged neatly on the two coffee tables. Grace crawled to one of the coffee tables and opened up the door at the bottom. Photo albums, neatly stacked in a row, beckoned to her. Unable to resist, she nabbed the first one.

Leaning against the couch, she flipped through the pages. She could only assume the little boy smiling out at her was Dominick. Continuing to turn the pages, she witnessed Dominick's first day of school to his first prom date and everything in between. Phoebe commented the same on every single picture: "Ah, cute."

"Can't you think of anything else to say?"

Phoebe chewed her bottom lip. "Really cute?"

Grace grunted in exasperation. The next photo album held pictures of Dominick's college years. Some of them made Grace blush.

"Look at those abs," Phoebe whispered. She traced a finger over them.

Grace slapped her hand away. "It's rude to molest people like that."

"It's a picture. I can molest whatever I want to!"

Grace turned the page and gasped. Molly and Dominick, locked in an embrace, beamed at the camera.

"Isn't that Skanky Maid from the wedding?" Phoebe asked.

"Yup and she's looking pretty cozy with our pal the carpenter."

Grace picked up the last photo album and stopped. Smiling back at her were Dominick and a blonde bombshell with ice-blue eyes and perfectly clear complexion. The tiny baby swathed entirely in pink was nestled in between them.

Several pictures of Dominick and who Grace assumed to be his wife, Carmen, exhibited the love they obviously felt toward each other. At the pictures of them kissing, hugging, holding their daughter, Grace's heart broke. How could she compete with his dead wife? Why would he want hamburger when he'd already tasted steak? Did he still love his wife like the pictures portrayed? Suddenly tired of memory lane, Grace replaced the picture albums, and they made their way down the hall and into the first room.

A computer desk with swivel chair, a dead house plant, a paper shredder, and a Bowflex machine crammed the room. Crawling over to the computer desk, Grace turned it on. She cursed. The computer needed a password.

"Untrusting country bumpkin!" Grace rifled through the loose papers on his desk. Nothing. "Doesn't this guy have any secrets?"

"Maybe he hides the dead bodies in the closet?" Phoebe half-jokingly suggested. Phoebe eyed the Bowflex machine. "I wonder if he works out without a shirt on."

"He probably works out in the nude."

"Ooohhh, you really think so. That is hot."

"You're strange."

Phoebe stuck her tongue out. "Like you don't think that's hot."

Grace rolled her eyes and entered the hallway again. They entered the bathroom and searched the medicine cabinet. Tylenol, a red toothbrush, Crest toothpaste, shaving cream and razor, and a bottle of Dominick's cologne shared space with a Tinkerbell toothbrush and toothpaste set. Grace lifted the bottle of cologne. XS. *Hmmm,* Grace thought as she snapped open the cover and whiffed. After Grace accidently sprayed some cologne on her shirt, they left the bathroom. Two doors remained on the ground floor. With a beating heart and racing pulse,

Grace pushed the door closest to the bathroom open. The smell of Dominick rushed out of the room, and Grace involuntarily shivered.

Phoebe giggled from behind Grace. "If we are like Goldilocks, we should probably try out Papa Bear's bed."

"All right, but don't roll around in it, and don't make out with his pillow."

"You first."

"Me? Why me?"

"Well, you're the one who wants him really bad. I'm okay with sloppy seconds."

Grace rolled her eyes. This might be the only time she ever found herself in Dominick's bed. When life hands you an empty bed, make out with the man's pillows. With a whispered curse, Grace began crawling onto the king-sized bed. The soft sheets invited her to cuddle right in, and the bed smelled strongly of him.

"Is it hard or soft?"

Grace screamed in shock as Dominick's voice addressed her from the doorway. "Run, Phoebe, run like the wind!"

Phoebe squeaked, jumped to her feet, blindly turned to run, and smacked directly into Dominick's chest, fainting dead at his feet.

Dominick bent down and checked Phoebe. With an exasperated sigh, he straightened back up and leaned his long body against the door frame. He turned his dark chocolate eyes on Grace. "And to what do I owe this pleasure?"

"Why are you home?" Grace demanded.

Dominick chuckled softly. "Because I live here."

Grace sputtered and stuttered, "But...we...cookies...Phoebe had to pee!"

Dominick merely cocked an eyebrow.

194

"We knocked." Grace announced. Her fists clenched as Dominick's other eyebrow reached his shaggy hair, and how she wanted to brush his hair out of his eyes. "Oooohhhh! You are impossible."

"You're the one who broke and entered into my house!"

Grace tapped her bottom lip and got to her feet. "We didn't 'break'; we simply 'entered'."

Giving into temptation, Dominick forgot his promise to Grace and in one swift movement was in front of her. He pushed her back across his bed. With catlike agility, Dominick captured her body with his. Panic and desire raced through Grace's body. Struggling to free herself, she called in vain to a still lights-out Phoebe. With one last effort she punched him in his right pectoral muscle with a free hand. "You said you'd leave me alone!"

"I lied." Dominick kissed her. His lips, urgent and rough, captured hers and forced them into submission. Her hands, with a mind of their own, wound around his neck and pulled him closer. Dominick moaned and Grace burned with a fire she'd never experienced before. His lips broke free of hers and started traveling along her jaw line, across her cheeks, and down her neck. His fingers tangled in her hair as he again claimed her lips.

Suddenly he froze. Grace pulled him toward her again. He placed his hands on either side of her head and looked down at her. She could feel his body shake with desire and in the soft daylight streaming through the bedroom curtains she could see the battle between passion and reason waging war in his eyes. With sudden tenderness, Dominick kissed her forehead.

"Get out," he whispered into her hair.

Grace blinked. "What?"

Dominick, still holding her hands captive, released them gently and kissed her wrists. "I hope I didn't bruise them."

Grace wanted to scream. What was he talking about? "What's happening here?"

"Nothing." With that Dominick rolled off Grace and kneeled down next to Phoebe. He gently tapped her cheeks. "Phoebe, you need to wake up now and take Grace home."

Phoebe grunted and slightly raised her head. Concentrating on the face before her, she suddenly squeaked, "What are you doing here?"

Dominick lifted Phoebe off the floor. "I live here."

"Right." Phoebe looked pleadingly at Dominick, "I brought cookies." Phoebe shook her head and anxiously scanned the room. "Grace?"

Grace sat up on the edge of the bed and shook her head. "Yeah. I'm right here." Completely ignoring the helping hand Dominick offered her, she grabbed Phoebe's elbow and swiftly escorted her out of the house, planting her in the passenger seat. Brushing her hands together as if to say, "Job well done," Grace cocked her head up and, with as much confidence as her shaky legs could muster, walked around to the driver side. "I'll take myself home," she muttered to herself as she yanked the door open.

Chapter Fifteen

Grace rose with the sun. Slipping on her running clothes and shoes, she started out on a fast walk. Excited for her first run in the countryside, Grace quickly accelerated into a medium-paced run. Her legs, slamming the gravel to the music of Beyonce, moved her up and over hills and down into valleys. Momma cows grazing on the dewy morning grass gave her little notice, but their babies seemed fascinated with her as they watched her approach with wide-eyed wonder only to dash away kicking up their heels as soon as she got too close.

The sun bore down hard upon Grace and sweat beaded on her body and fell in rivulets. Grace regulated her breathing and continued to run. Memories of the "cookie" debacle spun through her head. Ignoring the pain cramping in her side, Grace punished herself and ran harder. If anybody deserved to be punished, it was her.

A blush spread over her already beet-red face as she remembered her own stupidity. In fact, non-stupid moments for her were few and far between lately. Shaking her head with shame, she hurtled up the last hill. The pain in her side cramped viciously and she doubled over in pain. Sucking in a breath, she tried stretching it out. Grunting with pain, she sat on the shoulder of the road. Rest, that's what she needed.

Resting her head on her bent knees, Grace closed her eyes. Gravel dug into her butt but she didn't care. She was past the point of caring. She thought she could run away from her problems, but she had just created more. Dominick's face swam before her eyes and Grace instantly opened them. She didn't know which bothered her more, his rejection of her or her heartbreak over being rejected.

Hitching herself up, she did some abdominal stretches and started on her way home. The word stuck on her tongue. Phoebe thought it was a place to hang her hat. Grace just knew it was where the heart was. Her heart definitely wasn't at the old Victorian house. It was probably walking around, shoved unknowingly in the back pocket of a carpenter.

When Grace finally jogged into the driveway, sweat streamed down every surface. Her ponytail sagged in the humidity and the red dust mingled with her leg sweat, creating a paste. Wiping her sweaty brow with an equally damp forearm, Grace studied the house. The windows gleamed and men worked diligently on the new roof. Painters scurried up and down ladders and slowly, with meticulous attention to the small details, transformed the old place into a shining beacon on the prairie. Pride welled up inside Grace. Yes. Phoebe and she had made an excellent choice.

As she walked closer to the house, the sounds of progress met her ears. Hammers, drills, power saws, and nail guns created a cacophony of sound. It was beautiful. Grace smiled to herself, pulled out her ear buds, and began stretching on the porch. Mrs. Sloucombe sauntered up and began rubbing against her legs.

"Thanks, Mrs. S. Now the red paste on my legs is furry."

Mrs. Sloucombe purred and went off in search of trouble.

"Don't even think about finding the Chihuahua, Turbo, from down the road. I've called his parents."

Mrs. Sloucombe swished her tail, daintily stepped off the porch steps, and went off in the direction of a good time.

Grace rolled her eyes. "Kids nowadays."

Phoebe came out of the house, wearing a pair of short pink running shorts and a bright yellow top. Grace eyed her. "Going to the roller rink after a Cindy Lauper concert?"

"No. Wish I were though." Phoebe sighed and sipped at the glass of orange juice in her hand. "Those were the days, weren't they?"

"Yeah, because as babies we were such party animals."

"I don't know about yours, but my crib was certainly rocking."

Grace chuckled and leaned over to stretch her back. Her fingers swept the floor and blood rushed to her head. "So what did you do this morning besides have a doughnut and some juice?"

Phoebe guiltily brushed away the remnants of powdered sugar off her bright top. "Thought about running. Doesn't that count?" At Grace's grunted response, Phoebe asked, "So how many miles did you run today?"

Grace, still bent over, grabbed the pedometer off her shorts and handed it to Phoebe.

Phoebe studied the pedometer and gaped. "Holy snap, Grace! You ran ten miles."

Grace grunted and swayed back and forth, watching her pony tail brush the wooden planks of the porch. "No wonder I hurt."

"You're crazy, sis. Bona fide crazy." Phoebe chewed on her bottom lip. "Um, Mom called while you were out."

199

Grace continued stretching. "Jeeze. She's called us twice in one month. That's gotta be a record."

"She says she's doing just fine and hopes that we will soon grow some brains and come home."

Grace grunted. "Home? With her? Not a chance. I'd sooner move back in with Kevin."

"Mom says that when she final ties the knot with her new 'lover,' she hopes we will treat him like a father."

"Pft! She's drinking more than I thought she was." Grace slowly eased up vertebrae by vertebrae and faced Phoebe. "So, how old is this 'boyfriend'?"

"In his mid-twenties, I think." Phoebe shuddered. "Am I the only one who thinks that is totally disgusting?"

Grace rolled her eyes and slowly descended again. Her runner's high was slowly fading away and in its stead grew the tingling sensation of nerves. "Nope. That's pretty gross. Especially if she expects us to call him 'Daddy'! Never!" Grace leaned her body to the right and stretched her hamstring. "Did she give lover boy's name?"

"Leo."

"Figures." Grace continued to the left side and stretched the left hamstring. "I hope we never meet him. He's obviously after one thing. Dad did leave her with a substantial amount of money when he died. Don't know why."

Before Phoebe could agree, Dominick's voice intruded from behind Grace, "Are you wearing something you can get dirty in?"

Grace yelped and immediately straightened up. She glanced at Phoebe who was very preoccupied with fanning herself. She mouthed the word "yes!" Grace sent her a glare and turned around.

Dominick, dressed in his usual faded Levi's and T-shirt, leaned against the supporting post. That same sexy smirk played on his lips, but his eyes were different this morning. There was no smile there. Grace quickly wondered how long he had been staring at her derriere. Then she remembered she'd sat in dirt. Fighting the urge to wipe off her butt, she swallowed her embarrassment. Yesterday, now this! At this rate she could soon run for mayor of Loserville.

"Why?"

"I need to fix a small water leak. The problem is that it is under this porch. None of my men are small enough to shimmy their way under the porch. So, I need you to get under there, and I'll tell you what you need to do."

Flashes of creepy crawly things sent shivers down Grace's spine. She hid her shivers and forced a strained smile on her lips. "Sure. Just let me grab some breakfast, and I'll be right out."

Grace didn't wait for his reply and quickly escaped into the kitchen. Phoebe followed quickly and exclaimed, "At least he's still talking to you."

Grace poured herself a bowl of Special K cereal and skim milk and began eating it with a vengeance. "What am I going to do, Pheebs?"

Phoebe grabbed a handful of cereal from the box and began munching thoughtfully while fiddling with the pots and pans hanging from the rack suspended above the kitchen island. "Do you want to know what I honestly think?"

"No, please lie to me."

"No need to be snippy. Anyway, here's what I think. I think Carpenter Hottie really likes you enough to give you some space."

Grace groaned around a mouthful of cereal. "That really sucks."

"What? You are crazy."

"Don't you get it, Pheebs? I don't want him to like me. I don't deserve it." Once the words were out, Grace slid to the kitchen floor and put her head between her knees.

Phoebe sank down beside her and rested her head against the stainless steel oven. "Why? Why don't you deserve a good man?"

Grace's breath hitched and she wiped her nose on her bare arm. "Look at me. I'm broken. What exactly can I bring to a relationship? Nothing!" Grace looked at her sister through tear-filled eyes. Phoebe held Grace while she cried. The tears were different; instead of stinging, they seemed to sooth, and in their wake was calm instead of storm. Grace released herself from her sister's embrace and wiped away the salty moisture. "Sorry about snotting all over your pretty shirt."

Phoebe looked down at the smears. "Anything for you. Oh, and by the way, you look like crap."

Grace laughed and rubbed her hands over her face. "Maybe it will keep unwanted visitors off my property."

"Ha! Maybe Carpenter Hottie likes dirty women."

Grace stood with hands on her hips staring at the tiny black hole under the porch. A shudder ran through her body. Icky, nasty things lived down there.

"Ready?" Dominick asked.

Grace snatched the headlamp Dominick offered and placed it on her head. Grace sent a laughing Phoebe a death glare. "Shut up or I'll make you go into the creepy hole." Phoebe zipped her lip and just shook with silent laughter.

"Okay. When you get under the porch, there should be a pipe sticking out of the ground and into the side of the house. That is where the leak is. You need to tighten the elbow joint and then use this caulking very liberally around the ends of the joint. It might not hurt to check the section of pipe going into the house. Caulk that as well."

Grace puffed a few wispy bangs off her forehead. "Sure. No problem." *Yeah, right.*

Dominick handed her the pipe wrench and stuck the tube of caulking down the back of her shorts. Grace shot a look at Phoebe who was too busy fanning herself to notice the glare.

Grace gave a mock salute and started to wriggle her way under the porch. The cool damp ground felt good on her hot skin as she shimmied farther into the hole. Her headlamp sent a beam of light directly in front of her. Swishing her head from side to side, she checked for any wayward badgers, rabid skunks, mutant spiders, and sharks (just on the freak chance they lived under porches).

"You okay?" Dominick's voice sounded as if it were traveling through a tunnel. He tapped the bottom of her Nikes, "You're still halfway out. Need a shove?"

Grace thought about what remained outside the hole. "Nope. I'm good." She continued crawling military-style through the hole, and eventually her entire body rested uncomfortably under the porch.

"This really sucks," Grace whispered to herself. Directing the light toward the outside of the house, Grace spotted the water line. Sure enough, small droplets of water plinked to the ground with staccato fluency. "Found it!" she yelled.

Dominick repeated the instructions, and she gingerly slid through the mud toward the pipe. Taking the pipe wrench in one hand, she used her other one as an added weight to get a tight seal. The dripping stopped.

Grace used her T-shirt to dry the elbow joint and caulked the ends. Not proficient with the caulking gun, Grace ended up getting caulking in her hair, on her face, and somehow in her armpits.

"Crap!" Grace grunted. The coolness of the small hovel soon turned to an uncomfortable sauna. Sweat combined with the caulking; the caulking combined with the red mud. Grace crawled over to the outside wall of the house and checked the pipe entering the house. Nothing wrong there. She started backing up when the beam of the headlamp illuminated a large, furry, eight-legged creature crouched just inches from Grace's face.

Grace's breathing stopped. Her body tensed and she could hear a scream rip through her body. "Crap! Get me out! Now!"

The spider blinked its million eyes and sprinted toward her. Another bloody scream burst out of Grace and she flailed out with her arms. "Son of a ...."

Her curse was cut short with a tug on her legs. Grace kicked. There was no way that spider was going to carry her off to its lair and eat her alive.

"Stop kicking!" Dominick's sharp command ordered.

Grace felt herself being pulled by the ankles. As soon as she emerged from the hole she stood up, danced around, and brushed herself wildly from head to toe. "Get it off me!"

Dominick and Phoebe, with arms crossed over their chests, watched Grace dance wildly around.

"Should we help her?" Phoebe asked.

"Nope, I like watching her dance."

Phoebe grinned. "Yeah, she learned all her moves from me."

Dominick barked out a laugh. "Grace was right. You are crazy, aren't you?"

"One of a kind. Someone just needs to snatch me up while I'm hot." Phoebe batted her eyelashes. "You interested."

"Ooohh, sorry. No can do. Someone's already snatched me up." Dominick smiled sadly at the crazy woman still dancing the heebie-jeebie jig. "Problem is she doesn't know it yet." Dominick left Phoebe gaping at him with tears welling up in her eyes. Phoebe sniffled and wiped her nose on her very bright, very yellow tank top.

"Here, let me help you." Dominick approached Grace cautiously.

Her arm flailed out in an attempt to kill all the creepy-crawlies and whacked Dominick across the nose. Sucking in a gasp of pain, Dominick cradled his nose in his hands.

"That's it, woman. This is the second time I've gotten hurt trying to rescue you. Now hold still, or I'll shove you back under that porch and let the spiders adopt you."

Grace, too preoccupied with her issues, never heard him. He grabbed her arm and forced her to stand still. With rough tenderness, Dominick cupped Grace's chin in his hand and with the other fished out all the cobwebs from her hair.

For the first time since emerging from the hole, Grace looked at him. "You're bleeding."

Dominick carefully dabbed his nose. "Yup. Sure am." He went back to picking out other debris from her hair and wisely never showed her the huge spider he plucked off her.

"Why are you bleeding?"

"Some wild animal attacked me."

"Don't you just hate when that happens?"

Dominick stopped messing with her hair, turned her around, gave a cursory wipe over her back, and spun her to face him again. "Depends on the animal." Taking a bandana out of his back pocket, he carefully, and with a very steady hand, wiped the sweat and grime off her face.

With his face just inches from hers, Grace found it difficult to breath. Trying not to look directly in his eyes, she studied his jaw line where fine stubble had begun to sprout. Her eyes traveled to his scar. What would he do if she traced it? Grace's fingers yearned, and she stuck her hands behind her back. His minty breath fell on her face and somehow his cologne had survived the first humid morning of July.

"There. I think a shower should finish this up."

Grace shook her head. She hadn't heard a single word. His dang cologne was hypnotic. "What?"

Dominick studied her. "You. Shower. Wash. Clean."

"Yeah. Right."

Dominick's eyes held hers. That tiny smile didn't play on his lips, and his eyes were much too serious for her liking. "Thanks for helping me this morning." His hand reached out and brushed a stray piece of red mud off her nose. "I…um…just wanted to apologize for last night. I shouldn't have…you know…kissed you." Dominick looked at the house. Looked at the tree grove. Looked anywhere but at her. "It won't happen again, unless you…" He stopped abruptly and walked quickly into the house.

Grace, muddy and reeking, stared at the door Dominick had passed through.

"What did he say to you?" Phoebe asked as she approached her.

"Nothing." Grace gave her sister a defeated smile and a reassuring pat on the shoulder. "I need a shower. Then I thought we could get the cattle prod out and gently coerce some men into leveling off the ground for our gazebo. They were supposed to get that ready a month ago already."

"Sounds good. Oh, some exciting news about Dominick. He told me that he…"

Grace held up a hand, stopping the words from coming out of Phoebe's mouth. "It doesn't matter. It's nothing."

Before Phoebe could relay what Dominick had said, Grace walked to her bedroom, stripped, and de-bugified herself with a cool shower. After washing her hair three times, Grace felt fairly sure that all the ickies were gone.

Grace stepped out of the shower, wrapped a towel around her, and combed out her long auburn hair. Leaning toward the mirror, she inspected her face. *Is that a pimple?*

A soft tapping noise sounded on her bedroom door. Thinking it was Phoebe, Grace called out "Come in." The door opened and Grace walked out of the bathroom and came to an abrupt halt at finding Dominick in her bedroom.

Dominick, equally surprised to find Grace in just a bath towel, stared, and then quickly turned his back to her. "Sorry. I thought I heard you say come in."

"I thought you were Phoebe." Grace dashed over to her bed, grabbed the clothes she had setting out, and ran back into the bathroom. "I'll be right out."

Dominick let out a pent-up breath. Not knowing where to sit, he wandered the room, looking at the pressed wildflowers. He eventually seated himself on the window seat he'd made and looked out at the bright afternoon sky.

At the sound of the bathroom door opening, he quickly hopped up and rearranged the pillows he'd squished.

Grace kept the bed between them. "Did you need something?"

"Yeah. Actually, as you know, it's the Fourth of July this Saturday. Beacon usually has a big celebration and we, my friends, family, and I and Lilly, of course, get together and grill out and stuff." Dominick shuffled his feet and cleared his throat. "I was wondering if you'd like to join us, like you did at the lake."

"I'd love to spend more time with your daughter. I haven't been able to keep my tea appointment. I hope she wasn't disappointed."

Dominick chuckled. "No. She mentions it every now and then, though. You should plan on coming in tomorrow." Dominick's eyes crinkled with laughter. "She's the greatest thing to ever happen to me. Changed my life, actually. Her mother..." Dominick looked at his shoes. This was always the tricky part of telling people his story. He had to actually say what he didn't want to believe out loud. He forced himself to look into Grace's eyes. What he saw there didn't surprise him. He'd known from the beginning that she was a compassionate soul. "I met Lilly's mother when I was in the military. It was love at first sight. Marriage four months later. Baby nine months later." Dominick cleared his throat. "Carmen was her name. She died when Lilly was just three months old."

"I'm so sorry, Dominick. Losing someone is never easy."

Dominick cleared his throat and quickly changed topics. He was not ready to reveal his past and the fact the he was responsible for his wife's death. "So, um, did you want to come or not?"

Grace played with the wrought-iron bedpost. "I'll have to ask Phoebe, but we should be able to come."

"That's great. I mean whatever works for you. I'll let you know tomorrow the definite times and the place. It'll probably be at my place this year." Even though his face was still sober, a playful light danced in his eyes. "You shouldn't have any problem finding it."

Grace blushed and ducked her head. "That was all Phoebe's idea. But I am very sorry that we...I...invaded your privacy."

Dominick chuckled and made his way toward the door. "No worries. Oh, just a warning here. There's a huge storm brewing. If you have any problems, just give me a call. You won't hear the sirens from town in case of a tornado, so you need to keep your radio on and keep your eye on the sky." Dominick sent Grace a reassuring smile and quietly shut the door.

Grace sank to the bed, struggling to grasp what he had just told her. She'd seen the pain. Her heart broke for him. Straightening out the comforter on her bed, the realization that she was falling for him bowled her over. With a heavy sigh she collapsed on the re-straightened comforter. Not knowing what to do, Grace bowed her head for some much-needed one-on-one time with the Lord.

Chapter Sixteen

The air hung heavily over the plains of Kansas. Storm clouds brewed on the horizon and cattle shoved themselves into the corners of the fence. The grass wriggled in anticipation of a long, cool drink.

Grace sat on the porch swing Dominick had installed and watched the horizon flicker angrily with lightning; she could already hear the distant rumbling of thunder. Never a fan of storms, Grace clutched her bottle of beer and chewed her bottom lip.

"What county are we in again?" Phoebe called from inside the house.

"I don't remember."

"Doesn't matter. Everybody is under a severe weather warning."

"Awesome," Grace muttered. She continued to watch as the clouds heaved and breathed on the horizon.

Phoebe joined her on the porch swing. "I wish Dominick and his men wouldn't have left. It's a little scary being out here by ourselves with this storm coming."

Grace felt for her cell phone. She needed Dominick, and not necessarily for protection from the storm. She began dialing his number and stopped. She pressed the end button and put it to the side. She wouldn't be the damsel in distress.

"Burr, is it colder or is it just me?" Phoebe hugged her arms to her chest and rubbed her hands up and down her arms rapidly.

Goosebumps exploded on Grace's exposed skin. "No, it's much cooler." Grace's eyes darted to the horizon.

The angry black clouds flashed with lightning as the rumble gave way to a loud thunderous crack that shook the window behind them. "I think we're in for one heck of an evening, Pheebs."

As a perfectly-timed omen, the skies opened up, propelling fat raindrops into the ground. Mrs. Sloucombe, gray hair standing on end, flashed across the porch and sprinted to the tree line behind the house.

"Crap!" Grace jumped off the porch swing and watched as her cat disappeared into the trees. "I really need to go get her."

Phoebe grabbed her arm. "I don't think so. This storm is moving fast, and you'll get caught out in it." Phoebe pointed to the sky, "Look at that." The clouds, black and menacing, grumbled and swirled directly above the house.

"I'll make it. Trust me, I'll be fine." Grace yanked herself from Phoebe's grasp, and dashed out into the rain. Soaked within seconds, Grace splashed through puddles toward the tree line.

A slash of lightning followed closely by a clash of thunder caused Grace to scream and crouch close to the ground. "Bad idea, Grace. Very, very bad idea!"

Continuing on, keeping a wary eye on the blackening sky, Grace called continuously for Mrs. Sloucombe. "Mrs. S. where are you? Here kitty, kitty!" Grace heard a small meow from the tree closest to her. She looked up and there perched Mrs. Sloucombe, trying to keep a grip on the drenched tree branch.

"Hi, kitty. You need to come down now. Okay?" Grace raised her hands, hoping her cat would jump right into her arms. "Oh, you stupid cat! Just jump. I'll catch you."

Mrs. Sloucombe continued meowing down at Grace and clung to the tree branch. Another slash of lightning followed directly by a boom of thunder hit the tree. A deafening crack resounded in Grace's ears, and she watched in terror as the tree started to topple over. She tried to run, but her feet stuck to the sucking mud. With a quick prayer, Grace threw herself to the ground and covered her head with her hands. Darkness enveloped Grace.

Thunk. Ping. Crack. Coming out of unconsciousness, Grace yelped with pain and tried to protect the back of her head and the sides of her face from the hail that threw itself down at her. Fear gripped her insides like a demented cat. It was better when she'd fainted.

"Phoebe!!!" Grace yelled. With one last super-human effort, Grace tried tugging her leg free. No luck. "God, if you're going to help me, I'd like it to be very soon." Thunder crashed and lightning streaked in evil forks across the sky. "Okay. Never mind. Take your time."

Then somewhere in the midst of the howling wind and cracking thunder, Grace heard someone call her name. *Was it God!*

"Here!" Grace's voice cracked with emotion and waved frantically. "I'm over here!"

Phoebe skidded to a stop and knelt down next to Grace. "Are you okay?"

Grace could barely hear Phoebe over the torrential rain and howling wind. "No! There's a frickin' tree on me! Now get back to the house before something bad happens. Again."

Phoebe's tears mixed with the rain water pouring down her face. "I'm not leaving you. I called for help. He should be here soon." In an act of sisterly sacrifice, Phoebe covered most of Grace's body with her own. Never once did Phoebe yelp when hail stones as large as golf balls pummeled her back. Grace, cocooned, under her sister, knew for the first time, that not only did her sister look like Xena, Warrior Princess, but she also had the bravery of the renowned Amazon warrior. Phoebe protected Grace for what seemed like hours. And then finally, Grace heard a voice.

Even with the torrent of sound and rain and hail, Grace knew the voice calling her name. Emotions she had tried to stifle ever since seeing Dominick flooded her body, competing with the fear and terror. Grace couldn't put a name to many of them but she certainly knew which was the strongest.

"Grace!" Dominick reached her and knelt down beside her head. He pulled Phoebe off her, offered Phoebe a blanket, and placed one over Grace. Dominick wrapped his arms around Grace's torso and tugged.

"My leg!" Grace screamed in pain.

Dominick set her down gently and with studied calmness tried lifting the branch off her leg. The branch would not budge. He scanned the surrounding area. Kneeling beside her, he bent down next to her ear. "I'm going to need something to pry the tree off you; I'll be right back."

Grace watched through the torrential rain as Dominick's sprinting body disappeared in the darkness. Phoebe lay down next to Grace and covered them both with the blankets that Dominick had brought.

"Hang in there, Grace!" Phoebe shouted over the wind.

Grace clasped Phoebe's hand and squeezed it. No words could escape the constriction of her throat.

Before long, Dominick skidded to a halt with a crowbar and a wood block. "Okay, here's the plan," he yelled, "I'm going to try to get this branch up a few inches. Phoebe, when I do, you are going to need to pull Grace from under the branch. You will not have a lot of time, do you understand?"

Phoebe nodded her head and moved into position at Grace's head. Grabbing under Grace's armpits, Phoebe nodded her head again. "Ready."

Straining with all his might, Dominick leaned down on the bar. Instantly the block sunk into the soft soil. "Please, God, just a few inches," Dominick lifted is head to the onslaught of hail and rain and hollered to the Heavens. He put all his body weight on the crowbar. At that moment the block found solid ground and braced itself against the pressure of the crowbar, and inch by inch the tree began to lift.

"Pull, Phoebe!" Dominick grunted through clenched teeth.

Phoebe dug her heels into the sucking mud and pulled. Grace screamed in pain as her leg was finally freed from the grasping limbs of the tree branch. Dominick dropped the branch and reached for Grace. He lifted her up and carried her back to the house. Grace buried her face in his neck and breathed in his scent. Tears of relief flowed over, and her body shook with tremors.

Dominick stopped in the foyer. He looked at Phoebe, and for the first time that night smiled, "Phoebe, you did very well tonight. Grace certainly is lucky to have you. Now I need you to call 911. Then I need you to get some hot tea or something hot for Grace." Dominick shifted Grace's weight in his arms and studied Phoebe's face. "You took a beating out there. Are you okay"

Phoebe bit her lip and nodded. She gave Grace a swift kiss on the cheek and went in search of her cell phone.

Grace, exhausted, mumbled into his neck, "I'm so tired."

"I know, baby, I know. Just hang on for a second, and you'll be tucked safely in bed." Dominick carried her into the bathroom where he set her gently in the bathtub.

"Hey, what are you doing?" Shivering in the tub, Grace looked at him, confused and disoriented.

"I'm going to get some warm water running and start cleaning you up." With the utmost care, he gently washed the mud from her hair. Grace didn't put up a fight. His strong fingers massaged and caressed her head. Grace bit back a groan. At Phoebe's entrance, Dominick backed away. "Can you finish washing her up, please? I've got her hair clean."

Phoebe nodded silently and waited until Dominick left to strip off Grace's ruined garments. Phoebe finished and drained the water from the tub. Wrapping Grace in a towel, she called for Dominick again. He lifted her out of the tub and carried her to her bed. Without a word, he left again, gently closing the bedroom door behind him.

Grace shivered as she heard thunder crash over the house. "It's okay." Phoebe grabbed Grace's pajamas and slipped them on. She grabbed Grace's comb and began working out the snarls. "The worst of the storm is over."

Grace's leg ached, her face felt as if she'd been in a bar fight, and she couldn't stop shivering. Her eyes kept rolling to the back of her head, and she slowly lost the battle for consciousness. Phoebe sucked in a breath and ran for the door.

Dominick met her at the door, and his face paled at the look on Phoebe's face. "What's wrong?"

"Grace just fainted."

Dominick ran to Grace's side and grabbed her hand. He gently stroked the back of her hand and called her name. Her eyes cracked a small slit, and she turned her head toward him.

"Hi."

"Hi, yourself." Dominick turned at the commotion at the door. Paramedics began entering the room, and Dominick rose to leave.

"No, don't leave me." Grace's eyes filled with tears.

Dominick gave her hand a quick squeeze. "I'll be right outside the door if you need me."

"But I do need…" Grace was interrupted by the paramedics beginning their assessment of her. Dominick gave a reassuring smile and walked out of the room.

He shut the door behind him and sank to the floor. The fear he had squelched and had kept firmly chained suddenly ignited and broke free. Unwilling to sit idle, he stormed into the kitchen and poured the boiling water over the tea bag. He added some other ingredients and watched as the clear water turned brown. Placing his hands on the kitchen counter, he pressed against it with all his might. He turned sharply at a rap on the doorjamb.

"How is she?" His voiced cracked.

Phoebe entered the kitchen and put a hand on his shoulder, "The paramedics say she's fine. Her knee is twisted, and it'll probably turn a lovely color. Her face is pretty beat up, and she'll have a massive headache but nothing life-threatening. She didn't want to go with them, so they had her sign a release and recommended she see a doctor tomorrow." Phoebe breathed out a pent-up sigh. "She's just scared right now and really emotional. I told her not to go after the stupid cat." Phoebe pressed her fingers to her eyes. "She said she'd make it back before the storm got worse. When she didn't come back, I called you. The rest you know all ready."

Unable to speak, Dominick nodded his head and stared out the kitchen window at the rain snaking down the glass. Clearing his throat, he handed Phoebe the cup of tea. "Here, this is ready. I..um...I probably should get going. Will you tell Grace that I...ah..." Dominick paused and shuffled his feet. "Never mind."

Phoebe smiled. "Actually, you can take her the tea. She asked to see you."

Dominick quickly made his way to Grace's bedroom. With a soft tap on the door, he entered. Grace lay under the covers, her head resting on her pillow. She looked so frail and scared. Dominick's heart beat in his chest, and he covered the distance to her bed in a few strides.

"Hi." Dominick placed the cup on her nightstand.

"Hi." Grace gave a quivering smile. "I just wanted to thank you. I don't know what would've happened..."

Dominick reached to sit her up. "You need to sip on this tea at least. Warm you up from the inside out."

Grace reached for it and took a tentative sip. "Mmm. That's good." She peered over the cup at him. "What else is in this?"

"My little secret; trust me, though, you'll sleep like a baby."

Grace sipped again. Her eyes, struggling to stay open, tried to focus on him. Grace finished her tea, and Dominick set it aside. He laid her back gently across her pillow and tucked her in. "There. You'll be safe and sound. I'll tell the guys to come in the afternoon, so you can get a good night's sleep, okay?"

Grace nodded, and her eyes began to mist with tears. Dominick, choked by emotion, started for the door.

"Stay," Grace whispered.

Dominick turned around and nodded. "If you want me to; I'll just camp out in the parlor." he turned to leave again.

"With me."

Dominick stopped, hand on the doorknob, with his eyes closed. Swallowing hard, he slowly turned around again and gazed at her. "Are you sure?"

Grace smiled shyly. "Yes." An epiphany hit Grace. "What about Lilly?"

"I dropped her off with Annie before I came out here. She'll be okay. I'll send Annie a quick text." The glow of his cell phone illuminated his chiseled face. "There. My baby's taken care of." Without another word he walked over to the window seat, lifted it, and took out a comforter. After laying it on the floor next to Grace's side of the bed, he stripped off his damp shirt and damp jeans.

Before lying down, he claimed Grace's hand and squeezed it gently. "Oh, Grace, I drove like a maniac, thinking the worst," his voice cracked. Grace squeezed his hand. "And when I saw you lying on the ground motionless..." Dominick paused when Grace's hand slackened. A moment of fear raced through him.

Dominick darted up and looked at Grace. She was asleep. Letting go of his pent up breath, Dominick gently enfolded Grace's hand in his and studied it. With tenderness only love could create, he kissed every scratch. Dominick lay down on the floor and watched the lightning brighten up the sky. His mind reeled and he saw the flashes of the gun muzzles, smelled the gunpowder, and felt his world end as his wife and baby fell to the ground. He closed his eyes to shut out the heavenly pyrotechnic display. His body shivered as he remembered seeing Grace lie lifeless on the ground--just like his wife. His soul cried out to God, and his body cried for Grace. Carefully Dominick

218

lay next to Grace in her bed. He needed her warmth, needed to feel her breathe, and needed to see her chest rise and fall. So as not to wake her, Dominick gently situated himself so his arm lay over her stomach. He laid his head on her chest and listened to her strong heartbeat till he fell into a dreamless sleep.

Chapter Seventeen

Grace groaned as a brightening light pulled her from her dream. *Stupid sun, go away!* She wanted to stay in her dream. To stay in the arms of… Grace's eyes snapped open. Slowly, Grace maneuvered herself to the edge of the bed and peeked over the edge. No Dominick.

Disappointment and relief mixed in her stomach. A blush worked its way up her face. She couldn't believe she'd actually asked him to stay. It's a good thing he'd slept on the floor. She could never look at him again if she'd been allowed to take refuge in his arms and snuggle into his warm chest. What was she thinking? The thump to her head probably caused the momentary brain lapse. It couldn't be anything else. Grace rolled over on her side. Watching the sunshine stream through her window, Grace forced her heart to believe it.

Phoebe opened up the bedroom door. "Good morning, Sunshine. How are you feeling this morning?"

"Like I've been hit a truck. This time I think it was a garbage truck." Grace rolled over to look at her sister and gasped. "Phoebe! Your face, your hands!" Phoebe's face, littered with scratches, cuts, and bruises, was red and splotchy. Grace ignored her pain and sat up in bed. "Oh, my gosh! I'm sorry. I should never have gone after that stupid cat. Can you ever forgive me?"

Phoebe clucked her tongue at Grace. "I should beat you for that stunt you pulled last night."

"I know. I'm really sorry, Pheebs." Grace gently touched a scratch on Phoebe's hand. "Thank you for saving me last night."

Phoebe waved away the thanks. "Dominick's the one you saved you."

"You were the one who lay on top of me to protect me from the hail and rain; you were the one who called for help; you were the one who pulled me out. Don't insult your bravery, my dear little sister."

"I'm just thankful you are okay." Phoebe sat beside Grace. With tenderness, Phoebe brushed back Grace's hair. "You're going to have awesome coloring in a couple of days."

"Thanks, so are you," Grace stated ruefully. She could already feel that her face was puffy and very sore. She dreaded looking in the mirror.

"Do you think you can get yourself ready, or should I dress you?" Phoebe asked with a playful grin spreading across her face.

"I don't trust your fashion sense." Grace repositioned herself on the bed. "I think I can manage it; just don't expect anything pretty."

Phoebe got up. "Good because I'm taking you to the hospital in one hour. No arguments." Phoebe held up a warning finger. Satisfied that she had made her point, she left the room, closing the door behind her.

"I think she's serious." Grace chuckled. "Oh, even laughing hurts. Well, here goes nothing." She sent very slow messages to her muscles to respond. Cautiously, inch by inch she moved until finally she was sitting up, her legs dangling off the edge. She wrinkled up her nose as she examined her knee; it was the size of a grapefruit and had turned colors overnight.

"Lovely, just lovely," Grace muttered as she limped to the window. Everything outside shone and sparkled like diamonds when the sun's light hit the beads of rain drops. Grace opened the window and breathed in the fresh morning air. Revived and refreshed, she limped back over to the bed and, out of habit, began to make it.

All was going well until she got around to the opposite side when she tripped; pain shot into her knee, and catching the edge of the bed, just in time, she sat down. Rubbing her aching knee she saw what had tripped her up: Dominick's pillow. Grace used her good leg to move the pillow closer to the bed. She gingerly reached down and picked it up. Dominick's very familiar scent soothed her, and she indulged in placing her face in the fluffy surface and inhaling Dominick. A soft knock on the door had Grace jumping. Stashing his pillow back on her bed, she certainly didn't want Phoebe catching her sniffing a pillow!

Instead of Phoebe standing in the doorway, however, Dominick stood, his smile quickly melting into a frown.

"You shouldn't be out of bed yet!"

"I'm not an invalid!" She shimmied front and, just to prove her point, stood up, fighting back the urge to cry out in pain. She gave Dominick a huge triumphant smile.

"I never said you were an invalid. I just pointed out that maybe you shouldn't be out of bed. You did have a tree fall on you last night."

Grace sighed. Why did he always manage to get her back up? "Sorry. I didn't mean to get snippy. I just...I don't know..." Grace sat down on the bed. Feeling a desire to hug something, she grabbed for a pillow. Too late she realized what pillow she had grabbed as the scent whiffed up to her nose.

Dominick kneeled down before her and looked at her knee. "Pretty colors." He gazed up at her.

Grace's breath hitched and she forced herself to breathe normally. Her conscience upbraided her when she noticed the tiny scratches on his face. Her idiotic stunt had really brought everybody she knew and lov...her mind stopped mid-thought. She looked away from his intense gaze.

He gently turned her face back to his with his index finger. "Do I make you nervous?"

Grace nodded her head. "No. Yes."

That tiny smile played on his lips. "Which one is it?"

"I don't know." Grace tried pushing him away. He didn't budge.

"Grace, I know there's something between us. I feel it every time we're near each other. I can't get you out of my head!" Dominick smiled. "Problem is, I really have no idea what you want from me." Dominick held her gaze. "But I do know this. I'd like to find out."

Grace, held captive by his gaze, swallowed hard. "I don't know you."

Dominick sat beside her on the bed. "Okay, then. You want to know me?" At Grace's nod, Dominick began. "My name's Dominick Stephen Carson. I'm thirty years old and was born and raised right here in Beacon. I excelled at wrestling and football, dated the prom queen for a while and daydreamed in class. I decided I wanted out of small-town life and attended the University of Kansas. I hated every moment of it. So, I joined the Marines." Dominick paused and subconsciously ran a finger over his scar. "I met a girl...and well, you know the rest of that story. I left the Marines after my wife's death, and came back to live in the very town I escaped from. The end."

Grace sat mute.

Dominick gently captured Grace's chin in his hands. "I don't know why you don't trust me. But I promise you one thing, I'll never hurt you, ever." He lowered his head to hers and gently kissed her forehead. "Think on it. You know where to find me."

223

Grace watched as Dominick walked out of her room. Her forehead tingled where Dominick had gently kissed her. She waited for the doubt. She waited for the fear. She waited for the memories of Kevin. They never came.

What did come was a knock on the door followed by a bustling Phoebe. "Oh my gosh, you are not even dressed," ripping open the closet door, she grabbed the first thing she saw.

"Oh, Phoebe, not the pink sweatpants!" Grace groaned.

"Well you don't think you're gonna get into a pair of your tight jeans, not with that basketball of a knee. Besides you had plenty of time to get yourself ready, so you are in my hands now, and you know how I hate being late."

Wardrobe picked out and lying on the bed, Phoebe unceremoniously began to "help" Grace with her pajamas.

"You know, Pheebs, you'd make a lousy nurse." Grace flinched as Phoebe bumped into her bad knee while trying to pull a t-shirt over Grace's head. "Ouch, that hurts, you know."

"Sorry!" Phoebe's face suddenly lit up.

"What is wrong with you? Your face does not look like one who is very repentant."

Phoebe stifled a giggle. "Well, I don't feel too sorry for you beings you got to have some snuggle time with Carpenter Hottie last night!" Phoebe ignored Grace's stunned look and placed her hand on her chest. "He looked so cute, too, curled up next to you in bed."

Grace snatched Phoebe's arm and pulled her face close to her own. "What do you mean, 'curled up next to me in bed?'"

"Don't you remember?" At Grace's puzzled expression, Phoebe went into action. Excitedly and with much animation, she wove the story from Dominick's truck racing into the yard, tires screeching and gravel flying, to him running through the pelting rain and hail with Grace tugged against his chest, to him gently washing her hair and then tucking her into bed. And then you asked him to stay and he did. The end!" Phoebe, out of breath, flung herself on the bed.

"What do you mean 'the end?' I remember everything that happened except the part you didn't divulge! Where does the part about Dominick in my bed come in?"

"Well, before I went to bed, I peeked in to check on you and there he was snuggled right up against you, sleeping like a baby." Phoebe, imitating a baby sleeping on its hands, rested her head on Grace's shoulder.

Grace's temper tried to ignite but it fizzled out; instead a gentle smile played at the corner of her mouth then sprinted across her entire face. Phoebe stole a peek at her sister's face and smiled. Even the bruises could not tarnish the beautiful peace that rested there.

Chapter Eighteen

Dominick felt as if he were walking on air. He hadn't been this happy since before Carmen's death. Wham! It hit him so hard he gasped. *And how long will that happiness last when she finds out the truth about Carmen's death. You sure avoided that part of the story. The end, indeed!* The voice was not audible, but it was as familiar to Dominick as his own. It was the one he always heard whenever the fortress of secrets he had spent so much time and energy to build was threatened. His old friend, Fear, began to creep up his spine. Needing a moment alone, Dominick sprinted up the steps and into the old nursery. It was peaceful here, a perfect place for a battle. Dominick fell to his knees and fought. An hour later the battle was over. The truth had won. The lie that Dominick had come to believe, that he was responsible for Carmen's death, lay in wet puddles on the newly restored wood floor. Dominick now knew in his heart that an evil man had killed his wife, not him. Now he was ready to tell Grace the whole story; what her reaction would be he didn't know, but that was in God's hands now.

With a silent prayer of thanks, Dominick made his way outside to inspect the progress. It never ceased to amaze him how quickly things could be rebuilt. The old Victorian house, given a new lease on life, rose proudly into the prairie sky. After the equipment was gone, Dominick knew Grace would be on her hands and knees creating a landscape worthy of the old place. Knowing he and his men would soon be done with the house, a wave of uncertainty overcame him. What excuse would he have to see Grace? Until then, he had the house.

"Earth to Dominick."

Dominick turned and smiled at Noah. "Hey, what's up?" Dominick studied his friend closely. "I didn't think you needed to inspect anything today. What gives?"

Noah grinned. "Good to see you, too, my friend." Noah turned to look at the house. "You've done a mighty fine job. It's a good thing my dad gave Grace and Phoebe your number, huh?"

Dominick chuckled. Without Dickie Weasel, Dominick might have never met Grace. Now, he couldn't imagine his life without his little auburn-haired spitfire. Dominick stared at the toe of his steel-toed boots. "Those two women he sent my way are quite the pair, aren't they?"

Noah stared at one window in particular. "Yup. Colorado breeds weird but very intriguing women."

"You ain't kiddin'." Dominick slapped his buddy on the back, "So what does bring you out here, Mr. Fire Inspector, who has nothing to inspect?"

"It's not any of your business, but I'm here to inspect a very fine specimen, very rare and very difficult to handle --priceless, actually."

"Dude!" Dominick grinned devilishly. "You've got it bad!"

Noah hung his head. "I know! Ever since I saw her dump that soda on Roy's head, I was in..." Noah's jabbering stopped at Phoebe's shrill voice erupting from the house.

"That's it! I've had it with this old piece of crap. I know that Carpenter Hottie knows what he's doing, but I swear he left open nooks and crannies for every possible creepy-crawly to get in!"

Noah glanced at Dominick. "Who's Carpenter Hottie?"

Dominick shrugged. "Heck if I know."

227

"No, Grace, I will not calm down!" Phoebe continued on her tirade. "I found a mouse in my bathtub this morning and just now a spider as big as Mrs. Sloucombe climbed up my leg! And, just for the record, I can call Dominick anything I want."

Noah turned to Dominick. "I guess we found out who Carpenter Hottie is."

"Shut up, Noah!" Dominick blushed. *Good grief!* Before the men could catch their breaths, a whirlwind with streaming black hair and neon green shorts descended the front steps. Muttering to herself, she never saw Dominick or Noah, and proceeded to run right into the latter. On the cusp of a creative swear word, she looked up and stopped dead still. Her sapphire eyes darted nervously from a pair of chocolate ones to a pair of blue.

Phoebe retreated slightly. "I, um, was just telling Grace what an amazing job you've done, Mr. Carson. And, Noah, I hope I didn't crush your toes, as I am as large as an ox and as graceful as a water buffalo...or so I've been told." Tears pooled in her eyes, and she quickly retreated.

Dominick and Noah watched flabbergasted as Phoebe marched off in the direction of the pond. Occasionally they'd see her arms flailing as if she was chastising herself. Dominick cleared his throat and gave his friend a push. "Go get her, pal."

Noah smiled stupidly at the thought and trotted after her. Dominick watched as his friend caught up with Phoebe and slipped his arm around her waist. With a quick laugh, Dominick walked to his truck. If this house was ever going to get done, he needed to get more supplies. Maybe if he drove slow enough...

With the commotion of improvement, no one noticed the wicked grin spread across Leo Muldoon's face.

It was a face full of excitement and anticipation. He licked his lips. The time was near. He could feel it. As quick as the blood-thirsty look came, it left, leaving only the innocent, shy face of Andrew Carnegie.

Chapter Nineteen

"Does it hurt bad?"

Grace smiled at Lilly who was busy prodding Grace's elbow with a pink plastic stethoscope. "It feels much better now, Doctor Lilly." Grace studied the little blonde-haired girl and was glad that Dominick had brought her along. After having a tree-hug two days ago, she needed a little ray of sunshine. And the ray of sunshine was currently checking her big toe.

"You are a very good patient. Daddy never sits still for me. He says it tickles." Lilly scrunched up her nose. "Daddy is silly." Lilly stopped wiggling Grace's little toe and seemed to study her with a surprising wisdom. "I told Mommy I was coming here to fix you."

Grace felt her eyebrow shoot up to her hairline. What does one say to that? "And I'm glad you did come fix me."

Lilly continued to gaze at Grace. "Mommy said it was okay. Sometimes I wish I could fix my Mommy, too." Grace reached out and Lilly instantly crawled into Grace's lap.

Grace held the little girl who had somehow captured her heart. Would it have felt like this if she'd had a child? Could she be holding her own child if Kevin hadn't sabotaged her? Grace killed the negative thoughts and concentrated on holding Lilly. The little girl snuggled into Grace's shoulder. Grace sang into Lilly's hair and cried inwardly for the little one in her lap.

That's how Dominick found them. His heart skipped a beat at the sight of Grace holding his little girl. Both had fallen asleep on Grace's bed; Lilly's head, tucked up under Grace's chin, looked as if it belonged there. While part of his heart still mourned for Carmen and probably always would, he knew that the woman holding his child would make the perfect mother for Lilly and the perfect wife for him.

Dominick knelt down beside Grace's bed and studied Grace. Her auburn hair hung in rivulets, framing her oval face. One of Lilly's hands had snagged a piece of it and had fallen asleep still clutching the soft tresses. Dominick hoped that one day he could do the same. His eyes took in the bruises and scratches on Grace's face, but those wounds did not even come close to marring her beauty. Tiny freckles dotted the top of her nose and under her eyes. Dominick wanted to kiss every single one of them. And her lips, he knew enough about them to know he couldn't go without. At the memory of her pinned under the tree and hail pummeling her, his heart twisted in his chest. He could have lost her as well. He breathed a prayer of thanksgiving and risked touching a curl that had escaped and cascaded past Grace's right eye.

Grace's eye popped open. Dominick withdrew his hand and whispered, "Sorry. I didn't mean to wake you."

Grace looked down at the little girl in her arms and smiled so sweetly that it almost broke Dominick's heart. "That's okay," Grace whispered back. Her right hand lightly caressed Lilly's hair. "It's like silk."

"Her mother's hair was just like that." Dominick swallowed around a sudden lump in this throat. "In fact, if you want to know what Carmen looked like, all you need to do is look at her daughter."

"Carmen must have been beautiful." Grace didn't divulge that she'd already seen his gorgeous late wife.

"Yeah. Yeah, she was." Dominick softly cleared his throat. "How are you holding up?"

"My leg hurts, and my face feels like someone mistook it for a punching bag."

Dominick tenderly clasped Grace's free hand. "No, Grace. I'm not talking about that. How are you? "

That one hated question started it all. Grace felt the pricking behind her eyes, and the worst part was she couldn't stop them, couldn't stop the tears of regret, of fear, of loneliness. "Sorry. You probably don't want some blubbering woman to deal with."

Lilly squirmed in Grace's arms but didn't wake up. Instead she snuggled deeper into Grace and entwined both hands in Grace's hair. The tears which before had been a mere trickle, avalanched into a waterfall. And before she could press her mute button, Grace found herself spilling her emotional guts out all over Dominick.

"I never wanted to be a trophy wife! All I ever wanted was to be loved and to have someone love me. Is that too much to ask?" Grace whispered hoarsely. "I really can't explain the emotions that came over me when I saw Kevin, my ex, lace my yogurt with birth control pills. I had thought both us were on the same page. I went through a series of emotions. Betrayal, disbelief, and hatred. Hatred at Kevin. Hatred at God. Hatred at myself for becoming a mindless bimbo."

Grace angrily dashed away the tears. "My mother didn't think it was such a bad deal. I was supposed to live it up. And children really did put a hamper on one's social life. My father, God rest his soul, would have probably punched Kevin in the gonads if he'd known." A small smile lit up Grace's face. "Phoebe is really the only thing that I have in this entire world." Grace's smile saddened. She glanced down at the tiny fist in her hair. "Pretty pitiful life story, huh?

Dominick caressed the back of Grace's hand with his thumb and gazed into Grace's watery green eyes. "Do you know what I see when I look at you? I see a confident, independent woman who is forging a life for herself and who's not afraid to get a little elbow grease on herself along the way. You are stronger than you give yourself credit for, Spitfire." A blush crept its way up his neck. "And I think when the time is right, you will make a great mother."

Dominick paused and sweat beaded on his forehead. If any time was right, it was now. But Fear tightened around his stomach like a boa constrictor and squeezed. Dominick had certainly seen enough of those hideous snakes to know the damage they could wreak. The same would happen to him if he didn't confess to the woman lying before him. He took in her green eyes, so full of care, and dare he say it, love? Despite her bruises and scratches, he could still see the freckles that dotted the bridge of her nose. He prayed that someday he'd be able to kiss every single one of them. In order to earn that right, though, Dominick had a confession to make.

Taking a deep breath, Dominick went in for the plunge. "Grace, I need you to know something about me."

"Okay," Grace's kind smile settled his nerves.

"I...um...kind of left some essential information out of my little bio I gave you." Dominick watched as Grace's smile slipped slightly. "Remember that night at Reed's Diner when you accused me of being a mercenary?"

"I never 'accused', I simply guessed." Grace smoothed Lilly's hair.

Dominick smiled wryly. "Well, you weren't quite on the mark, but you were close." He took a deep breath. *Here it goes!* "I have killed before, Grace."

"For money?" There was no judgment in her eyes, but Dominick her smile disappear entirely.

"No!" Dominick suddenly fell to his knees by the side of the bed and clasped her hands in his. "I was a Marine. Special forces. It was part of my job, at times, to take out the enemy. And I did. It was my enemy that took my wife. I was there when my wife died. She died protecting Lilly. I couldn't save her." Dominick released her hands and gently twirled a piece of Lilly's hair around his calloused index finger. "I just thought you needed to know before we...well...I just needed you to know."

Grace placed her hand on his stubbly cheek and gently turned his face toward hers. She tentatively traced his scar. He closed his eyes as she ran her finger up and down the fine line. "Is this where you got this?"

"Yes." Dominick met her eyes. "Do you hate me now?"

"Hate?" Tears pooled in Grace's eyes. "No! I could never hate you. Ever. I'm sorry you had to witness your wife's death. I'm sorry you couldn't save her."

"Me, too. Her death crushed me. Almost killed me, actually. If it weren't for little Lilly, I'd have probably become an alcoholic. But God provided me with my baby girl. He saved me with her."

Grace smiled and caressed his scar again. He smiled and the scar puckered slightly under her fingers. "I'm glad you had Lilly. She's truly a precious gift." She tilted her head slightly and took in the scent of Lilly's bubblegum scented hair.

Dominick stopped Grace's caressing fingers by placing his hand over hers. "Thank you for understanding...for not turning your back on me. I can barely stand to look at myself in the mirror some days. I don't know what I would have done if you'd..."

"You served this country, Dominick. You had a job to do, and you did it. I'm not saying that killing is right, but every kill you made was a righteous one. Remember, I love another man who also had that burden to bear as well."

"Your father."

"Yes, my father. Roy Muldoon was not his first." Grace wiggled her hand out from under his and placed it over his beating heart. "What you have inside of you is much more powerful and important than the targets you were ordered to take out. I'm not a naïve child, Dominick. I understand there are some terrible jobs that have to be done, and there are only a select few men and women who are gifted with the resolve and bravery to do them."

Dominick felt tears prick at the back of his eyes. He didn't care. He allowed them to fall down his face as Grace's words soothed his broken soul. "You, my dear Spitfire, are a true wonder."

Grace ducked her head and blushed. "I don't know what to say."

"Say you'll consider me more than a friend. I...I..."

Lilly stirred in Grace's arms, yawned, and rubbed her eyes. Her face lit up when she saw Dominick. "Daddy!" With a squeal she launched herself out of Grace's arms and into the waiting arms of Dominick.

Dominick whispered in Lilly's ear. Lilly smiled, nodded, and turned to Grace. "Are you coming on Saturday for the 4th of July? That's..." Lilly counted the days left on her left hand. "One, two! There's two days left 'til then!"

"I wouldn't miss it for the world."

Lilly beamed a smile and gathered up her doctor's kit. "I need to find Phoebe. She said painting is a pain. She needs fixing, too." With that, she bounded out of the room.

They both watched as she bounded out the door, calling for Phoebe. Dominick shuffled his feet, suddenly nervous to be left alone with Grace. Had he screwed up by asking her to be more than friends? Dominick cleared his throat. "You are still planning on coming, right?"

"Of course. I never break my promises."

"Good. Lilly would be very disappointed if you couldn't make it." He ran a hand through his hair. "Well, I'll let you get back to resting. Take it easy now and don't worry about a thing." On impulse he bent down and kissed Grace's forehead. He quickly left the room, leaving Grace to stare at his retreating form in wonder.

Grace awoke to screams tearing through the house. Phoebe. In one motion Grace flung herself out of bed and sucked in a gasp of pain as her bad leg impacted the floor. Ignoring the pulsating throbs, Grace grappled for her handgun tucked safely in her nightstand drawer. Another scream pierced the air. Grace hobbled to her door and silently turned the doorknob. Trying to calm her racing mind and roiling stomach, Grace inched her head out of her door and froze.

Two dead raccoons lay in the hall, blood pooling around the carcasses. The words "Prepare To Die" covered every inch of the beige hallway. Everywhere Grace looked, the dripping raccoons' blood sent her the same message. Grace felt her own blood pool to her feet. Her head, light and airy, felt as if it would pop right off her neck and skitter across the ceiling. Phoebe's scream sliced through the fog in Grace's brain, and her brain kicked into overdrive.

Grace signaled for Phoebe to stay put and with deft movements made her way to the front door. One look at the alarm keypad told Grace everything. Someone had disarmed the alarm. There was no evidence of tampering.

"Phoebe," Grace hoarsely whispered, "call the police."

"Think!" Dominick instantly regretted the harshness in his voice. He so desperately wanted to kiss Grace's tired eyes and wanted to kiss away the dark circles. He needed to get her away from this, get her to safety. Instead, he filled Grace's coffee cup. Phoebe, leaning against Noah's wide chest, looked like an 80's punk rocker with a hangover. "Sorry. I just don't know who would do this to you! So, I really need you to think. Who have you given your security code to?" Dominick tried to keep judgment out of his voice.

He watched as Grace shut her eyes and cradled her head in her hands. Slowly and tentatively Dominick reached out an unsteady hand and caressed the hair that fell down her back. He felt her tense under his touch. Reluctantly, he moved his hand from her hair, only to be surprised when she fell into his side and began to sob. Not knowing what to do, he looked at Phoebe for help. An unsuccessful mission, as she, too, blubbered into Noah's already soaked shirt. Gently, Dominick lifted his arm and cradled Grace against his side and buried his face in her hair. He didn't say anything. There was nothing to say. He simply caressed her hair.

Grace promised herself a few minutes tucked up against Dominick. He was warm and sturdy. He was what was allowing her to stay somewhat close to sane. Ten minutes and two dried up tear ducts later, Grace sniffled

237

and hiccupped. She really wanted nothing more than to stay in Dominick's arms, but her dignity called and she had to answer.

"Sorry about that." Grace grabbed a tissue and clumsily swiped at the drool and tear marks staining Dominick's grey t-shirt. "I tend to get a little leaky when emotional."

"She's right, ya know." Phoebe dabbed at her red-rimmed eyes. "When you two get married she'll be a puddle of happiness."

"Phoebe!"

Phoebe shrugged. "Whatever. It'll happen." She pushed herself off Noah's chest. "You know, those that think crying is for sissies don't know what they're talking about. I'll tell you, whenever I've had a good cry, I end up feeling a little stronger and a little meaner afterward. I don't know about you, sis, but I'm so ticked off right now I could kick a kitten."

"No need to hurt little puffs of fur, Phoebe." Dominick pulled a small notebook from his pocket. "What you two need to do is make a list of everyone you remember giving the code to."

"But I haven't," Grace argued.

Grace, Dominick, and Noah all turned to Phoebe. Phoebe dropped her head and started messing with the hem of her shorts. "What!" At their continuing stares, Phoebe quit fiddling. "Okay, okay. Jeeze. I only gave it to a couple of men when they forgot something in the house. It's no big deal, right?"

Grace bit her tongue. "Phoebe, who did you give the code to?"

"Oh, I don't know. I had to give it to Randy the other day because he forgot his cell phone. Steve needed it the other day for his wallet. And Andrew." Phoebe looked pleadingly at Grace. "Don't you remember several weeks ago when I gave him the code so he could get his wallet. I can't think..."

Grace bolted off the couch and instantly sat down in pain. "Andrew!"

"Just because you don't like him, Grace, doesn't make him a criminal. Besides, he's too ho..." Phoebe stopped herself. "Nice. Yeah, he's too nice to do anything like this."

Noah leaned toward Grace. "What made you pick Andrew out of the list Phoebe gave you?"

"Oh, I don't know. Ever since he asked us for the job right after we bought the house, I just keep getting this uneasy feeling. It could be nothing."

"No." Dominick quickly to his feet and paced the newly renovated and decorated front parlor room. "We need to look into this. I'm going to talk to the sheriff." With that, Dominick marched from the room, leaving Grace and Phoebe in the protection of Noah.

"Do you think Grace and Phoebe are in danger, Sheriff?" Dominick stood on the front porch of Grace and Phoebe's house next to the man he'd beat in wrestling at the State Championship their senior year. *Wouldn't know it to look at the guy now,* Dominick thought sadly as he surveyed his old opponent. The buttons on the navy blue button-up hardly contained Sheriff Clarkston's drooping belly. It was truly a miracle that his toothpick-sized legs could support the man. Dominick immediately pictured a pregnant Gumby. Add a gallon-sized white Stetson to the mix and the match would be identical. Dominick quickly squashed the vision and turned back to the matter at hand. "First with the dead squirrels and broken window, now the dead raccoons and bloody death threats, what's going on?"

Sheriff Clarkston removed his Stetson, revealing a receding hairline too large for a man of only thirty. He wiped his brow and tugged his hat back on. His physique had certainly diminished since the glory days, but Dominick knew under that huge hat lay a mind as sharp as a razor. His Grace was in good hands. *His?* Dominick's heart thudded in his chest. When had he started thinking of her as his? He struggled back to reality and tried to pay attention to whatever Sheriff Clarkston was explaining, "...posted around the house. No one would be stupid enough to try anything right now. But we'll have to be extra vigilant. You might want to convince the ladies to leave the premises for a while, maybe even leave Beacon 'til all this settles down."

Leave? Dominick swallowed. Yes, she had to. There was no doubt about that, but the thought of her leaving, if only for a short amount of time, caused his heart to fall to his feet.

"No!" Grace huffed and planted her arms across her chest and glared at Dominick. "I'm not leaving my home." Much to Grace's embarrassment, her voice hitched at the word "home." Clearing her throat, she continued, "And you can't make me, Dominick Carson!"

"You are not listening to reason, you stubborn woman. Don't you see you and Phoebe are in some kind of danger?"

"Like some loser with a penchant for killing small animals is going to hurt me." Grace forced a calm she certainly didn't feel into her voice. She would have much rather preferred to scream and cry. "I will not let some person ruin the only good thing that has ever happened to me, don't you understand that?" Grace gestured to the finished foyer with its glistening hardwood floors, polished front desk, ornate floor rugs, and glinting glass windows, "This is the first place I've ever been that has felt like home since my father died. This is the first place I've ever been able to be myself. I will not leave it. Do you understand me?"

Dominick reached for her. Grace retreated a quick step back. Dominick didn't seem to care. He kept advancing on her, and before she knew it, Grace was pinned against the front desk. He placed his two large hands on the top of the desk behind her, successfully pinning her in between his arms. She knew from practice there was no way out now. Unless...she brought back her right foot a few inches. She'd only aim for his shin this time. But before she could even begin her forward motion, he stopped her with an electrifying kiss that sizzled her insides and turned her bones to jelly. Her head told her to kick and kick hard; her heart told her to kiss and kiss hard. Her heart won.

Dominick broke the kiss first, but he only receded a centimeter. His breath came warm and fast on her face. She gazed into his eyes and tried to remind herself to breath. "I want you to go, Spitfire, because if something happened to you, I don't know what I'd do." Grace opened her mouth to retort but was shushed by his calloused finger on her lips. That wicked little grin played on his lips, and Grace stifled the urge to bite his lip, in punishment of course. "You see, Miss McIntyre, somewhere between seeing you kill an innocent window shutter to finding out you wear days-of-the-week underwear, I fell in love with you. So it's high on my priority list that you are safe. Do you understand me?"

Well. Grace opened her mouth and snapped it shut. *Well.* Grace darted her tongue out and nervously licked her lips and she tasted Dominick on them. "I...I...well...I..."

241

In panic, Grace pushed herself away from Dominick and ran.

Chapter Twenty

This had been the opportunity he'd been waiting for. All day he'd watched the police buzz around the house like worker bees. Too bad for them, they would find nothing. And now his prey, his quarry, was coming straight at him. He knew the trees would hide him well if he chose to stay hidden, but today was not the day for hiding. Today was the day for revenge. Grace McIntyre would pay for her father's sins. Reaching around to his back, he grabbed his favorite hunting knife from the waistband of his jeans. Sitting back on his haunches, he sat and listened with heightened excitement to the quick footsteps bringing Grace to him.

Grace ran. Ran from Dominick. Ran from the house. Ran to the woods. Grace's knee was throbbing but she was bound and determined to get to the woods. Dominick's words reverberated in her mind: "I fell in love with you." In vain she tried to skew their meaning but it was no use. The fact was that he loved her, and she couldn't escape the realization that she loved him too. She just didn't know what the heck to do with it. The humidity and her bum knee quickly zapped her strength, and Grace slowed down to an awkward hippity-hop gait. Before she realized it, she found herself deep within the little woods behind the house. The only other time she had been in the woods was when she had come to inspect that weird light she'd seen the first few days after arriving. All the weird phenomena that had happened in the last month collided in Grace's mind. The weird light in the woods, the dead squirrels, the dead raccoons--it all led to one conclusion: someone was targeting them. Maybe Dominick was right. Maybe she and Phoebe did need to leave for a while and come back when this nightmare ended.

Grace turned to head back to the house when she heard it--a single footstep. Grace knew she wasn't alone. Grace swallowed the bile that had erupted up to her mouth. Fear snaked through her body and constricted her heart as a wisp of cigar smoke assailed her senses. And she suddenly remembered. She remembered the sticky, hammy hands which had manhandled her and her sister in the panel van. She remembered the green couch. She remembered the stench of the same sweet-smelling cigar smoked by the fat man who'd taken her from her home.

"Grace."

Grace closed her eyes in resignation. *So this is it.* Turning slowly, Grace faced the man which intuition told her would kill her. "Andrew."

"Leo. Leo Muldoon." Gone was the shy cowboy. In his stead stood a seething human body of hatred and malicious intent. Leo's grey eyes looked almost green in the filtered light of the woods. Perspiration glistened on his face and ran in rivulets down his arms. Grace watched as one tiny river of sweat beaded down his arm and then ran down the hilt and then the blade of a very large, very scary looking knife. "You like my equipment?"

"Never been a big fan of knives, to be completely honest." Grace tried to sound nonchalant. As if there weren't a single problem with her being in the woods with a man who looked at her the way a cheetah does a gazelle. She swallowed the rising bile.

"I don't think this experience will cause you to change your mind." Leo giggled to himself. "Do you remember me?"

Grace shook her head. "No, Leo. I was only a little girl when your father kidnapped my sister and me. Why are you doing this?"

"The sins of the father are to be laid upon the children." Leo's eyes danced with insanity.

Grace clutched on to this one opportunity to distract him. Maybe if she could keep him talking, Dominick would come looking for her. But, why would he? She'd basically slapped him with another rejection. Only a very patient man could take no for an answer as many times as she'd doled them out. No, Dominick would not come looking for her. That thought alone made her blood freeze. The sweltering humidity crushed her, her leg and head ached, and she fought to stay on her feet. If today was her day, she'd go down fighting. She'd get her punches in.

"The Bible also says that one should not kill and that we are to forgive one another."

"Shut up! An eye for an eye! That's what I believe in." Leo's face split into a slithery grin, "You ready to meet this God you seem to believe in?"

Yeah, she was, Grace thought. But just maybe, today was not her day. Grace turned on her good leg and prepared to run, but before she could make a break for it, Leo was on top of her. Grace cried out in pain when he kneeled with all his weight on her bad knee. He forced her over on her back and pinned her viciously to the ground. His free hand grabbed her hands, and in one swift motion he tugged her arms above her head and stuffed a dirty handkerchief into her mouth. His eyes sparked with insanity and a slow smile slithered across his face. "And here is the part where you're probably going to really hate knives."

In horror Grace watched as Leo Muldoon sliced downward with his knife. A split second later Grace's body bucked in agony. She felt her eyes bug out of her head and her stomach spew forth the last thing she ate. She tried to spit out the foul gag but couldn't and was forced to swallow the vile tasting stuff. Escape was impossible now. Pain which seemed to melt her very bones pulsated from the very center of her hands where Leo had staked them to the ground with his knife. Grace struggled and vomited again from the pain. Every movement, almost every breath caused the knife to slice a little more into her palms.

"You should be more careful, Grace." Leo kneeled down beside Grace's head and gently, maliciously brushed a strand of hair out of her eyes. "The more you struggle the more it will hurt."

Looking into her attacker's eyes, Grace knew what it was to look into the eyes of a shark: cunning, cruel, and deadly.

"Why!?" Grace's muffled question seemed to humor her attacker.

"Why!?" Leo leaned his face an inch away from Grace's and shouted, "Because your father killed my father and left me with nothing!" Regaining his composure, Leo sat up, his face catching the last rays of the setting sun under the canopy of trees. "It was my job to watch you and your bratty sister so you two didn't make a sound. My father needed me; I was important." Leo's voice rose in hysteria, "I watched. I watched as your father killed mine." Slowly, Leo pulled a gun from the back pocket of his jeans and caressed it up and down Grace's cheeks. "Your father gunned down my father, who was only protecting himself, protecting me."

'Click'. Grace nearly passed out as the gun pressed to her temple clicked on an empty chamber. Leo smiled at her terror and leaned over and whispered in her ear. "I have another secret, but I'll wait for the finale. You're going to love it!"

Tucking the gun in his waist band and producing a length of baling twine from his pants pocket he tied Grace's wrist together and with one swift movement wrenched the knife from her hands, freeing them from the ground. Thousands of tiny white stars slammed into Grace's vision. The knife being pulled from her hands was almost worse than the going in. She could feel the dampness on her hands spread down her arms and into her armpits, her own blood. Grace fought to stay conscious. She had to. Doing otherwise would certainly be a death sentence.

Leo held the bloody knife in his shaking hand and skittered it up and down Grace's cheeks. Not hard enough to break skin, but just enough to leave tiny white scratches in a tic-tac-toe pattern. "And now for my little secret. Do you remember the day your father's horse came back into your yard with your dead father slung over the saddle?"

"You sonofa…" Grace's mumbled curse ceased as Leo's large fist smacked into her face. Tears she'd been holding back broke the dam and cascaded down her cheeks. Her poor father.

"He was only the beginning. Your mother's new fiancé? Well, she fell easily enough for such a shy young cowboy. Now don't go getting all teary-eyed on me," Leo admonished as he noticed Grace's tears. "I'm not going to kill your mother, yet. First I need to comfort her when she gets the news that her two precious little girls are dead, the only descendants of Jeremiah Wallace gone. Oh, who will get all that money?" Leo leaned into her face again. "When I ask you a question, I expect an answer. Who…?" Leo screamed in her face.

"You," Grace mumbled as her eyes shot spears of hatred at him.

"Very good, Gracie." Tenderly he traced her jaw line with the dull edge of the knife. "You really are beautiful; too bad I have to kill you...but before I do..." Leo ripped the handkerchief out of her mouth and smashed his lips down on hers. Suddenly he screamed in pain.

Grace, tasting the blood from the gaping hole in his lip, sprang into action. Ignoring all pain and fear, she flung up her tied wrists and whacked Leo on the head at the same time she rolled out from under him. Free at last, she began to army crawl, but she didn't get far.

Enraged, Leo grabbed her around the waist and unceremoniously sat her up against a big tree, bashing the back of her head against the trunk. "You little bitch, you bit me." He yelled at her. "Just for that, you can die first. But I want to you die knowing that I will make Phoebe's death a torturous one." Sitting on her knees, he grabbed a hunk of her hair and bent her head backwards, exposing her long, slender, ivory neck. Seemingly fascinated, he watched the rapid pulsing of the artery which was transporting warm, life-giving blood throughout her body.

Grace finally gave up the fight and closed her eyes and prayed. Prayed for forgiveness. Prayed for protection for her sister. Prayed for Dominick. A sudden peace settled upon her, and she thought about seeing her father again. Suddenly all her senses came alive. She felt Leo's hand release her hair, and his body slide sideways off her legs. She smelled her blood and his body odor. She tasted her own vomit and the salty flavor of his blood still clinging on her lips. She heard the gentle rustle of leaves as they danced in the breeze and breathing that wasn't her own. This was not heaven!

Looking down she opened up her eyes and saw the empty eyes and gaping mouth of her attacker. Looking up she saw Phoebe brandishing a large tree limb held high in the air. Her wild black hair streamed down her back and her sapphire eyes glowed with angelic light. Phoebe, Xena, Warrior Princess look-a-like, lifted her sneakered foot and gave a swift kick to Leo's face and stomped it in the dirt.

Phoebe violently rolled Leo's inert body off of Grace's legs and flung herself next to her sister and quickly pulled the gag out of Grace's mouth. Tears streaked down Phoebe's face as she gently caressed Grace's hair back. "It's going to be okay, sweetie."

Grace tried to speak but her throat burned, and she suddenly didn't have the energy. She brought her hands in front of her face to inspect the damage, and both she and Phoebe turned snow white when they saw Grace's hands.

"That...that...son of a..." Phoebe stopped herself and simply leaned down and kissed Grace's tear-soaked cheeks. "He'll never, never hurt you, again. Not on my watch." With that Phoebe yelled with all her might, "Help. Grace needs help! Call 911. Now!"

Chapter Twenty-One

Sunlight streamed through the hospital room window. Flower arrangements and stuffed animals crammed every nook and cranny. An entire corner of the room was reserved for the mountain of boxed chocolates. A mindless talk show host on the television jabbered about some new miracle diet. Phoebe lay lightly snoring in a cot on the opposite wall.

Dominick noticed none of it. He only noticed the sleeping woman lying in the hospital bed next to the chair he'd yet to vacate for the past four hours. In his hand was one of Grace's bandaged ones; in his lap lay a Bible open to one of his favorite Psalms. He'd lost count after reading it twenty times. He'd been down in the valley of the shadow of death so many times he assumed that's just where God wanted him. Bowing his head, he prayed for the woman he loved. And for himself, that he could someday be worthy of her and her trust.

Grace opened her eyes. She saw white walls, colorful flowers, prettily packaged candy. The massive headache driving spikes into her brain kept her from shaking her head in confusion. Her gaze slid to her left, and her heart leapt.

"Hey." Dominick's soft smile soothed her jumbled thoughts. He scooted his chair closer and laid his calloused hand on the thick bandaging of her left hand. "How are you feeling?"

"Like I've been steamrolled," Grace croaked. Dominick grabbed her water glass and held the straw so she

250

could take a sip. Grace exhaled. "Better." She studied the IVs sticking out from her right arm. She purposely ignored looking at her hands.

Dominick tucked an auburn curl behind Grace's ear. "The doctor says you'll be fine. The knife did a little damage, but they fixed you up really well. With a little therapy, you'll have full use of your hands again." He brushed a stray tear trickling down Grace's bruised and scratched face. "He won't hurt you, again. Phoebe took care of that." Dominick shuddered. "Oh, Grace, I don't know what I would do if Andrew...Leo...whatever his name was..."

"Was?" Grace sat up a little too quickly and pain shattered in her head. She clutched at it with her bandaged hands to try to stop the cascading torment.

Dominick quickly stood up and helped Grace lay her head back on the pillow. He stroked her hair, avoiding the bandage circling her forehead. "Take it easy, Spitfire." Dominick kissed her bandaged head and sat back down again. "Phoebe's whack to his head killed him, Grace."

Grace, unable to reply, simply nodded her head. Grace couldn't help but feel a twinge of pity for him. After all, he was a victim of his father's crimes just as much as Grace and her family were. The only difference was that by God's grace they had made better choices than Leo had. Grace looked at Phoebe still snoring on the hospital cot. Pride shone in Grace's eyes, and she watched Phoebe twitch a little in her sleep, a trait which had bothered Grace to no end when they had to share a bed as little girls. No more would Phoebe's quirky ways annoy her; she'd relish them and store them in the tiny treasure chest in her heart.

Dominick's hand on her hair had her turning back to him. "I'm so sorry, Grace. I'm sorry I drove you to run away. If it weren't for me, you wouldn't be here. You'd be

251

safe…" Grace opened her mouth to protest, but Dominick laid a finger on her lips. "Let me say my piece." Dominick cleared his throat and continued to touch her hair. "I'm sorry I hired him. I'm sorry I granted him an opportunity to get close to you."

As if suddenly trapped, Dominick began pacing by her bedside. He jammed his hands in his hair and seemed to be trying to contain a loosely-leashed rage. Grace said his name, tried to get his attention. He halted and turned to her with tears in his eyes. "I'm sorry; I'm a coward!"

Grace knew better than to sit up again, but her voice certainly conveyed her astonishment, "What?"

"I should have run after you. I should have taken better care of you. I failed to protect you, just as I failed to protect my wife." As if suddenly tired, Dominick collapsed back in the chair and laid his head on the Grace's bed.

Grace awkwardly caressed his head with her boxer glove-like hands. "Don't do this to yourself. You can't control me anymore than anyone else. Just ask my sister."

Dominick lifted his head and loosely held on to Grace's hands. "When you left the house, I watched until I saw you enter the woods. Concerned, I started after you, but Phoebe stopped me. 'Don't go after her,' she said. I protested, but Phoebe's was adamant. 'Trust me,' she said, 'she needs her space and you'll only make things worse. Believe me I know.'

"So I tried to busy myself around the house. About five minutes later, I glanced toward the wood and saw Phoebe disappear into it. Relived that you wouldn't be alone, I decided to tackle those shelves in the cellar storage room. I lost track of the time; that's when I heard the men scrambling and yelling about something. They told me Phoebe was yelling from the woods, something about 911." Dominick paused here and scooting as close as possible, he leaned his elbow on the edge of the bed and laid her hand against his cheek.

"When I heard those words my heart stopped. I ran, Grace. I ran as fast as possible. And when I saw you covered in blood..." Dominick's face whitened, and Grace feared he'd faint. "Let's just say, I've never fainted before in my entire life, but right then and there I thought I'd fall like a tree. Grace I thought I'd lost you...again!" His voice cracked, but before Grace could respond, he forged ahead, "Then I saw you move," gently he reached up and touched her cheek; Grace sighing, leaned into it, "and I thought my heart was going to burst...you were alive. Phoebe was quick to get me up to speed on the situation. It wasn't until then that I noticed Leo's body on the ground. When I checked for a pulse there was none."

"You cannot blame yourself. You didn't know what he was, what he was capable of." Grace pleaded with tear-filled eyes, "He would have gotten to me anyway, Dominick. Please don't blame yourself."

Dominick bent down and kissed Grace's wrapped hands. His eyes sparkled with unshed tears when he looked back into Grace's face. He ran his thumb over Grace's chapped lips. "I'm sorry my stupidity caused you such pain. I pushed you when you didn't want to be pushed, and for that, I'll never forgive myself. But I'm begging for a second chance. I'll wait for you until you're ready." Dominick played with a tendril of Grace's hair. "I'll have you know that I'm not like Kevin. If you want me, my spunky, quirky, little Spitfire, you will have all of me forever."

Grace closed her eyes against the onslaught of tears threatening to drown her and nuzzled her cheek against the warmth of his hand. The calluses scratched a little, but Grace didn't care. Her stubbornness and mistrust had nearly killed her. She knew exactly what she wanted. She locked gazes with Dominick. Turning her head slightly, she kissed his palm. Even under the influence of pain killers, Grace's insides liquefied when she saw Dominick's eyes darken with desire. A little smile played at her lips. "If you ever break your promise, I'll just send Phoebe after you."

As if on cue, Phoebe snorted, shot her butt up in the air, and plopped down on her other side. Dominick grinned. "I'm terrified."

"Surprise!" Lilly bounded into Grace's hospital room two days later with a fistful of dandelions. "I brought you flowers."

"Why, thank you. This is a very nice surprise." Grace smiled and brought the proffered weeds up to her nose to take a big whiff.

Dominick followed closely after his daughter with an apologetic look on his face. "She insisted on bringing these we…"

"Beautiful flowers." Grace beamed at Lilly. "These dandelions mean more to me than any bouquet of flowers in this room. "

"Even more than these?" Dominick brought his arm which had been tucked behind his back into view. A simple bouquet of wildflowers shook slightly in Dominick's extended hand. He leaned over and kissed Grace's lips. "Beautiful flowers for a beautiful woman."

Grace clutched both bouquets to her chest and gazed at the man and little girl in front of her. "Dominick, I…"

Phoebe and Noah rushed in the room. "Good news, Grace! You get to go home. Today!" Phoebe jumped up and down and shook her booty.

Noah brought her to a stop by promptly planting a kiss on her mouth. After Phoebe was romantically and permanently subdued, Noah turned back to Grace. "Sorry. That's really the only way I can get her to settle down."

"Must be such a hardship," Grace stated ruefully.

Noah winked. "It's a hardship I'm sure I can endure." He tucked Phoebe against him. "As soon as the doctor gives you your final check over, you are free to leave. You will be so amazed when you get..." A puff of hair escaped his lungs as Phoebe's elbow made contact with his ribcage. "What you do that for?"

"It's a secret!" Phoebe whispered. She exhaled. "It's a good thing you're so darn cute."

Grace smiled. "What's this?"

"No, no, no, Miss McIntyre. You will not weasel it out of any of us." Dominick picked up his daughter, "Right, princess?"

Lilly simply stared at Grace. With the accusing voice only a four-year-old can muster, Lilly stated, "You missed the 4th of July."

"Oh, Lilly, I know. I'm sorry." Grace glanced down at her hands, white and bulky with wrappings.

As soon as Lilly saw the bandages, she squirmed from Dominick's hold and scampered to Grace's bedside. "You have big owies. I need to fix them."

"You sure do. Why don't you bring your doctor kit over to my house, and you can fix me up."

Lilly began to climb onto Grace's lap. Dominick reached for her, but Grace waved him off. Lilly carefully picked her way up Grace's legs and laid her head on Grace's chest. "There's a drum inside you. Daddy has one, too." Grace rested her cheek on Lilly's soft hair. Lilly brought her head up quickly. "I wanted to save a firework for you. Daddy wouldn't let me."

Grace laughed. "With you around, I'm not sure I need fireworks."

255

Lilly scrunched up her face and plopped back down on Grace's chest. "I'm not a firework. I'm a princess."

The four adults in the room burst out laughing. Dominick reached for his daughter. "You sure are." He handed Lilly to Noah and bent down to whisper in Grace's ear, "What were you going to tell me before we were so rudely interrupted by the love birds?"

Grace bit her lip. "I'll tell you tonight."

"Promise?"

"Promise."

Chapter Twenty-Two

"Is the blindfold necessary?" Grace leaned into Dominick's arms he guided her across the gravel driveway.

"Trust me."

Grace simply smiled. She would. Somewhere along the line, her heart had learned how to trust again. Not that her heart didn't hurt slightly whenever she thought of Kevin, but the man beside her had slowly and annoyingly, at times, conquered her heart and destroyed the dragon lurking there. Grace sent a prayer of thanks to Heaven for sending her a knight who loved her enough to fight for her.

Whispers and a slight commotion tore Grace away from her reverie. She listened carefully, yet could not pick out any distinct sounds, just whispers, a few stifled giggles, and shuffling feet. Dominick stopped and the next thing Grace knew she was standing by herself in the artificial darkness. Cocking her head like bat trying to get a better radar signal Grace listened, trying to make out the muffled voices.

"Go ahead, Grace. Take off your blindfold." Dominick's voice reverberated with excitement.

Grace slowly slipped the blindfold from her eyes. Her breath caught in her throat, and her heart stopped beating for a millisecond. With tear-filled eyes, Grace beheld the sight before her.

No more construction equipment. No more scaffolding. No more noise; there was just the once dilapidated Victorian standing proudly in the center of the peaceful Kansas prairie. The new windows sparkled and the newly painted buttercup yellow smiled at her, seeming to welcome its new owner to finally call this place home.

Grace looked at the smiling people surrounding her. Her questioning gaze turned to Dominick.

"It's done."

"All? The whole house is done?"

Dominick smiled and tucked a piece of wayward hair behind Grace's right ear. "Yes, Spitfire. Your and Phoebe's house is completely done." Dominick winked. "You no longer have a need for me."

Grace stood on tiptoes and whispered in his ear, "My need for you has just begun!" Grace turned to Phoebe and Noah. Phoebe plied herself from Noah's arm and rushed to Grace and wrapped her in a bear hug.

"We did it, Grace. You and I. We conquered it." Phoebe let go of Grace and gestured to the house. "It's not a nightmare anymore, is it? Do you think Dad is proud of us? Do you think he can finally rest in peace?"

Grace wrapped her arm around Phoebe. "He's always been proud of us. It's just that this time, *we* can be proud of us. He never needed the peace. We needed it. But we fought our demons, Pheebs, and made something glorious out of something ugly."

Dominick looped his arm through Grace's and made a grand sweeping gesture toward the house. "Shall we?"

Grace nodded and had to hold herself from running up the porch steps. Phoebe opened the door, and Dominick ushered Grace through the threshold.

"It's absolutely amazing!" Even though the majority of the house had been completed the last time Grace saw it, there had been the dust, debris, and clutter that construction creates. That was all gone. Nothing remained but beautifully stained floors, perfectly painted walls, crisp crown molding, and beautifully woven rugs. Almost in a trance, Grace slowly made her way through the entire house. The guest rooms, each done in a different color, created a soft rainbow that would be sure to welcome Grace and Phoebe's future guests.

The men must have been cleaning into the wee hours of the night, Grace thought as she inspected her clean finger after running it along the mahogany mantle of the fireplace in the master suite. Appreciation welled up inside her and came out as tears.

"What's wrong?" Dominick snaked his arm around Grace's waist.

Grace laughed through her tears. "Nothing at all. This is all just too much to take in. You all must have worked so hard." Grace looked at Phoebe, Noah, and Dominick. "Thank you."

Phoebe hugged Grace. "Let's just say you owe me a lifetime of Blizzards." Phoebe scrunched up her nose. "I think I actually named my dust rag. We were buddies."

Dominick smoothed Grace's hair. "There's something else I have to show you."

"Aren't you coming, Pheebs?" Grace asked when Phoebe didn't follow them out of the room.

Phoebe grinned from ear to ear as Noah wrapped his arms around her. "Nope. I think this is a surprise just for you."

Grace barely caught the wink that Dominick gave her sister. Curiosity simmered in her belly. She turned to Dominick as they reached the bottom of the steps. "What's the big surprise?"

Dominick grinned mischievously. "Good things come to those who wait. Close your eyes." He placed his arm around Grace's shoulders and led her out the backdoor and down the back porch steps. "Go ahead. Open them."

Grace obeyed and gasped at the sight that met her eyes--her gazebo. Red geraniums in white flower boxes circled the top white railing of the rounded turreted structure. Fresh sod added a vibrant carpet of green, and red and white geraniums ran parallel on both sides of the cobblestone walkway which led down to the small pond, perfectly blue and sparkling in the sunlight. Behind the gazebo and pond lay the small patch of woods which had twice harbored danger for Grace. Instead of feeling fear, she felt hope. Hope for her future.

She knew now that no matter what or who threatened her happiness or survival, there was always her Heavenly Father to bring her through. He would never remove the dangers; He'd simply hold her through those and put people in her life to support and love her through them as well. She inhaled a deep breath and absorbed everything--the scent of the geraniums, the fresh paint, the earthy smell of the sod, the delicious cologne from Dominick. And she exhaled everything she'd been holding in for a very long time--the bitterness, the distrust, the anger. A smile split Grace's face. She was finally home.

"Oh, Dominick," Grace whispered, "it's perfect."

Dominick licked his lips, and his chocolate brown eyes turned to molten fudge as he gazed into hers. "Not quite yet, however, you are the only one that can make it perfect."

"I don't know what I can do. You did it all. I don't know how, but you fixed it. You made this place a home for me, Dominick, and for that I'm eternally grateful."

Dominick cleared his throat. His eyes darted toward the resurrected house and then back to Grace. "I was kind of hoping that this place wouldn't be your home."

Confusion clouded Grace's face until Dominick's comment truly sank in. "Are you...what...?" Grace's mouth opened and shut several more times until Dominick gently brought her lower lip to her upper lip with his index finger.

"Yes, my lovely Spitfire, I'm asking you to someday consider being my wife and a mother to Lilly." Dominick's eyes danced with passion.

Grace's face fell slightly. "Why aren't you asking me now?"

Dominick laughed. "We could get married by the justice of the peace right now if you wish, but I'd like to date you first. I've yet to take you on an official date. And all-you-can-eat shrimp night at Reed's Diner doesn't count." Dominick lightly ran his thumb across a colorful bruise on Grace's face. "Besides, I want you to be sure about this. I don't want you to regret marrying me."

Love for the man in front of her swelled and threatened to overcome her. Never had a man, besides her father, put her first. Never had a man been willing to wait for her, to have patience with her. Tears spilled freely down her face. "I'd never regret marrying you, but a date does sound nice."

Dominick gently curled a tendril of her hair around his finger. "What were you going to tell me yesterday in the hospital?"

Grace batted her eyelashes. "I think you already have your answer to that, Carpenter Hottie!" Grace brought his forehead down to touch hers. In a soft whisper she finally allowed the words to rush out, "I love you, Dominick. I love you for who you were, and who you are now." Aware of the tears on his face, Grace playfully tickled his ribcage. "You wanna go for a swim? Remember, you don't have to wear a swimsuit."

Dominick's eyes flashed. Before Grace knew what was happening, Dominick captured her lips with his. It was a kiss of possession. It was a kiss with a promise. It was a kiss that brought her home.

About the Author

Jessica Berg uses her writing to share her love of the Midwest, family, and her savior, the almighty God. When not teaching high school English, Jessica strives to create worlds surrounded by her beloved prairie through inspirational romance. She currently resides in South Dakota with her husband and three children.

Jessica invites you to see what inspires her on her website jessicabergbooks.com or her blog jessicabergblog.wordpress.com.

Jessica loves to hear from her readers. Contact her via twitter @jessicaberg2003 or her facebook page facebook.com/jessicabergbooks

Made in the USA
Lexington, KY
10 October 2017